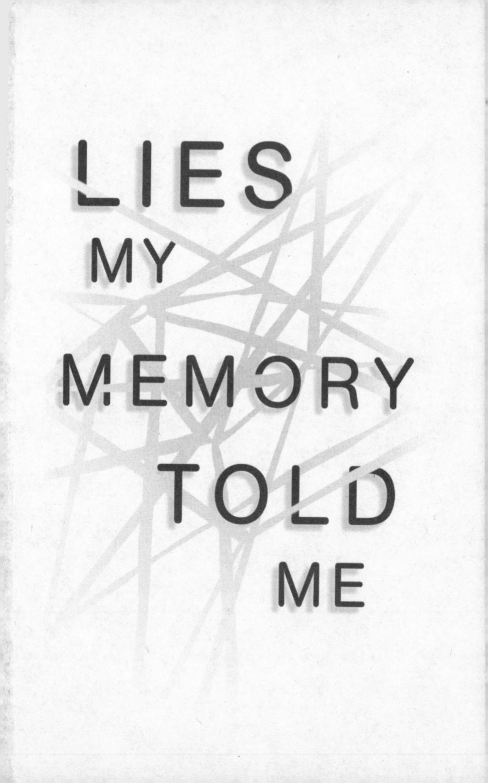

LIES
MY
MEMORY
TOLD
ME

SACHA WUNSCH

LIES MY MEMORY TOLD ME

ISBN-13: 978-1-335-01827-4

Lies My Memory Told Me

This edition published by arrangement with Harlequin Books S.A.

For questions and comments about the quality of this book, please contact us at CustomerService@Harlequin.com.

Inkyard Press
22 Adelaide St. West, 40th Floor
Toronto, Ontario M5H 4E3, Canada
www.InkyardPress.com

Printed in U.S.A.

To Tammy—thanks for the spark!

prologue

The platform was a hundred and fifty feet up.

I tried not to look down.

I hadn't even known I was afraid of heights until the moment I stood up there.

The stranger came up to me, grinning. "You're going to love it," he said.

I swallowed.

My entire body was sweating, most notably my palms, slipping as I tried to grip the safety harness.

Was I really going to do this?

No. I was going to get unclipped, turn around, and simply climb back down what felt like the millions of stairs stretching below me.

And then, just as I started to turn, someone pushed me off the platform.

I screamed as I dropped, nothing but air beneath me.

And then…I started to glide.

The scream kept coming a few seconds more, but my heart did a flip before it could reach my mind. I was soaring. Over the treetops. Whizzing along the zip line at high speeds. It was the best thing I had ever felt.

I had never been this free. Which made sense, I was essentially flying, after all.

Giggling was very much not in my nature, but there I was, giggling anyway. I closed my eyes to get a better sense of the wind on my face, but when the sweet scent of fresh-blooming flowers greeted me, I opened them again. Sure enough, the trees several yards below my feet were blooming some kind of large purple flower.

I sucked in a breath, wishing I could inhale the whole scene, wanting to appreciate it as much as I could—savor it—knowing it wouldn't last forever, and landed gently on the other side.

I did not have to be pushed off the second platform—barely able to wait my turn to jump again. I soared from platform to platform, wishing nothing more than for this to go on forever, grinning all the way, and realizing only at the last second that the final landing platform wasn't a platform at all, but a deep, cooling pool.

I sucked in a breath, and with a final burst of adrenaline, I splashed into the crystal clear water.

TWENTY MINUTES EARLIER

"Come on, open it," Mom said, beaming.

I held the small, beautifully wrapped box, unable to imagine what it was. My parents knew I wasn't really that into jewelry, and neither were they really, but what else could be in such a tiny box?

I tore into it and flipped the lid open.

Which confused me even more. It wasn't a ring or a pendant, just a small metal disk.

Dad sensed my confusion. "Give it a second," he said, beaming even brighter than Mom.

In a blink, a form emerged, a hologram above the disk. There was no sound, but it looked like the person in the hologram was gliding through the tops of trees high in the air.

"This is...really cool," I said, and meant it, but couldn't help but feel like I was missing something.

Mom was practically bouncing. "We wanted to do something special for your birthday."

"Thank you," was all I could really think to say. The disk was pretty cool, but what the hell was with their enthusiasm?

"You're welcome, Nova," Dad said. "But this isn't the whole thing. It's the experience of it that's the real gift."

"The experience of it?"

Mom had gotten up and gone to the desk by the front door. She picked up another box, this one unwrapped, and pulled something from inside.

"Here, you put this on," she said, handing me a clunky set of headphones plugged into a small handheld device about the size of a phone.

"The disk goes in there," Dad said, and showed me how to open it, setting my new present inside.

And then I experienced my first ever zip line.

★ ★ ★

As the experience ended, I blinked my eyes open, a hundred percent sure I'd be soaking wet, but I was sitting right back in my living room. The sensation was a bit disorienting but my parents were staring at me like they were about to explode.

"What was that?" I asked, grabbing the hem of my shirt, which I couldn't quite comprehend being dry.

"That was Enhanced Memory," Dad said, but the look on his face said so much more—like if he'd had feathers, they'd be plumaged out like the most badass peacock of the bunch.

"What did you think?" Mom asked, clasping her hands like she had so much energy whizzing through her body she had to do something to hold it in.

"Well, obviously it was amazing, but by the way you two are acting, you already know that." I couldn't help but grin. They were just so cute sitting there all proud of themselves. "But seriously, what is this? What is Enhanced Memory?"

I'd seen 3D movies and had even tried virtual reality once, but this was way beyond either of those. This was next level.

"It's simple," Dad said. "The headphones are equipped with dozens of...well, let's call them electrodes for sake of ease, though really, they're more advanced than that."

"Okay," I said, mostly with him still, although knowing Dad it wouldn't be long until the science-y droning took hold and steered him right off the layman's term trail.

"And these," he said, taking the disk out of the machine and holding it up, "are Memories."

"Memories."

Mom nodded. "We discovered a way to extract memories and reproduce them."

"Wait, you guys created this?"

Mom nodded, her smile huge and eyes wide. "This is what we've been working toward all these years."

My mouth dropped open. I knew my parents had been working on some kind of project for a long time, but I guess I hadn't really been that interested in what it was.

Mom laughed at my stunned expression while Dad came over to give me one of his signature kisses on the top of my head.

"Happy birthday, sweetheart," Mom said, beaming.

I mean, they were scientists and science was basically the last thing I wanted to pay attention to, so I never really asked many questions.

But this was way beyond science. This was…actually kind of awesome.

A smile crept across my face. I couldn't wait to try it again.

1

The last bell rang and I hurried out, hoping to avoid the after-school rush to the lockers, but as always I was hit by a surge of people—some of them backing out of the way as I passed. Most of the time I felt like I had three heads when I walked through the halls. In a smallish place like Marinville, I guess the new girl will always be the new girl. Especially the new girl whose parents invented "the coolest thing on earth"—at least that's what I'd been told approximately one hundred and thirty million times, anyway. I swear, I knew exactly what it was like to be a fish in a fishbowl.

I glanced up and accidentally made eye contact with one of them.

"Hey," Chase Mason said, with a sideways grin and a slow gaze up my body—his deodorant body spray a strangling, pulsing entity invading my personal space. He was known for being a player.

I shot him an ultraquick smile as I hurried past, trying to

make it clear it was for courtesy purposes only. Still, I could feel him watching me as I sped away, tucking my books closer to my chest.

"You could do worse than Chase Mason," Andie said as she slid up beside me, clearly having seen the whole display. "I've heard he's a lot of fun." She grinned, turning to walk backward and giving Chase a little tip of her imaginary hat for his attempt, before turning back around to walk with me, tucking a strand of hair behind her ear. She was the only person I knew who could wear her hair short in the back, long in the front, color it a deep, rich maroon and not only get away with it, but look like she was born to wear it that way, striking against her pale, almost translucent skin. She definitely had a look all her own, unlike me who was all basic brown hair, gray eyes, average white skin—definitely not the kind anyone would ever comment on like they did Andie's. She was also one of those people who could be friends with anybody. I don't know how she did it when it was a miracle I had even one friend in this place.

I sighed. "I know, but that is not the kind of fun I'm looking for."

She rolled her eyes. "You are wasting all your good high school years on books and old people."

"Whatever. You work there too."

"Yeah, but for me Golden Acres is a job. For you it's like... a lifestyle or something."

She wasn't wrong. The long-term care facility on the east side of our small city was a reprieve. A chance to just be myself. A place where nobody really cared who my parents were. Honestly, I was lucky that Andie had helped me get the job.

We eventually got to the edge of the schoolyard, but neither of our parents was there yet.

"I'm just saying, all these guys are dying to get into your, let's say…business," she said, making herself chuckle. "It wouldn't kill you to give one of them a chance."

I raised my eyebrow at her.

"And while you're at it you could, I don't know, wear something that isn't five sizes too big, or is, you know, a little more exciting than all black, all the time." She tugged at the sleeve of my oversized sweatshirt. "I know you've got the goods under there."

I rolled my eyes. "No thank you. I like being comfortable."

"And by comfortable, you mean hidden," Andie said.

I shrugged. "It's what I like."

We sat on the grass as people passed, getting into vehicles. A kid whizzed by on a skateboard.

"Haven't seen one of those in a while," Andie said.

"No kidding," I said, watching as he nearly ran into a parked car. "Seems unnecessarily risky."

Andie nodded as a girl who I thought was named Ashley came up to us. "Hey, guys. I don't know if you heard, but I'm having a get-together this weekend and it would be great if you could both come." She looked expectantly from me to Andie and then back to me again.

I was, as usual, at a total loss for words.

"Yeah, maybe," Andie said, used to doing most of the talking for both of us.

"Okay, great. That would be great," Ashley said, smiling as she turned away.

I waited a few seconds before I spoke. "There's no way I'm going to a party."

Andie feigned shock. "What? Nova Reynolds *doesn't* want to go to a party? I'm utterly flabbergasted!"

I shoved her with my shoulder and smiled. She smiled back and we fell into a comfortable silence for a minute or two.

"It would be nice if you gave everyone a chance though. I know it's weird for you with who your parents are and everything, but most people here are pretty decent."

I nodded. "I know. I just…I don't know, I'm never comfortable around them. I feel like I haven't been comfortable since the day I moved here. Like…I don't know, I can't even find a way to be *me* here. Do you ever just…feel off? Like you can't figure out who you're supposed to be in your own skin?"

Andie gave me a look.

"Oh god, sorry," I said, burying my face in my hands.

Of course Andie knew what it was like to not feel comfortable in her own skin. I always envied how comfortable she was with herself—so at ease around everybody—that I almost forgot that when I first moved here, it hadn't been that long since she'd transitioned. I couldn't imagine how difficult the process must have been, but she was so utterly herself now, that it was hard to remember things used to be different.

And all she was trying to get me to do was wear jeans that fit and go to a party.

"Don't worry about it," Andie said. "Honestly, it's the reason we're such good friends, I think. They want to be nice and inclusive and everything, but they don't quite know what to do with me and they don't quite know what to do with you either. We're the famous outcasts." She shrugged.

I nodded, not sure if that made me feel better or worse.

"Did I ever tell you that it was partly because of Enhanced Memory that I decided to come out?"

I looked at her, searching. Shook my head.

She gazed out into the parking lot. "It just started making things easier. People would use all these EMs, and of course lots of the original memories that were duplicated had come from people all over the gender spectrum."

I nodded. Enhanced Memories were just that. Memories. And those memories came from people. I'd seen a ton of articles and news stories about it. A collective empathy and understanding had begun to form, sort of by accident. Being inside someone's memories, inside that lived experience, gave people tiny glimpses of what it was like to be in that person's shoes. Like truly be in their shoes, literally feeling the things they felt, the nuances of living a life you would never otherwise know.

It wasn't a cure for ignorance, of course—people so easily went back to who they were—but acceptance and understanding had made huge strides since EM's release.

"People just started to understand a bit better, I guess," Andie continued. "As much as movies and TV and social media could tell someone's story, EM let people *feel* what it was like to be someone, if only for a moment. It made the world a safer place for me. For so many of us." She turned her gaze to me. "I wasn't as scared to be who I am."

Tears sprang to my eyes as I imagined my best friend stuck, feeling like she had to pretend all the time.

"Anyway," she finished, straightening her shoulders as if to shake off the heavy conversation. "Who would even want to be the same as everyone else, right?" she said, and this time it was her turn to give me a shoulder shove.

I nodded, blinking the tears back to where they came from, and we sat in silence for a minute, each lost in our own thoughts.

"So how are your lines coming?" she asked after a bit.

I leaned back on my hands. Truthfully, I'd had my lines memorized since about two days after we got our parts. I don't even know why I was so excited—it was just a silly school play and I didn't even have that big of a part, but this was the first time I'd ever been brave enough to try out for any kind of production and I was excited. And okay, it was definitely Andie who made me do it, but still.

I actually did it.

"Good. I think I've got most of them down," I said, picking at the grass.

"Ugh, I wish," she said, digging in her bag. "I don't know how I'm ever going to remember mine."

"Yeah," I said. "Must be super terrible to have almost all the lines in the whole play," I said, grinning.

"Well, I mean, true, but it's still hard," she said, mock pouting. Her mom pulled up and she stood. "We're Face Chatting later to run lines. I need all the help I can get."

"You're so bossy," I said, but of course not minding for a second.

"And seriously, think about the party. It might actually be fun."

I nodded and waved as she got in the car.

The parking lot was starting to clear out. I checked the time on my phone and sighed.

And yeah, I knew things were super busy for Mom and Dad, but honestly, if they didn't want the responsibility of a kid, why did they bother having one?

As I waited, I checked my feeds.

Enhanced Memory Takes World by Storm.

I did it more by force of habit than anything else these days. I used to check all the news about Enhanced Memory because I thought it was so cool that my parents had invented this huge thing, and I guess I just never stopped. Maybe because the articles never stopped.

EM was a part of pretty much everyone's life now. People always seemed amazed at how fast the tech became a household thing—articles always freaking out over how it moved even faster than when smartphones became the thing everyone had to have. This tech my parents actually helped invent—and truly made the real breakthroughs in the brain science part of it—was becoming so huge, and I couldn't help but smile as I looked over at a couple kids sitting ten yards away who had EM headphones on. As much as my parents being who they were was a huge pain in my ass, I had to admit this thing that they had done was still pretty cool.

And it wouldn't be this way forever. After graduation I could move anywhere and no one would have to know where I came from.

But as always, I clicked the link and turned up the volume.

"Not just for race car driving and bungee jumping anymore. Enhanced Memory could be the miracle cure for what ails you," the reporter began. *"With all the benefits the world is seeing from this advanced new tech, don't be surprised if it is.*

"What started off being marketed as an ultrarealistic entertain-

ment experience is truly becoming a life-hacking system. Not only can you 'download' instructions on how to fix a sink or change a tire right into your memories, but this may also be the medical marvel you've been waiting for.

"'Not just for entertainment,' Experion Enterprises CEO Jackson Davies says, touting his fastest-selling device as a miracle cure for almost anything a person can suffer from.'"

I recognized my parents' boss on the screen.

"People all over the world have been discovering the myriad ways that Enhanced Memory can be used that go beyond what even we first imagined."

The video jumped to a woman telling her experience.

"At first, I didn't know what to make of this…thing," she said, holding up her Enhanced Memory device. "My kids gave it to me. They live far away and I was always bored, you know? With no one to talk to all the time and everything. But because of this little device, my whole world has changed. What I didn't tell my kids was that I wasn't just bored, I was lonely, but now, because of Enhanced Memory, it's like a whole new world has opened up. I have plenty of experiences and people in my life now. My mental health has never been better."

The newscaster came back on-screen.

"There are seemingly endless ways Enhanced Memory can be used. Companies are experiencing increased employee satisfaction, as EM has become a leading tool in corporate sensitivity training as well as in the restructuring of hiring practices. People with addictions report getting off drugs and alcohol with this simple-to-use device, and still others are living in whole new worlds they couldn't even imagine before."

The video changed to a woman sitting in front of the most gorgeous landscape paintings.

"I've never had the money to travel, but it's always been a dream of mine to gather inspiration for my art from all over the world." She stopped, her eyes glistening. *"But now I can, and because of it, I've been able to sell my paintings to others who travel through EM and want to show their friends all the places they've gone. I'm finally able to make a living off my art, which is another dream come true."*

The logo for the station popped up and the video ended.

The videos and articles were usually news clips, but every one of them was always so enthusiastic, they were almost more like a marketing campaign. As usual with these videos, goose bumps popped up on my arms. I still couldn't believe this was something my parents had done…this thing that was changing the world.

Twenty minutes later I started walking. Having such high-achieving parents had its pros, but it definitely had its cons too.

I pulled out my phone and texted Andie. Guess what, the parents never showed.

She immediately sent back the shock-faced emoji. Are you okay? It's scary out there. Do you need us to come get you?!

I had a habit of forgetting that people couldn't read my intentions over text. No no. I'm good, just complaining. Should have finished with the eye roll emoji. Sorry.

Okay…if you're sure.

Yes, I'm sure. Thanks though! ☺

Honestly, I just shouldn't text people. It was a beautiful day and the walk was actually kind of nice.

When I eventually made it home, Mom and Dad were both in the living room with Enhanced Memory headphones on.

I'd been hearing nothing but how I had to get off my phone and limit my screen time because I wasn't living in "real life" for years, but like all the other rules my parents thought were so important, apparently they applied only to me and not to them. I tried my best not to roll my eyes, not to mention thank them for the nonexistent ride home.

But they had their reasons, even if it was inconvenient for me. With the spring season of new releases coming out in the next few months, there was tons of beta testing to do, and my parents were very hands-on. I didn't even bother jolting them out of their Memories.

I was tired from walking. And I was tired of doing everything myself. I was tired of feeling like…well, like I was on my own. I just wanted to relax and not think about it for a while.

If Mom and Dad could spend all afternoon doing it, I deserved a session too, especially after that walk home. I headed to my room and soon I was in another place, another time.

The crowd roared and I let their energy soak into my skin. These people worshipped me, adored me even. And all I had to do was sing. I was good too. Good enough to deserve all the attention. I had worked so hard and it had all come down to this moment.

The band started playing the intro to my biggest song and I started to groove to the music, knowing that I could do no wrong in the eyes of my fans. And the clothes—all glitter and bare skin and tightness—looked amazing, and I felt amazing in them too, the confidence of the singer melding with my soul. That was the magic of EM—for a little while, you could blissfully become someone else.

I drank the energy. Feeding it back to the crowd with my lyrics, believing so deeply in every word that I sang and wanting nothing more than for them to believe in the words as much as I did.

For those five minutes I sang and danced and gave everything I had to my people—and I had never been so alive in my life.

As I took the headphones off, adrenaline pumped through me, giving me the same rush as if the Memory had actually happened to me. My worries from before somehow seemed further away. I was lighter…happier, even. It was a feeling I never wanted to let go of.

My parents had created this amazing thing. And yeah, maybe they were more focused on their work than I would have liked, but it wasn't for nothing. In five minutes my mood had gone from completely shitty to this rush of adrenaline… like I could do anything and be anything I wanted. It gave me something to aspire to…to try for. Not the singer part, of course, but that shot of motivation that maybe I'd be something important someday. Here I was bitching about the little things that didn't matter when they were working hard to make people's lives so much better. So much more interesting.

This was all so much bigger than me.

Enhanced Memory was this huge gift, a complete game changer, and my parents had given it to the world.

2

I woke up early the next day so I'd have enough time to walk to work, and was surprised to find my dad downstairs on the couch. If he hadn't changed into his pajamas at some point, I would barely have known that he'd even moved, still sitting in the same position, his Enhanced Memory device beside him.

I thought about sitting down, or at least saying good-morning, but just kept walking straight out the door. He didn't like it when he was disturbed from a Memory.

As I walked, I couldn't stop thinking about how it was possible a company could make someone work that much. Or why my parents were so willing to put up with it. I was kind of lost in the thought of it, I guess, so when the bike came careening past, the kid speeding like there was some kind of emergency, I practically jumped out of my skin.

"Hey, watch it!" It was so weird to see someone on a bike. I couldn't imagine what would make anyone actually ride one in real life and risk all that danger when it was so much safer to get the experience through an Enhanced Memory. I shook my head as he pedaled off in a blur.

As Golden Acres came into view, I thought about the first time I'd walked in, knocking lightly on the office door I'd been pointed toward. Genie sitting behind the desk. She was all business, dark hair pulled back, polite pearl necklace, and reading glasses balanced on the end of her nose. When she heard the knock, she looked up, smiling politely.

"Nova!" she said, sounding far more excited than I probably would have been in her position.

Interviewing some kid for an entry-level job did not seem like something that was worthy of that kind of smile. She was obviously a lot better at people than I was. Which instantly made me even more nervous.

"Sit!" she'd said cheerfully, the smile still in full swing. "I'm Genie. So nice to meet you!"

I tried to smile through the roiling of my stomach, hoping it wouldn't like, loudly gurgle or something.

I sat.

"So, tell me about yourself," she said, after she sat as well.

Which was of course the absolute worst thing she could have asked. I never really knew how to answer that question. It seemed like it should be obvious. Sixteen. Quiet. Not much to tell.

But I took a deep breath and let my rehearsed answer seep out. "I'm in grade ten and I used to work in a grocery store and, um, my parents work for Experion Enterprises," I said, self-conscious, as if that had anything to do with my accomplishments at all. "Um, and I would really love to work in a place like this. It seems like I could really learn a lot." I thought about what Andie had told me about Golden Acres, and about the impact my parents were making on the world. "I'm really interested in quality of life and I feel like that's an important aspect of what you do here. And I like helping people." I pulled my chunky cardigan tighter around me, realizing too late that my crossed arms might make me look nervous or closed off or something. I uncrossed them as casually as possible, setting my hands in my lap, which felt even more awkward.

Genie leaned back in her chair, thankfully still smiling. "It certainly is," she said, shuffling through some paperwork on her desk.

She asked a few more questions about schoolwork and whether I did chores at home and things like that. I guess she was satisfied with my answers because after that she got up. "Come on, let me introduce you to some people."

"Okay," I said, unsure what that meant. Was I...hired? I mean, I knew Andie was going to put a good word in for me, but I wasn't sure if that really meant anything or not.

We went down a long hall to a staff room.

"I hear you guys know each other," Genie said, opening the door to where Andie had been sitting at the table eating wheat crackers and hummus, with a side of...chocolate cake. Typical Andie—health food with a generous side of sugar.

"Hey!" Andie said. "No offense, Genie, but it will be nice to have a little company my age around here."

Genie rolled her eyes. "Yeah, I always think to myself, poor Andie, never seems to have any attention, definitely needs more socializing."

As if on cue, Andie's phone dinged with an incoming text. Then just as she was about to open her mouth to retaliate, it dinged again, so she grinned instead. "Touché."

I'd grinned at the exchange. As all business as Genie had seemed when I stepped into her office, she was relaxed and on friendly terms with the staff.

Another check mark in the right direction.

After the staff room, we'd headed to a common area with a TV and a bunch of tables set up for visiting or playing games.

The place was surprisingly hopping. Several people gathered around a table, all with coffees in front of them and an amazing-looking selection of home-baked treats in the middle. A few others were watching the news and a couple more were in the back corner of the room playing cards.

"It's usually better to introduce new people one-on-one," Genie said. "Otherwise you could be here for hours getting grilled. I just wanted to give you an idea of what it's like here during the day. If you decide to join us, your shifts will start a little later, after school and into the evening, and things aren't quite as busy in the common areas then. But it's good for you to get a sense of the different scenery."

I'd nodded as we headed back toward Genie's office. On the way, an older man, a resident, I assumed, passed us in the hall. I couldn't stop staring at his eyebrows, so thick and bushy they were more like two caterpillars loitering there, a single long hair poking from each one, almost as if they were about to high-five each other.

"What's up, Genie?" the man said, a huge grin spread across his face, which made him look much younger than he was, almost like a mischievous kid.

He looked curiously at me.

"Uh-oh, watch out for this one," Genie said. "Clyde never lets up on the poor staff around here. Clyde, this is Nova. She might be coming to work here."

Clyde looked at me with a surprised little expression, which seemed a bit melodramatic—though somehow it worked on him. Like he prided himself on being a comedian.

"Well, welcome!" he said, with a side of overexaggeration. "Another player in the game of life." He grinned and winked. "Nice to meet you."

I smiled back, appreciating that he was comfortable doing the talking. Usually if people wanted to take up most of the space in a room, I was more than happy to let them have it. It was so much easier than trying to constantly come up with something to say.

"Ah…" he continued. "The strong silent type." He squinted his eyes playfully. "You remind me of my daughter," he said. "Always quiet as a mouse, but nothing could get past her. Smart as could be."

"Um, thanks," I said.

"Just don't scare her off, Clyde," Genie said.

Clyde made a mock face like he was terribly offended. "Genie, that hurts," he said, then turned to me. "It was very nice to meet you, Nova, but I better get going. The ladies aren't going to flirt with themselves. A man's gotta keep up his reputation, after all." He wiggled his eyebrows and headed into the common room.

Genie shook her head and laughed. "Clyde's one of our more…entertaining residents here."

I smiled. "He seems happy."

She nodded. "He does a pretty good job of keeping everyone's spirits up." We made it back to Genie's office. "So, what do you think?"

"About...working here?"

"We'd love to have you," she'd said, smiling.

Was it really less than a year since I'd had that interview? It seemed so strange. The people here had become like a second family to me. Andie and I had gotten so much closer, planning activities for the residents together—trivia, charades, bingo...we'd even planned a speakeasy party a few weeks back. We watched a bunch of videos to learn this old dance, the Charleston, so we could teach it to everyone, but the joke was on us since they all already knew it and completely schooled us on the dance floor.

Still, the night had been a huge hit, all the residents having a blast and sipping on mocktails all night. I even saw Clyde pull out a flask and slip something into a few willing residents' glasses as they all giggled and looked over their shoulders to make sure no one would catch them. Clyde had quickly become one of my favorite residents at Golden Acres. I'd heard more than one nurse say he was "full of piss and vinegar" and wasn't really sure what, exactly, that was supposed to mean, but it must have been a good thing because Clyde was always smiling and trying to get everyone else in on it too. I had no idea what the residents thought would happen—last time I checked there was no maximum drinking age, but I pretended to be oblivious anyway. I didn't want to ruin their fun.

I had no idea what I would have done without Genie lately either. For the past few months she'd been helping me with my math homework during break. Thankfully, Genie was pretty much a math whisperer and could somehow explain it in a way that my brain would actually absorb. Honestly, it seemed like a million years since that awkward first meeting.

I put my stuff in my locker and started my shift with the usual list of rooms needing to be cleaned. I finished a few while the residents were out doing morning activities, but when I got to Mae's room, she was still in the bed.

"Good morning, Mae," I said.

It was the practice at Golden Acres to acknowledge each resident to make sure they were doing okay before starting our cleaning. It helped them feel like you weren't just there to get a job done and you actually cared about how they were doing.

"Oh," she said, startled, looking up from the paper she was holding. "Oh hi..." She paused a moment, glancing at my nametag. "Nova."

"How are you doing today, Mae?"

"Oh okay, I guess." She smiled, though she seemed a bit distracted. Usually she couldn't wait to visit, but today she turned her attention back to the note in her hands. After a moment, she put the paper down on her night table.

"That's good," I said as I began dusting her room. "Are you heading out to the common area at all?"

I hoped she wouldn't stay cooped up in her room all day. That never seemed to be very good for anyone's mood.

"Oh yes, I'm sure I'll get out there."

"Good," I said, making my way over to the table and catching a glimpse of the paper she had set down.

Dear Mae,

I know you always worry, but just this once, please try to stop. Yes, things are confusing right now but we have a plan.

Science has found a way to help us with our memories, even though we're starting to lose them. The nurses can help get you started with your Memory machine. It allows you to replay all of the best memories from your life so you will never forget all the important people and places.

We are taking good care of us. Honestly, it's okay. Trust me.

Love,

Mae from Yesterday

I swallowed. I'd never really thought about how hard it must be to not even be able to fully trust your own mind anymore.

I put my hand on Mae's, not sure what else to do.

"Are you one of the nurses who can help me with the Memories?" she asked, gesturing to the note.

I wanted nothing more than to be able to help her, but I wasn't sure where everyone's Memories were stored. I didn't know all the details, but Golden Acres was an Enhanced Memory health facility. Most of the patients here suffered from memory loss issues. I wasn't sure how it all worked, but somehow they were finding ways to preserve people's memories with the help of the company my parents worked for. I made a mental note to ask Genie more about it.

"I'm afraid not," I said, trying to sound more cheerful than I was. "But I can definitely go find someone who can."

She smiled. "Okay. But maybe in a little while. If you can stay and visit for a bit, that would be nice too."

"Of course," I said. "What should we chat about?" I asked, already knowing the answer.

Mae loved to tell stories about her time as a dancer.

"Have I ever told you about when I was a showgirl in Vegas?"

I smiled. "I'd love to hear about it. Do you mind if I do a little straightening up while we're talking?"

"Oh of course, dear, whatever you need to do."

I squeezed her hand one more time and started with my chores while she happily explained about when she was one of those scantily clad ring girls at a boxing match. She beamed as she told it, closing her eyes as if reliving the whole thing.

3

The last thing I wanted to see when I came home was a sink full of dishes, a mess in the living room, and bathrooms in desperate need of a scrub down. And honestly, I'd never really noticed that kind of stuff before, but these past few weeks, it had been getting kind of gross and I couldn't really take it anymore.

I straightened up as best I could in the living room, making sure to work around my parents, who were zombied out inside their EM machines. Tiny boxes marked "beta" were scattered all around them so I had to be extra careful not to touch them or make too much noise. When they were beta testing new experiences, being interrupted was a huge distraction. Dad had explained how a beta tester could never get that first impression of an experience back if he had to start over and try it again, and nothing, *nothing!* was more important than that first impression.

It was important work, but sometimes I worried that Experion was piling way too much on them. Whatever happened to work-life balance, anyway?

Eventually Mom emerged from the Memories.

"Hi, honey, did you straighten up a bit?"

I nodded, thinking it was a heck of a lot more than "a bit." Especially considering I was still at the sink doing the dishes that wouldn't fit in the dishwasher. "It was getting a little out of control."

Mom's shoulders slumped. "I'm so sorry. The upcoming release is going to be the end of me. I'm so far behind in everything." She gave me a look that said she felt terrible about the whole thing. "Thank you for doing that. I promise this isn't going to last forever." She came over and I thought she was going to hug me, but she squeezed my arm instead. I had a strange suspicion that she thought I was too old for hugs now or something. She didn't seem to offer them anymore and yeah, it wasn't like I was a baby anymore, but sometimes I just…wanted my mom. Wanted to be the little kid for a minute.

"I know," I said, and smiled. "I don't mind doing it once in a while."

"I don't know what I'd do without you," she said as she headed back out of the kitchen.

"Mom," I said, before she got too far. "You'll still be able to come to the play, right?"

Mom looked confused for a second and then her eyes lit up. "Oh right, your school thing! Of course we'll be there, honey. We know how hard you've been working. We wouldn't miss it."

I'd put the tickets for the play up on the fridge last week and sent them each a text with the time and day. I had never been brave enough to do anything like it before and I was kind of excited. I wanted them to see a different side of me, I guess. Show them how I was, I don't know, becoming my own person or something.

I suppose I wanted to make them proud.

"Literally all my work money goes to these little beauties," Andie said a few days later at school, holding up one of her Memory disks. "Honestly, my parents should start giving me my college money now. There's no way we won't be able to get our full education in half the time with these soon enough."

I raised my eyebrows. "I hadn't thought of that," I said.

Andie shrugged. "It only makes sense. Why would you bust your ass trying to learn something new when you can buy a Memory from someone who already understands it? I mean, I understand so much more about so many things since I started using Enhanced Memories."

I nodded. "I guess. I feel like I know what it's like to ski and dance and sing and everything. Like I have the muscle memory to do all of it—even in real life if I wanted to. Not that I'd want to. Who needs to risk embarrassing yourself?"

"Exactly. I swear the next big thing in EM is going to be education. In fact…maybe we should skip today."

I rolled my eyes. "Was that a whole speech just so you could get me to skip? Because you know me better than that."

She sighed and shook her head at me. "I actually wasn't, but honestly. It sucks that we're going to be the last people to have to endure going to real schools. I bet by the time we graduate the whole system is going to be overhauled."

"I doubt it will happen that fast."

"Still...imagine how much time we're wasting here."

The bell rang, putting a punctuation mark on her point.

"Well, until then, I'm going to keep going to class," I said.

She reluctantly collected her books and tucked her Enhanced Memory device away. "At least we have drama fifth period."

Drama was about the only class Andie actually liked. She practically lived for it, and when fifth period finally came, I could tell it was going to be an interesting one. Ms. Bailey had asked us each to imagine a place we'd never been before and describe what it would be like to be there.

"Describe the setting in detail," she instructed. "Use your senses. What are the smells, the sights, what do you hear? Most importantly...what do you feel? It's important to be able to portray these feelings when acting...to be able to conjure moments and places in your mind, interacting with the space as if you are really there."

Everyone looked excited, like places were instantly coming to mind and they were sure this was going to be an easy assignment. I thought I was being especially clever about mine, assuming everyone was going to describe a specific building or nature spot in their setting description, but mine would be especially good because it was more of a setting "experience." I was going to describe my first time on the zip line, using all the scenic details as I "moved" through the scene.

Ms. Bailey looked pleased as we all got started. After a few minutes she began to stroll around the room, looking over a few people's shoulders as we wrote. She paused over me, lingering over my paper.

"This is interesting, Ms. Reynolds," she said. "You're describing this place as if it's somewhere you've actually been."

I smiled. "Nope, never been there. Just in a Memory."

And then Ms. Bailey made a noise, then turned to address the class. "Show of hands—how many of you are describing a place you've been in an Enhanced Memory before?"

Every hand in the room went up.

Ms. Bailey's shoulders dropped a little, then she straightened. "I should have been more clear about the assignment. The point here is to use your imagination," she said. "In a drama production, you are not always going to have the benefit of having been in the situation or setting before. We must consult our minds to visualize what it might be like. So please, flip to a new page and begin writing again, this time with someplace completely new to you in every way."

There were a few groans and everyone flipped to a blank page.

No one started writing.

Ms. Baily moved around the room again. "I know, it can be difficult to begin, but really, this can be anyplace in the world. Heck, it doesn't even have to be in the world, you can imagine what it might be like to be on the moon, or in a totally different fantasy world. It could be a different period in time, even. The possibilities are endless!"

I felt kind of bad for Ms. Bailey then. She seemed so excited, like she really was trying to make class fun for us, and we were just sitting there, letting her down. After a while, a few people started writing tentatively, but then some scribbled their words out again. But it was better than the rest of us, who couldn't seem to find a single thing to say.

After about six million years of staring at that annoying blank sheet of paper, my mind unable to go anywhere besides all the Memories I'd done, the bell finally rang and I swear the whole class breathed a collective sigh of relief.

By this time, Ms. Bailey had gone back to her desk, looking rather frustrated. "And don't forget to study your lines," she said, calling after us as we filed out of the classroom. "I'm serious, people! Do not spend the entire night on Memories!"

We had our big production of *The Wizard of Oz* coming up and we were all practically living it every spare moment we had. Lately it seemed like I all I did was eat, sleep, work and study the play. I barely even had time for Memories these days, which was kind of a tragedy. Especially since Mom and Dad were always bringing home so many good disks. I'd picked one up the other day of a safari in the plains of Africa.

"This looks amazing," I'd said to Mom.

She nodded enthusiastically. "It is sooo good. I can't wait to get it out in the world."

But I reluctantly set it back down. The play was the priority.

The big night came shockingly fast. I'd been focusing on my lines for weeks, and had even dictated them into my phone so I could listen whenever I had a minute, to really get them to sink in. I was playing Aunt Em, and a lot of my lines were at the beginning of the play, so I was really getting nervous. Honestly, I wasn't sure why so much was riding on this one silly show, but it somehow meant everything to me. It was so far out of my comfort zone and, I don't know, I was kinda proud of myself. In drama class, Ms. Bailey was always instructing us to "become the character," and honestly I didn't know what that was even supposed to mean. I tried to imagine what it would be like to be Aunt Em—a farmer's wife in Kansas. But I just kept thinking about how I'd sort of known the basic *Wizard of Oz* story since I was a kid, but I'd honestly never thought much about Aunt Em, or why Dorothy was even being raised by her aunt and uncle, for that matter.

For the past several weeks though, it was all I could think about. Like what had happened to Dorothy's parents? Were they dead? It was so weird that they never really mentioned it. At least not that I knew of. And why was Aunt Em raising Dorothy? Had they always been close, or had she been the only option?

So here I was, playing this motherly woman who had agreed to raise another woman's child. And she was supposed to be this strong, even mildly aggressive person, telling off the neighbor lady and all that. And as hard as I'd tried over the last little while, I couldn't remember having a moment of aggression in my life. I was always just going along with what I was supposed to do, not really even considering doing anything else.

And, honestly, how was someone supposed to push themselves aside while they were pretending to be this other person? I was terrified that when the time came, I wouldn't be able to clear myself out of my own head.

I tried to shove the nerves away, finding a quiet spot behind the curtain to go over my lines, saying them aloud quietly as I paced backstage.

"Oh my god, my parents aren't here yet," Andie said, scar-

ing the crap out of me as she peeked out the curtain ten minutes before showtime.

She looked amazing all done up in her stage makeup, braids,
and apron dress. I, on the other hand, looked like a frumpy
potato in my body-covering sack of a dress, which I kind of
loved. Why did skirts like this go out of fashion, anyway?
They covered everything. It was fantastic!

I peeked out beside her. The seats matching the tickets I
had purchased were empty too. But my parents had promised
they'd be there...all six times I asked them. "I'm sure everyone is on their way."

Andie nodded. "I don't know why my family is always late
for everything," she said, rolling her eyes. Which was ironic
since Andie was also always late for everything and never
seemed the least bit concerned about it.

My parents, on the other hand, were always early for everything. At least they always used to be.

Five minutes later, Andie and I watched from backstage
as her family piled into the theater, making a huge commo-
tion. Her little brothers argued loudly as her mom ushered
them into their seats and tried to shush them, her dad falling
in behind as if nothing at all was happening. He was simply
a man heading to his seat.

"Oh good lord," Andie said, closing her eyes and shaking
her head a little. "That is so embarrassing."

As her family began to settle, Andie's phone dinged. She
showed me the text, still shaking her head. So sorry. Got stuck
at train. Here now.

"As if the whole damn auditorium didn't know they were

here now," she said. "My family moves around like they're attached to elephants."

I laughed, and a few people in the audience actually looked up to where we were standing. My nervousness must have been coming out, along with my ridiculous laugh. Sometimes when I laughed too hard, it came out sounding a little wild, almost like I was faking it even when I wasn't. I cleared my throat and checked my phone.

Nothing.

The play started, but there were still two aggressively empty seats in the theater. I was able to get lost in the play a little, pushing my parents out of my mind for brief moments, and it was the strangest thing...I was somehow able to get out of my own head and it was suddenly easy to become a whole different person. I didn't feel like a rural farm wife from Kansas, exactly, but I did feel like someone else. Almost like I was able to channel someone who knew how to act. And weirdly, this feeling of becoming someone else felt comfortable, felt... easier than being myself somehow. I could see why people chose to do it for a living.

But when they still hadn't arrived by intermission, I started to get worried. And kind of pissed that they had missed most of my lines.

They never missed this stuff. Every piano recital and soccer game, they'd been there. Something must be really, really wrong.

I grabbed my phone for a quick second in the midst of the intermission backstage chaos. Where are you? Is everything okay?

I watched my phone, waiting for the reply bubble to pop up, but after a minute or so I put it away again.

When the play resumed, I was distracted.

Had the train that Andie's parents been waiting at derailed or something? Maybe they were stuck across town and unable to get here because of it. Or maybe something even more catastrophic had happened. Maybe one of them was hurt. Or sick or something? They wouldn't miss it. They promised.

But that would mean they'd have to be so hurt or so sick that they couldn't even shoot off a quick text.

I really didn't want to think about that. But the play was starting again and I didn't have time to figure out what my next move was supposed to be.

I couldn't concentrate. I tried to watch Andie and the others, and get ready for my cue. Just listen for the cue, I told myself. Just listen for the cue.

And then I completely missed it.

Someone shoved me lightly, knocking me out of the horror daydream I was having of my parents getting hit by a car that I'd been replaying in my head for the last few minutes.

"There's no place like home!" Andie was saying from the stage, loud, and a bit annoyed.

I rushed out onstage. "Wake up!" I shouted, too loudly. I cleared my throat and tried not to look at the audience. "Wake up, Dorothy." My face was hot under the high collar of the lacey shirt. I tugged at it, trying to find more air.

I somehow stumbled through the rest of the scene and made it through the applause at the end. Thankfully no one made me feel like I'd completely ruined the whole thing, even though I was pretty sure I had.

When I finally got offstage I couldn't take it anymore. I ran straight to my phone, already stripping off jewelry and my wig and making my mental plan to somehow get to them as quickly as I could. They could be anywhere between home and the school, or maybe even at a hospital. I glanced at my phone as I hauled my coat on right over my costume.

Hey honey, what's up? Just got done with some betas. What do you need?

I stared at the screen, blinking.

They forgot.

Even after my frantic texts, it hadn't registered to them what day it was.

They had been working. Beta testing more Memories.

It took everything I had to keep the tears that were stinging behind my eyes in check as the rest of the cast came into the dressing area, all hopped up on the applause and adrenaline and excitement of having pulled it all off.

I don't even know why I was so upset. It was only a play, but I guess I built the whole night up in my head. Made it more important than it really was. I was being selfish. My parents had always been there for me—they were allowed one screwup, right?

I started to change, no longer in a hurry to get home.

"Hey," Andie said, finding me.

She knew I was upset. At least I *hoped* she knew I was upset and didn't mess up that bad for no reason.

I buried my head in my hands and groaned. "I am so sorry."

She sat beside me, bumping me with her shoulder the way

she always did. "Don't be sorry. And do not worry about the play. It was fine. It all worked out. But…are you okay?"

I shrugged. "It's fine. They're really busy."

Andie nodded. I didn't know if I hoped she'd leave after I said I was okay, or if I wanted her to stay. She chose the latter.

"I'm just going to sit here for a minute, if that's okay."

I nodded. I wanted her to stay, but I also didn't want to break down over something so silly. Except someone being there was kind of too much. Made me more emotional. Which was also ridiculous. I should be able to control myself.

"Things change, I guess," she eventually said. "People disappoint us without even meaning to."

I nodded.

"Sometimes it's not even their fault. It's just the way life turns out. Like with Ami and Mason. We used to be inseparable, you know? Did absolutely everything together. We've been friends since kindergarten."

I nodded. "You guys still hang out a lot though."

Andie laughed a little. "We do, but it's not the same as it used to be. I don't even know when things changed really, but at some point they did. You'd think it would have been during my transition. You expect that stuff to be hard, but that wasn't the way it happened. If anything they made an extra point to include me back then, but now…I don't know. They've gotten closer and I'm kind of a third wheel. And it's not like it's anybody's fault. People get close and people drift apart." She shrugged.

"But you guys are still friends."

She nodded. "Yeah, and they're great. I don't mean to complain. It's…not the same as it used to be, I guess. They just seem to have more in common. I don't know. Sometimes I feel like I'm a little too much for some people."

I made a face. "Well, you're definitely not too much for me."

Andie looked up at me. "Thank you for saying that. And I'm sorry, this was not supposed to turn into an Andie-the-oversharer moment."

I laughed. "No, it's good. I usually don't share enough. Is that a thing?"

Andie shrugged. "Everything's a thing sometimes."

"I know what you mean though. I had kind of a situation like that too," I said. It had been a while since I'd thought about back home. "Where I used to live it was always me, Alyssa, and Jess. For years we did everything together."

Andie was nodding, probably already knowing where my story was going. It felt weird telling it, but it felt good too, like it was nice that I finally had someone I was close enough to tell it to.

"Or at least that's what I thought, I guess," I continued. "I found out later that their families always did stuff together. Like Alyssa's mom and Jess's mom were good friends and they went on a camping trip every summer that they never told me about. And I guess it's nice they didn't want to hurt my feelings or whatever, but it was kind of a shock when I found out they'd been doing it for years."

"How *did* you find out?" Andie asked.

I laughed a humorless chuckle. "In the most cliché way possible. I was in the bathroom at school and they didn't know I was in there. Jess was talking to Alyssa and was all, 'I don't know why she always has to come to everything, anyway.

We're the real friends. She's just an annoying little tagalong.'"
I tried to make my voice sound light, like the whole thing
hadn't been as devastating as it was. That pathetic loser feeling that I'd felt in that bathroom years ago was creeping up
all over again, but I didn't want Andie to think I was still that
person. "Alyssa was nice enough not to say anything mean.
She just said, 'Well, at least we have our camping trip next
month.'" I shrugged. "I made the mistake of stepping out of
the stall and after that, I don't know. I guess they were too
embarrassed that they'd been caught. We didn't really hang
out anymore."

Andie sighed. "That's rough. I'm sorry."

I tilted my head. "It's fine. It's not like it scarred me for
life or anything."

She raised an eyebrow.

I laughed. "Or maybe it has. I was never good at making
friends after that. But I don't think I was super spectacular at
it before either."

A grin spread across her face. "Seems like you're fine at it
to me."

I smiled back. "Is this what it is to be friends? Sharing hor-
rifying and embarrassing stories for camaraderie?"

She laughed. "I guess sometimes you can't count on people,
you know? I wasn't sure if my parents would make it either,"
Andie said, then tilted her head. "No, I don't know why I
said that. I knew they would make it—they would probably
risk mortal injury to make it to this kind of a thing. It's just…
kind of embarrassing when they do finally make it. All chaos
and flusters and letting the *entire world* know they have arrived!" She smiled.

I laughed a little.

"But seriously, I'm sorry yours didn't make it. That sucks."

I let out a long breath. "Yeah."

Andie smiled. "I don't think people mean to do some of the things that they do. They just...I don't know. Everyone's the star of their own life, you know? They spend so much more time thinking about their little worlds than they do about anyone else's. Like my parents. The fact that they always show up to these things—and always show up late and make a huge scene on top of it—I think it might be more about everyone knowing they're there so they have this 'perfect parent' persona than it is about actually seeing me in the play, you know?"

I wasn't sure I believed her. I didn't really know Andie's parents that well, but they seemed totally into their kids. A pang of something shot through me. Not jealousy exactly, but maybe something jealousy adjacent. I'd had that once. My parents used to be all about spending time with me, real time—even when I was a little kid. But they couldn't now... not the way work was.

I nodded anyway, thankful that she was trying to make it seem less weird. "Yeah, maybe. But I still think your parents are great. They remind me a bit of how my parents were before..." I said, trailing off.

We sat in silence for a minute or two, until Andie finally broke it. "Hey, what are you doing now?"

I shrugged. "I don't know. Maybe going home to read or something."

Andie shook her head. "You're coming with me."

I laughed. "Um...okay?"

"Everyone's meeting up at Visto." She checked her phone. "You have to come."

I'd never been to Visto before. It used to be a place where you had to be old enough to drink, but bars had started letting in all ages a while back. After Enhanced Memories came out and it was so much easier to experience all the same things from the comfort of your home, the bar scene started dying out. Turned out, though, that bars didn't care about selling alcohol as much as they cared about making money, and some places, like Visto, figured out pretty fast that there was a lot more money to be made in the Enhanced Memory business than there ever was in the alcohol business.

And since there was no age regulation for EMs, there weren't any restrictions for entry anymore either. Not that I'd gone to any of these places very often. Andie had dragged me to one before and it had kind of been fun, but the music had been so loud that conversation was even more awkward than usual—so much screaming of the word *what*.

"Oh, uh...I don't know," I said. I really couldn't see myself being great company.

"Come on—it'll be fun. It's not like you have much else going on, right?" She smiled, and she had a smile that was hard to resist.

"I guess," I said. Honestly, I was out of excuses and I wasn't in any particular hurry to get home.

"Awesome," she said. "Meet me in the lobby in twenty?"

"I'll be there," I said, even though I wasn't a hundred percent sure it was a good idea.

I quickly changed and fixed my stage makeup into normal makeup, then waited for Andie in the lobby.

"Sorry," she said, rushing down the hall, several bags slung over various places on her body, one of those people who really tried but never quite seemed to get organized. She also seemed to spread out wherever she went, carrying so many things with her and always needing a couple extra chairs to set everything on.

"Ami and Mason are already there, so we can head over," she said, breathless.

"Perfect," I said, grabbing one of her bags that looked especially precarious as we headed out.

4

It was still kind of early, but the club was lined up. Andie waltzed straight up to the bouncer and whispered something in his ear while I stood there looking everywhere except at the dozens of people standing in line. He motioned us through—to the extreme discontent of everyone else.

"How in the hell did you do that?" I whispered in awe as she smiled at the guy. Honestly, this girl was way too cool to be my friend.

We headed in and she shrugged. "Just gotta have a little flair and confidence—" she raised one eyebrow "—and maybe an older cousin with connections." She grinned a sly little grin and started bouncing to the beat as we walked.

The music was a physical being, hitting me in the chest as we entered. It was impossible to talk, so I followed Andie as close as I could, an intense urge to grasp onto her shirt, but realized that might look a little desperate. Childish. My heart raced a little with the constant flow of movement around us and I had to make a conscious effort to stay calm with all the sensory inputs being thrust my way. Flashing lights, pulsing beats, people invading my space. I wasn't someone to avoid crowds completely, but I wasn't really someone who loved them either.

Andie seemed to know exactly where she was going though and within a couple minutes we found Ami and Mason and also, thankfully, a place to sit. Not something to take for granted in a place like that, but they had saved a couple seats for us.

They were deep in conversation and didn't notice us walk up.

"...got it on the black market," Ami was saying, kind of bouncing in her chair a bit. "He seriously couldn't stop talking about it."

Mason's mouth flopped open as he hung on her every word.

I purposely "by accident" bumped the table, pretending that I hadn't heard anything. The last thing I needed in my life was some kind of drug gossip about people I probably didn't even know.

Ami clamped her mouth shut.

"Hey, deadbeats!" Andie said, enthusiastically oblivious to any weirdness and dropping all her bags on the floor dramatically in true Andie fashion.

"Hey," I said to the others and tried to settle in and relax, giving myself a second to adjust to the atmosphere, trying to sense the rhythm of the place now that I was out of the main thrust of the crowd. I closed my eyes so I could feel the place from the edges rather than have it forced at me.

I started to sway with the music a bit, a smile even creeping onto my face now that I was settled a little. I couldn't help but think that it would be nice if there was an easing in to places like this. Like a quiet hallway that slowly waded you into the crowd, music getting incrementally louder, giving you a minute to prepare yourself.

"Harlow!" The word sounded far away, but the person was insistently trying to get someone's attention. "Harlow! Harlow!" And then something touched my shoulder and the word, loud, right by my ear. "Harlow!"

I turned and blinked, suddenly staring into one of the most interesting faces I had ever seen. The guy was striking with his brown-gold eyes, thick lashes, and warm brown skin, but more than that, there was something about him. A sense that I knew his face. I had the strangest urge to reach out to him, like there was some kind of weird connection between us. Maybe I'd seen him in a magazine or a Memory or something.

"Hey," he said, smiling.

"Um. Hey," I said back, keenly aware that his hand was still touching my shoulder softly.

But his expression changed after a moment. "You don't know who I am," he said, looking confused and somewhat horrified.

"Should I?" I asked, wishing I did know him.

"I—I guess not," he said, disappointed.

I couldn't help but be a little disappointed too.

"Was that you saying Harlow?" I asked.

"Yeah," he said.

"Well, uh…I'm Nova," I said, giving him one of those half smiles reserved for when you don't know what else to do. "And don't worry, people are always mistaking me for someone else," I said with a wave of my hand like it was no big deal.

"Huh," was all he said, then he tilted his head and walked away, looking more confused than ever. Almost dazed.

It was one of the strangest encounters I'd ever had in my life.

And with the awkwardness that I usually brought to any situation, that was saying something.

Andie leaned in. "Who was that?" She was staring after him as he walked away, clearly as enamored as I was.

"I have no idea," was all I could say, even though it was the only thing I really wanted to know all of a sudden.

We ordered a drink, but I was distracted. The encounter with the guy had left me unsettled in a way I didn't quite understand. A woman selling Enhanced Memory disks came up to our table, snapping me out of my thoughts. Ami and Mason pulled out their cards and bought a couple. Ami took some kind of movie star scenario, and Mason wanted to try whitewater rafting. Andie decided to grab one too.

"Actually, I'd love a hot-air balloon ride," she said, handing over her card. "You only live once," she said to me with a little shrug.

And you know what? I decided she was right. After the disappointment earlier in the night, I really needed something to take my mind off everything. I glanced at the Memories the woman had left in her tray.

Which wasn't a whole lot.

The big-draw Memories always went first—things like the

hot-air balloon ride that Andie snagged, or amusement park rides and stuff like that.

Fun stuff.

But there were as many kinds of Enhanced Memories as there were kinds of memories, so there were still a lot of disks, just not any of the super fun ones.

"Can I interest you in a wine tasting?" the salesgirl asked.

I scrunched my nose. Wine was about the last thing I wanted to taste a bunch of.

"Maybe something a little more thrilling?" she asked, raising an eyebrow.

I knew she was trying to "sell" me, but I had to admit, she was pretty good at her job.

"I'm listening."

"Well—" she leaned in close "—people always go for the obvious stuff, but really, how many bungee jumps can a person do, right?"

I nodded. It was true. After my fifth one, the excitement had kind of worn off.

"But there are way more experiences than that. The spectrum of human emotion is enormous. It seems silly to only experience excitement."

"True," I said, intrigued.

The girl studied the disks that were left and finally plucked one out. "I think you should do this one. It has guaranteed intensity."

She held the disk up and the hologram started to play showing people screaming then dissolving into giggles.

"What is it?"

The girl gave me a conspiratorial smile. "A night in a haunted house."

"Are you serious?" I said. "That doesn't sound fun."

"Come on, you saw them giggling. It's scary at first, but in that way that a scary movie is awesome. Really gets the adrenaline pumping."

I supposed she had a point.

"Okay," I finally agreed and got out my phone to pay.

"You won't be disappointed. It's wild," she said, shooting me a wink and heading to the next table.

Everyone else had already started their Memories and had smiles on their faces, so I quickly settled into my chair to start mine. The disk was different than the ones I was used to. The ones Mom and Dad always brought home were heavier, more solid somehow. It was like this one was made out of mostly plastic, but no one else seemed to think anything was weird, so I inserted the disk into my EM device and the world went black.

Fear. That's all I could feel. I had a sense that something horrible had happened, but had no idea what. My heart pounded and I tried to catch my breath as I ducked down, crouching low, trying to stay out of sight, not knowing what I was trying to stay out of sight from.

And then the whispers started. From everywhere and no-where—frantic, urgent whispers. I couldn't understand what they were saying, just heard snatches of words like *forever... darkness...death.*

I put my hands over my ears, but the whispers didn't stop. Like they were coming from inside my head.

And then a scream.

It jolted me out of my mind, and for the first time I opened my eyes. There was nothing but darkness and it took a moment for my eyes to adjust. I was…in a closet, maybe? The scream had come from somewhere outside of my hiding space, but it was impossible to tell how far away it had been. It sounded both far and echoey, yet somehow close too.

A knife was clenched in my hand.

I loosened my grip a bit, my hand sore from grasping so hard. Every muscle in my body was tense, fear cinching me like an eighteenth-century corset.

For several minutes I sat, working up the courage to do something. It had been silent outside the closet for a while, and I couldn't sit there forever. I slowly stood and moved my ear closer to the door. Still nothing. I turned the knob carefully, making no sound, and peeked out. The room was a bit brighter than the closet, but still pretty dark. Shadowy outlines of furniture peppered the room, which appeared to be a library. I'd never been in a house with an actual library before, so I assumed it was some sort of mansion or something.

I took a few steps, trying to calm my breathing. It was so loud inside my head, I was afraid I'd miss other noises that might alert me to trouble.

And then, even though I hadn't moved a muscle, a book seemed to fling itself off the shelf. Another scream. Far away, but definitely still in the house. I clutched my chest, nearing the closed door of the room.

Get out. Just get out of this house in one piece, was all I could think. I gripped the knife harder, not entirely sure what I thought I was going to do with it, but still, it gave me enough courage to keep going.

As I turned the knob, I kept reminding myself that all I had to do was find a way out.

On the other side of the door was another large room, which was even emptier. There was some furniture, but mostly around the edges, with a huge open area in the middle. A ballroom?

I spent what seemed like an eternity wandering—the knife shaking in my hand—moving from room to room with a few hallways sprinkled in. Screams and thudding noises echoed intermittently. It was like there was an endless supply of spaces and the more rooms I went into and through, the more panicked I became.

Finally, I opened a door that gave me hope.

A long hallway stretched ahead, then a set of grand stairs leading down. I breathed a sigh of relief. The foyer. At least that's what I thought these grand entranceways were supposed to be called. It wasn't like any of my friends had giant foyers or anything.

I crept toward the stairs, the old floors creaking under my feet so loudly I might as well have been sending out a radio beacon. But I moved quickly, as light on my feet as possible, which was more difficult than usual.

Enhanced Memories could be strange. You didn't exactly have control over what actions you were taking—these were, after all, re-creations of actual moments that had happened in a person's life and couldn't be changed—but you could still think for yourself. It was disconcerting as I moved down the hall—my gait was off, like the person who'd made the memory was really tall, making my perspective feel off, and it took me out of the experience a bit. Which, given the circumstances of the Memory, was maybe a good thing. I wasn't sure I wanted to be totally immersed in this one anymore.

I made it to the stairs and began the slow descent, one creaky step at a time.

I just wanted the Memory to stop, but Enhanced Memories didn't really work that way. It wasn't impossible to break out of a Memory, especially if someone from the real world touched you or something, but inside the Memory there was a sense of not being able to get out. Like a dream, but way more real.

As I reached the ground floor, I began to get excited. So close to being out of this awful place, so ready to breathe some fresh air and have this experience done with.

I ran for the door, not caring anymore about the noise I was making.

But the running seemed to take forever. Five steps away... four...three...

And then something came at me from behind, knocking me over and landing on top of me. It was all I could do to get flipped over to defend myself.

I closed my eyes and swung the knife, screaming. It glanced off the thing on top of me once, then instinctively I changed the direction of the knife and stabbed. Over and over, praying to get out alive.

I was stabbing and stabbing, sickening, sucking flesh noises coming from the end of the blade—my own mind trying to fight the Memory—wanting the whole thing to stop. What if I could never "un-remember" the moment I became a killer? But I couldn't break all the way into the Memory either. I couldn't convince my mind it wasn't real. The experience was both distant and terrifyingly close at the same time, like I was floating somewhere outside of my body—a body that didn't even feel right—and it was all so out of my control.

And then suddenly all the lights in the foyer turned on at once, the light both terrifying and a relief.

And then…cheering.

Cheering?

I opened my eyes, the knife still deep in the side of the thing that had knocked me over.

A crowd gathered around clapping and smiling.

I felt sick. And crushed under the weight of the thing on top of me.

A pig carcass.

I let out a breath, a tiny cry of relief. I wasn't a murderer after all. But then came the anger. Whoever these people were, this crowd, wanted me to think that I was.

"Congratulations," someone said. "You've completed the Haunted House and come out a winner!"

A winner?

The voice continued. "You've faced your greatest fear and discovered how capable you really are!"

The people cheered some more.

Wait, what? This was all some sort of…contest?

I heaved the carcass off and stood, making my way the last few steps to the door, as if the world was stumbling around me instead of me stumbling through it.

The Memory ended.

I blinked back into the club, which was unsettlingly quiet. The music had stopped and all my friends were gone.

Only a few stragglers remained, all still wearing their EM headphones, lost in Memories.

I pulled the disk out of the EM device and checked the back. Most Enhanced Memories weren't that long, maybe twenty minutes or so, and I wanted to kick myself that I hadn't checked this one before I started it.

I had wasted two hours of my life on that awful...whatever that was.

5

I walked out of the club somewhat disoriented. It was strange—the EM clutter usually took only a second or two to shake off, but this was lingering, like a head rush that wouldn't go away. I held the door frame for a second on the way out, letting the world fall back into place.

The EM had really rattled me and all I wanted was to be at home where it was safe. But looking around I realized being outside a club after closing might not be the safest place in the world. A guy was looking at me, and I accidentally met his gaze. He started toward me.

Dammit. What made guys think some accidental eye contact meant *please come over*? I ducked my head and started moving in the opposite direction, but the guy was not deterred.

"Hey," he said, sidling up beside me.

I looked around, but the street was empty ahead. I had two choices. Keep going and very likely have this guy continue walking with me, or stop where I was and hope having other people around would be the safer option, even if it did seem like I was giving him more attention.

"Hey," I said, not really hiding my frustration very well. Not that I should have to.

He looked me up and down, which did not ease my mind. I didn't know if I would ever get used to this as I tried to hunch into myself. I couldn't remember it happening to me back home, but ever since I'd gotten here, people seemed to be looking at me more. And it wasn't like I'd changed or anything. Maybe I was just something new here. A novelty.

In any case, it did not sit well with me. Life was much better when I could fade into the background.

"So…" the guy said, drawing out the word as he continued to look at me without really looking at my face.

I took a step back.

He was undeterred. "You uh, heading out or something?" he asked, still not having the decency to look in my eyes while he was talking to me.

"Um," I said, not knowing what to say to that.

There was no good answer, really. If I said no, he'd want to hang out, and if I said yeah, he'd probably ask to go with me. Or "follow me to make sure I was safe." I never did understand how someone thought it made sense for someone to "feel safer" walking with a complete stranger—particularly one who was acting all possessive and creepy, but here we were.

I tried to swallow the building sense of dread.

"Hey, Nova," a voice said. "Are you ready to go?"

I looked toward the voice. It was him. The guy who'd called me by the wrong name inside the club.

"Uh, yeah," I said, then looked one more time at the guy in front of me. "Definitely."

I don't know what it was that made this other guy seem much less threatening, but I'd never been so happy to walk alone into the dark with a stranger before. Maybe it was because he had kind eyes, or that weird sense of familiarity I'd felt before, but I did not get the same creep vibe I was getting from the other guy.

After we'd walked a bit he looked back, making sure we were out of earshot. "Sorry, it looked like you could maybe use some help back there."

"Um, yeah. Thanks," I said. "I didn't really know what my next move was going to be."

He nodded. "I've seen that guy around here before, always talking to girls. But only the ones who are by themselves."

"Yeah, that was kind of a reckless move on my part," I said. "But my friends just kind of left me there. I'm sure it would have been fine. He was creepy, but probably wouldn't have followed me if I'd walked away."

He nodded, not looking all that convinced. Not that I blamed him. I wasn't all that convinced either.

"I'm actually glad I ran into you again. I'm sorry about—" he shook his head "—whatever that was in the club. I was caught off guard. I should have introduced myself. I'm Kade." He held out his hand and smiled, friendly now. Much less... caught off guard, I guess.

I was still walking, heading in the direction of home, and he kept walking right alongside me.

"Nova," I said, shaking his hand.

"Right. You said that inside. And I, like the fool that I am, totally left you hanging and walked away."

I smiled. Something about this guy was charming—the self-deprecation, the mild goofiness...those brown-gold eyes. Had I ever in my life actually thought of anyone as charming?

"So you're leaving?" he asked.

I looked around. We were still walking. "Uh, yeah, I guess. It's kind of winding down in there."

He nodded and put his hands in his hoodie pockets. "Just the diehards," he said, grinning. "Must have been a heck of an adventure you were on to stay so late."

I shrugged. "It was...an experience, I guess." Truth be told, I was kind of glad I wasn't walking alone after that Memory. "I didn't check the length of it before I started."

He nodded and we walked a bit.

"So uh, what kind of experience did you do tonight?" I asked him, trying to break the silence.

"Oh I didn't. I'm not a huge fan of Enhanced Memories. I come more for the crowd...the energy, the dancing."

"Really?" I said, unsure how to process that. It was kind of unheard of. Everybody loved EM.

"Sorry, no offense if you're into it. It's just not my thing."

"No worries, it's fascinating though. To find someone who hasn't jumped on the bandwagon."

"Oh I jumped on it," he said, taking a deep breath. "I jumped on it a little too hard."

"Too hard?"

"Yeah, it kind of overtook my life. And then when I decided to stop, I started looking around at everyone else and it...well, it's scary how fast it's growing, I guess."

"It's definitely taking the world by storm," I said, thinking about all the headlines.

"More like taking *over* the world," he said, and I looked at him, confused.

His face was so serious. But then he smiled and gave me a little nudge with his shoulder as we walked along. I briefly wondered if it was too overly familiar a gesture from someone I'd just met, but somehow it seemed natural coming from him. I was already starting to feel comfortable with Kade, which made me a little nervous since I was definitely not one of those people who makes others comfortable when they're around me.

"Interesting," I said. "I guess I've just seen a lot of good stuff come out of it." I shrugged.

"I didn't mean to offend you," he said quickly.

"You didn't." I smiled, hoping to lighten things. "It's okay to have differing opinions."

Even if his is wrong, I thought.

"I mean, I used to be totally on board with EM, but it kind of scares me now. After a while it made me feel…I don't know, not myself or something. But that doesn't stop everyone from telling me I'm missing out, so I get that it's an unpopular opinion." He looked at me, as if gauging my reaction.

"Does it seem like you're missing out?"

"Not really. I mean, I guess I can't say I've been to Paris or Berlin or like, the top of a mountain in the past couple months like everybody else, but the thing is, in the end, they can't truly say that either."

I paused, thinking about this, deciding if it was true. The

Memories felt as real as being there. "I guess *technically* they can't, no."

"Give me a real memory any day. The good, the bad, and the ugly—I want it all. At least I can have it with me forever."

That part was true at least. EMs tended to fade after a while. But I thought about the residents at Golden Acres and how their memories were fading. "I suppose," I said.

We walked a bit farther, and he sensed I was lost in thought. "What?"

"It's just that…forever is a long time." I looked at him, trying to see inside him.

He looked back—half smiling and half confused, waiting for me to continue.

I sighed. "I have a part-time job at this sort of…nursing home, I guess."

His face softened. "You keep getting more and more interesting by the second, girl who looks like Harlow."

I furrowed my brow wishing he didn't have to bring that up again. "So what's the deal with this girl that you thought I was. Are you in love with her or something?"

I pulled my coat tighter around me. I was being more forward than I normally would be, but that Memory had put me on edge. I felt like, I don't know, pushing at something. Poking. And even though I was monumentally intrigued by this guy, he still happened to be the thing that was in my line of sight.

But he laughed as if it was the most natural thing in the world for me to ask. "Definitely not. We were just good friends."

"Just good friends," I said, the suspicious tone still there, even though everything in me wanted to believe him.

"Yes, just good friends. We were way too different. She loved the spotlight and I was more of a 'keep to the shadows' kind of guy."

I squinted at him, a half smile on my face. "You don't really seem like a 'keep to the shadows' kind of guy."

He thought about that for a minute. "You're right—I guess I'm not. I like to be in the middle of the action most of the time. But—I don't know how to explain it—I want to be there, but I don't like, want people to know about it. I guess maybe things seem more important, more real, if you're not doing stuff just to see what everyone else thinks of you after you've done it. So yeah, you're right. I'm not a 'keep to the shadows' guy. I guess I'm a 'do what means something to you, not because of what other people will think of you' kind of guy." He laughed at himself.

I snuck another look at him as he laughed. He was the one who was becoming more interesting by the second.

Kade suddenly stopped, looking off in the distance.

"Hey," he said, a small grin forming. "Do you want to do something?"

"Something?" I said, raising an eyebrow.

He chuckled. "Yeah, like make a real memory."

"Aren't we doing that now?"

"Definitely," he said, "but I was thinking of something a little more…interesting."

I was basically up for almost anything if it meant spending a little more time trying to figure Kade out, but it was also really late.

"I'd love to, but I have to get home."

I didn't mention the fact that it was probably a bad idea to sneak off in the dark with a stranger, no matter how weirdly comfortable I felt around them.

He nodded, and a little jolt zipped through me when he looked a little sad. "Fair enough," he said. "Maybe we could start slower. Like a coffee sometime or something?"

"That sounds perfect. I actually know this really cool spot," I said, hoping it didn't sound like I was desperate to impress him, even though I kind of was.

"How about tomorrow?"

"Um, sure?"

He chuckled, I assume because of the way I had awkwardly phrased it like a question. Like I wasn't sure. Which, to be fair, I wasn't. My brain was telling me that this guy was a complete stranger, but everything else in me said that I desperately wanted to see him again.

"Perfect," he said. "Text me the place you want to meet."

He handed me his phone and I added my contact info. He sent me a text right away so I'd have his number too.

I nodded again, not wanting to say anything. Not wanting to screw anything up.

"So, you're fine to get home from here?"

I nodded again. "It's not far. I'm good, thanks."

"Okay, great," he said, gracing me with his amazing smile one more time. "Until tomorrow then," he said, turning to head back in the direction of the club.

I waited until he was out of earshot. "Until tomorrow," I replied quietly.

6

I couldn't fall asleep when I got home, thinking about Kade and tomorrow and that awful Memory I'd done at the club. I was still so tired when the alarm went off, but it was Saturday and I had work.

I got ready and put on my nametag. We didn't have to wear a uniform or anything, but the nametag was always mandatory. With many of the residents suffering from memory loss, it was a relief for them to be able to see your name. So much of the anguish of memory loss was the pretending—trying to cover up that they didn't know exactly who you were. I wasn't sure why people felt pressured to pretend there was nothing wrong when they knew that there was, but I suppose it's human nature not to want to mess up. Not that that's really a mess-up, but I guess to the residents it felt like one.

"Hey, hon," Genie said, giving her usual greeting as I clocked in.

She was only half paying attention to me, focused on the little TV in the staff room.

"Another one bites the dust," she said.

"Another what?"

"Another local business. The go-cart track."

"That's weird," I said.

She shrugged. "Not really. A lot of businesses are struggling. With everyone's entertainment dollars going toward Enhanced Memories, real experiences have gotten so expensive. Not to mention the unnecessary danger."

"Right," I said. I guess I had seen that the travel industry and anything that had even the slightest hint of danger or learning curve, which of course was everything, had been struggling lately. I'd just never really thought about it before. It made sense though. Why struggle with something or risk injury when you could safely do it and have the "memory" of being amazing at it right from the start?

"Ah well, that's the cost of technology, I guess," Genie said. "And Enhanced Memories really do even out the playing field. It's so much easier and cheaper. Everyone has access now."

"Definitely," I said, then thought of Kade. "Although it's kind of sad that all those places are struggling. Sure, Enhanced Memories are a lot easier, but what if they're different than real memories?"

Genie shrugged. "They don't seem different. Especially with authentic extracted Memories."

This piqued my interest. I'd heard of "authentic" Memories, of course, but I didn't get why they were such a big deal.

"I guess I don't really understand the difference. I mean,

don't the developers take the extracted authentic Memories and synthesize them so they can start mass producing?"

"Yes, that's mostly the way it is, but the authentic Memories themselves can also be purchased."

"What do you mean?"

"Like the originals. The ones that have been extracted directly from another person."

"What's the difference?"

"Oh it's huge," she said, her eyes widening. "The synthesized Memories are...I don't know how to explain it, sort of like once removed. They are very cool Memories of doing very cool things, but there is this...distance in them. Almost like a dream. Not exactly like a dream, obviously, but that's the best way I can explain it. But the authentic Memories, they are something else."

"So that's why they're so expensive?"

She nodded. "And also because they're so rare."

Suddenly I wondered if all the Memories my parents had were the authentic ones. Was it possible I'd never used a synthetic Memory until the night at the club? It did look different. Plastic. Cheap. Was that one of the reasons the whole thing had been so unsettling?

The house smelled amazing when I walked through the door after work.

I headed to the kitchen. It had been a while since Mom had made a home-cooked meal, and she seemed to have forgotten how. The kitchen was a crime scene of tomato splatters, unidentifiable spills, and bloody, oozing meat.

"Hey, honey," Mom said brightly, wiping a stray hair from

her face with the back of her wrist, her hands (and now fore-head) covered in flour. A thin sheen of sweat shone above her lip. "I'm making your favorite."

"What's the occasion?"

Mom's shoulders slumped and she pointed to the unused play tickets still on the fridge. "I was just sick when I realized what we'd done. I wanted to see you so badly."

I nodded, swallowing. A lump was forming in my throat.

"You were texting and texting and I just blanked…" she said, trailing off, blinking as her eyes started to water a little.

Which of course made my eyes start to water a little too. Mom turned back to the counter to knead her dough, giving herself—and me—a second to get it together. We weren't re-ally the kind of family who breaks down and cries in front of each other. I honestly couldn't remember the last time I'd seen my mom cry. Which just made trying not to cry even harder.

Mom cleared her throat. "So I really wanted to do some-thing nice for you. I know Dad and I haven't been the most reliable lately. And by the way," she said, turning to me again. "Thank you so much for how well you've been figuring all this out. Getting to school and work and helping out around here. I don't know how it's gotten so out of hand. Work… kind of takes over, I guess."

I nodded. "It's all good," I said, not really knowing what else to say.

Besides, I hadn't had lasagna in forever, and she really did seem to feel bad.

"We're so lucky to have such an independent daughter."

I smiled. "So where's Dad?"

"He's stuck at the office for a little longer, but should be back any minute. Food will be ready in about half an hour, and I've got something special for dessert."

"He's working on a Saturday?" I said.

"I know, sweetheart, but with the spring releases coming up, we're so behind right now."

I nodded. "Yeah, makes sense," I said, though I couldn't help but think that there was always some kind of release just around the corner.

I headed to my room to get some homework done, but my mind wasn't really on it. I know Mom meant for the meal to be a nice gesture, but it kind of got me thinking about how different things had been lately. Once I figured out the bus system, the rides to and from work kind of stopped. Nobody but me seemed to mind that it took forty minutes out of my day every time I had to do it, when a ride would have taken ten.

I sighed and shut my laptop. I still had twenty minutes before supper, and I really needed to just…get away for a bit. I slipped downstairs and rifled through some of the Enhanced Memories that my parents had brought home from work. EM was definitely the best way to get lost and not have to think about anything.

But nothing was catching my eye. It's funny how after you've done enough EMs, everything starts to feel a little boring. Even things like cliff diving and parasailing become kind of mundane. And then I remembered how much I had really loved my first EM. The zip lining.

I headed back to my room, dug out my old birthday gift, put it in the EM machine, and sat back to enjoy the ride.

The Memory went through all the same motions. Stand on

the tower feeling nervous. Except this time I didn't feel half as nervous as I had the first time—that first time I hadn't really understood what was going on and my emotions were so intense because of that unknown, but this time I already knew exactly what I was in for. And that tiny adrenaline moment when I was pushed off didn't give me that life-or-death rush that I'd gotten before. Sailing through the air was still amazing. I honestly could not get enough of that, but even still, the flowers didn't smell quite as sweet, and the wind didn't feel as exhilarating on my face.

I put the disk away, realizing why Mom and Dad were so busy all the time. If EM experiences faded like this after the first play, the need for increasingly exciting activities would be endless.

A twinge of guilt crept through me. What my parents were doing was important. A lot more important than me taking a little extra time to get to my job or some silly school play.

I opened my door and the scent of lasagna hit me again. And they were "making it up to me" on top of everything else. I might just be the most selfish person on the planet.

I headed downstairs as the front door opened.

"Sorry I'm late," Dad said, rushing to get his coat off and get to the table.

I thought he was going to come and kiss me on the forehead like we always used to do when we sat down as a family for supper, but he just gave me a quick shoulder squeeze and turned away, making me feel a little silly for even expecting it and being so needy.

"It smells delicious in here," he added.

We dished up and started eating. Things were quiet for

a while until Mom finally cleared her throat. "So, how is school going, honey?"

I shrugged. "It's fine, I guess."

"Lots of homework?"

"Not too bad."

"Good. That's good," she said, nodding, and Dad was nodding, as if he was *really* interested in my answer too.

We continued to eat, forks and knives clinking loudly against the plates.

"And work? How is work?" Dad asked after a bit.

"Um, yeah. It's good," I said, finding myself mimicking their head bobbing.

The clinking continued.

When the lasagna portion of the evening was finally over, Mom brought out the "big surprise." And really, it was only ice cream, but it was my absolute favorite ice cream.

Tiger Tiger.

"I had to go to three different stores to find it, but I really wanted to do something special."

"I haven't had this in forever." I was practically drooling, remembering how I used to love Tiger Tiger so much as a kid. I was embarrassingly touched that Mom actually remembered. Something about the orange mixed with the black licorice taste just…went together. I never wanted to eat one without the other.

I couldn't shove that first spoonful into my mouth fast enough.

Mom was looking at me so intently with this veil of expectation, but as I swirled the icy goodness around in my mouth, something was wrong. What used to be the most amazing, delectable flavor on earth tasted like I was putting straight dirt in my mouth.

I swallowed, trying not to show the disgust on my face. She had worked so hard for this and she had that expectant half smile on her face that parents get when they're hoping for a certain reaction.

I smiled.

Mom took a spoonful. "Mmm, this is just like I remember it. Takes me back to all those summers at the lake."

Weird. I thought for sure they'd changed it or something, but if Mom thought it tasted the same, then what? Maybe if I tried the flavors separately. I carefully spooned some of just the orange ice cream, which was absolute heaven. Then I tried the licorice on its own and there it was. The most disgusting flavor I could imagine. It didn't just taste like dirt, it tasted like burned dirt.

Was it possible my taste buds had changed that much? I guess that was a thing? I knew lots of people who liked stuff now that they didn't like as kids—but I didn't realize it went the other way too. So many things were turning out to be more complicated than I was expecting lately. I guess I thought I'd be, I don't know, better at life by now or something, that it would all be...different from the way it was turning out.

I didn't want to ruin the moment, so I carefully picked around the licorice and then leaned back in my chair. "I don't think I can manage the rest," I said, patting my stomach. Which was probably a little over-the-top. Our drama instructor was always saying how the worst acting was when it was too over-the-top, and suddenly I felt ridiculous.

But my parents didn't seem to notice, just kept smiling and enjoying the Tiger Tiger.

"Thanks for dinner, Mom," I said, heading straight upstairs to brush my teeth.

7

I got to the coffee place and grabbed a Soy Latte before I sat in my favorite spot. The place had a cool vibe to it, and smelled amazing with the in-house baking and constant coffee brewing, but it was the travel pictures hanging on the wall that were my favorite, and what I thought Kade would like so much. They were for sale, but none had sold in all the time I'd been coming to the shop. I sat below a picture of the Eiffel Tower and after admiring it for a second, wondering when I'd get back there again—I'd just had a Paris experience on EM the other night—I started scrolling through my phone while I waited, clicking on a video that caught my eye.

"In a new trend, employers are beginning to complain that they are unable to get some of their workers to come in for their shifts. Several workers have been calling in sick, though it's becoming increasingly evident that this wave of 'sicknesses' is really more of an Enhanced Memory absence. It seems some users are beginning to show signs of

distraction, letting their EMs get in the way of their responsibilities. More to come as this story develops.

"In related news, the government is proposing a new tax break for small businesses. As more and more of our expendable entertainment dollars are funneled into the Enhanced Memory sector, many other businesses are suffering, particularly locally owned recreational businesses such as ski facilities, swimming pools, and even movie theaters."

I stopped the broadcast as a couple sat nearby. The woman got super excited when she saw the pictures on the wall. "Oh! I was there last night," she said, beaming and pointing to the photo of Venice. "You know, when you were doing the drum solo thing. It was soooo beautiful. Floating on the canal was amazing!"

"Oh I should travel somewhere tonight," he replied, then stood to get a better look at the photos. "I haven't gone anyplace in a while. Maybe here," he said, pointing to a photo of the Great Wall of China. "The views must be spectacular."

"Is it bad it bothers me that they're bragging about going someplace even though it's not really real?" Kade asked quietly, sliding into the chair across from me.

I smiled. "It is a little weird, I guess, but I love the pictures."

He checked out the selection on the wall and grinned back. "Me too. This place is great," he said. "Really great."

A little zip of adrenaline rushed through me.

"So have you ever gone anywhere fun for real?" he asked.

"I wish," I said. "But my life has thus far been about as boring as they come."

He got a strange look on his face then. A searching look. I didn't mean to, but I shifted in my seat, unsure of what I'd done to warrant the look.

He shook his head. "Sorry. I was lost in my own little world there. I do that sometimes."

"I do that too," I said. "Sometimes I wonder whatever happened to daydreaming, you know?"

He nodded. "And imagination. It sorta seems like the world has lost some of that."

I thought about that day in class when Ms. Bailey was trying to get us to write something original. I didn't mention that I hadn't been able to come up with anything original either.

"It all seems to be a regurgitation of everything that came before it," he continued. "It's like we've all gotten to this place where our brains are too lazy to be creative anymore."

"But how important is it to even be that creative anymore? I mean, we have access to all these Memories now. We can just live it instead of trying to imagine the way things could be."

"So what happens with original thought then? There would never be anything new, anything to move the world forward. We'd all just be standing still."

I didn't want to agree with him, but I had to wonder. As a kid I used to paint pictures of places I had never visited, imagining what they would be like to see for the first time, but I hadn't even thought about painting for a while.

I glanced over to the corner of the shop where an older man was putting Enhanced Memory headphones on. "It really is everywhere now, isn't it?"

Kade twisted in his seat to see what I was looking at and sighed. "Yeah." He turned back and sort of gave his head a little shake as if shaking off some bad juju. "I'm gonna grab a coffee," he said, pointing at the counter. "I just wanted to let you know I was here, and then we got to talking, but that coffee is smelling better by the second." He grinned and jumped up.

It was super sweet for him to come over and let me know he was there. He could have easily waved from the counter or whatever, but he came all the way over instead. It seemed especially considerate. People didn't seem to do that sort of stuff anymore, at least not with me.

He came back with an extra-large cup.

"What did you get?" I asked, always the worst at small talk, but at least I was able to speak.

"Lavender Latte."

"I've never had one of those—are they good?" I asked.

"I've never had one either," he said, taking his first sip. He tilted his head for a moment, deciding. "It is good. I wasn't sure if I'd like it, but I always try to find something new wherever I go."

"That whole real memory experience," I said.

"Always," he said and smiled. "Am I that transparent?" he asked, smiling again. He had a really great smile.

"Not at all," I said. "Well, maybe a little."

He chuckled. "Yes, I probably am."

"It's kind of fascinating that you don't like EM," I said. "I don't think I've ever met anyone who thought it wasn't the best thing ever."

"Well," he said, taking a sip, followed by a deep breath. "I used to think it was the best thing ever, and that was kind of the problem."

I tilted my head. "What do you mean?"

He squinted at me like he was trying to decide something. "Do you really want to know?"

Honestly, I wanted to know everything about him. "I really want to know."

He let out a long breath. "I don't usually talk about it," he said, and shifted a little in his seat.

"You don't have to," I said. "I was just curious. But I don't want to make you uncomfortable."

"No, it's fine. That's the thing. I don't feel uncomfortable at all around you." He cleared his throat. "I kind of feel like I've known you for a while." He looked at me then, like he was watching what my reaction would be.

I nodded. "Yeah, it's weird. I usually don't get into conversations this deep with people I barely know, but it's like somehow I know you aren't judging me." I paused for a second. "Sorry, that probably sounds strange."

He shook his head. "It doesn't sound strange at all. I feel it too."

He looked at me then, and it was like he wanted to say something, but wasn't quite sure how to say it. "So," he finally said, "in the hopes that the nonjudging thing is true, I guess I'll just tell you." He paused for a breath. "I sort of used to have a problem with Enhanced Memory."

"Okay," I said, still unsure about what he was getting at.

"I used to like it a lot. Too much. It kind of took over my life."

I furrowed my brow. "You said that the other night, but I don't really get what you mean."

"Not a lot of people do," he said, nodding. "Even though EM has been around for a couple years, it's still pretty new and the long-term effects of it haven't really been studied."

"There are some studies going on," I said, knowing that Experion was always conducting research.

"True," Kade said, "but they haven't really been going on long enough to come to any definitive answers or conclusions yet."

"Okay, fair enough," I said, honestly not knowing enough about it to argue one way or the other.

"Anyway, I guess most people are able to handle it a lot better than me, but I kind of got addicted."

"Addicted?" I said. "It's not like it's a drug or something."

Kade raised an eyebrow. "And that's why most people don't think it can be harmful. But you know that rush you get when you first try a new Memory?"

I nodded. I knew it well.

"It's like…it gives you a little hit of adrenaline or dopamine or something. So it actually does work a lot like a drug would in your system."

I scrunched my face. "But it's not like it's altering your body chemistry like drugs do," I said.

Kade shrugged. "I actually think it sort of does, and that's what some of the studies are trying to determine now."

"But it wouldn't be on the market if it wasn't safe. And besides, everyone uses EM. Why aren't people all over the place having problems?"

He shrugged. "Unfortunately, I found out that I have an addictive personality. Like to the extreme, I think. Once I got that first EM high, I literally couldn't stop myself."

"But…it's just an experience."

He let out a slow breath. "Yeah, but it does something to me. It was like it reacted differently with me than with some people. Most people, maybe. I couldn't think about anything else besides getting that next Memory into my mind."

"That's absurd," I said, then realized how terrible that sounded. I felt tangled by his words—by him—like his ideas were so foreign, but at the same time, I couldn't help but wonder if that was only because I'd simply never thought about it. "Sorry, not absurd, it's just…I've never heard anyone say stuff like this before."

"I know, and it does sound extreme, but it really was extreme. I guess I was sensitive to it, maybe? And then it seemed like the more Memories I used, the more and more I needed them to get through the day. And after a while I literally couldn't stop. And I know a bunch of other people that have gone through it too. It's a small group, but it hits some people harder than others."

"I had no idea that could happen," I said, and if I was being honest, I was still a bit skeptical. And it wasn't that I didn't believe Kade—I did—it's just…Enhanced Memory was such a miracle. It helped so many people. It was kind of bizarre to think that it could hurt people too. "It's so weird. I've done EM tons of times and it seems so harmless."

He nodded. "It does. And that's exactly how it snuck up on me. I convinced myself for quite a while that I didn't have a problem, but then I started lying to everyone, saying anything that would get me to that next Memory. I was paranoid all the time. The guilt was really getting to me, I guess. It got pretty bad, actually. I stole money from my parents. It was…well, it was bad."

I squirmed a little in my seat.

"Sorry, that was way too much information. I shouldn't be bugging you with this."

"No, thank you for telling me. That couldn't have been easy for you. I'm…I don't know. Processing, I guess."

Kade smiled, and it was like the heaviness of the conversation lifted immediately. "But I figured it out and got help and now I just stick with regular old authentic experiences."

"That is kind of amazing, really. I don't know very many people that still…do stuff," I said, laughing at how ridiculous that sounded.

"That's me. The guy who does stuff," Kade said, grinning that grin that I could look at all day.

"Seriously though, thanks for telling me."

He shrugged. "I feel like I can trust you."

"Thanks," I said, and smiled even though I felt like a complete jackass.

Because after he had just trusted me with this hugely personal thing, there was no way I could tell him that my parents pretty much invented the thing he thought had practically ruined his life.

8

As I headed down one of the residents' hallways the next day, I ran into Clyde coming out of his room.

"Hey, kid, having a bit of a day?" he asked.

I smiled. Clyde was named exactly correctly because he was about as big as a Clydesdale horse, but as gentle as the tamest one you ever met.

"Just lots of things to think about, I guess," I said.

"Ah, it'll be okay, kid," he said.

I kind of hated when anyone else called me kid, but when Clyde said it, it wasn't so bad. It seemed more like one of those terms of endearment from his generation than it was a "label." Like, that old movie with the line "Here's looking at you, kid," almost like a playful fake punch on the shoulder should accompany it.

"I'm sure it will," I said.

"No really. It will be okay. I mean, here you are, in one

of the most wonderful places on earth, and with some of the best company you can keep." He grinned and glanced at me out of the corner of his eye.

I knew he was joking—that was the only way with Clyde—but still, it was like he didn't know how true it really was. It didn't matter how crappy of a mood I was in, when Clyde was around, that mood was going to do a one-eighty in a matter of minutes.

"Did I ever tell you the funny story about my daughter?" he asked.

He had indeed told me dozens of stories about his daughter, but every story was so fun to watch him tell, the way his eyes sparkled as he talked, I didn't even care if this was going to be one I'd heard before. I shook my head and sat on one of the benches that lined the hall. There were seating areas everywhere at Golden Acres and sitting for a chat was always encouraged, even for the employees.

Clyde sat down beside me and a reminiscent smile crossed his face. "Well, one day Jenny and I decided to go for a walk in the rain. Jenny's mom had just finished baking apple pies, but we weren't allowed to eat them, which really is a special kind of torture, especially for a four-year-old." He glanced at me. "And, if I'm being honest, it might have been a bit of a problem for a thirty-two-year-old with a sweet tooth too." He grinned, patting his belly.

I grinned back and settled into the chair a bit. This was a new story that I hadn't heard before.

"The pies were for when company was coming over that night, so my wife sent me out with Jenny, even though it was raining, so we wouldn't be tempted, smelling that cinnamon-sweet goodness. Or maybe she was afraid we'd dive into one of them while she was in the shower." He rolled his eyes dramatically, as if that were so uncalled for.

I giggled, suspecting that his wife was more than justified in her assessment.

"Anyway," Clyde continued. "Jenny and I were walking along in the park. She was wearing her little yellow raincoat and little yellow galoshes."

I smiled, imagining her tiny boots, running to keep up with Clyde's long legs.

"It was fall and the trees were all changing color and the path was scattered with leaves. Jenny and I made a game out of kicking the leaves, and then she'd run off the path and jump into a puddle." He turned to me again. "By this time we were both soaked from head to toe."

I nodded as he looked out into nothingness, remembering.

"And so we turned back around since I knew we'd both have to get changed before our company arrived, and just as we were leaving the park, a gust of wind came up and blew the most perfect maple leaf you ever saw from the tree above us, and the best part was, Jenny scooped it up right out of the air." He looked at me again. "You should have seen it. She was so excited."

My smile grew, imagining the joy on the little girl's face.

"And she clung onto that leaf as we walked, studying it like it was the most intriguing thing she'd ever seen. And finally she looked away from the leaf and up at me and said, 'What I don't understand…'" He paused his story to address me for a second. "She was always talking like that, you see, like she was a grown-up in a little kid's body. So smart, that one," he said, shaking his head a bit. "And anyway, she was holding this leaf and looking up at me, and said, 'What I don't understand, is how the leaves get all the way back up into the tree in the springtime.' And it took me a second to realize that she thought the same leaves that fell to the ground somehow climbed their way back up into the trees after winter, and it took everything in me not to start laughing because it was so darn cute, you know?"

I nodded. It really was pretty adorable.

"But somehow I kept a straight face and explained how new leaves grow every year, and this look came over her... almost like she was sad that the leaf in her hand wasn't going to get a second chance at life or something. But she was such a determined little thing, and she put that leaf on her nightstand, and I'd be darned if that poor thing didn't stay there for years after that."

He sat back and crossed his arms over his belly, an amused satisfaction on his face. I sat back and crossed my arms too, sighing happily.

"I like that story," I said. "It makes me think about when my dad and I used to go for walks out at the lake."

Clyde nodded, still looking utterly content. "Those are the best kinds of days," he said, and I nodded along with him.

Genie started down the hall toward us and Clyde jumped up, though it was less of a jump and more of a heaving himself out of the chair about as quickly as you might imagine an eighty-something person to do. "Better not let the boss lady see me slacking on the job."

I giggled. I couldn't help it. And today I'd needed something to giggle about, if only for a minute.

"Clyde, are you bothering poor Nova again?" she asked, beaming. She knew as well as everyone else that having Clyde around was never a bother.

"Only always," he said, making an attempt at running away, though it was more of an over-the-top jovial shuffle that made me laugh even harder, and Genie laughed right along with me.

"Don't forget you have your appointment in twenty minutes," she yelled after him.

He waved in acknowledgment.

"Where does that man get the energy?" she asked.

"I have no idea," I said, with a happy sigh. "I hope I'm as optimistic as he is when I'm his age."

"Don't we all, hon. Don't we all."

I really did have the best job in the world. Or maybe it wasn't the best job exactly—I mean, cleaning rooms and changing sheets wasn't particularly glamorous—but I definitely had the best people to work with. And that included the residents. Even the snarky ones. And sometimes they were the best because I always had hilarious stories to tell my friends—all names kept private, of course.

"What happened to you the other night?" I asked Andie when I ran into her on my break. "One second you were there, and the next you disappeared into thin air."

"I waited for a while," she said, "but Mom was texting me repeatedly, and it didn't look like your Memory was anywhere near being finished. I told Ami and Mason to wait for you."

I raised my eyebrows. "Well, they didn't."

"Are you serious?" she asked, looking mildly alarmed. "Was everything okay?"

"It was fine, mostly. I guess I felt a little abandoned because the Memory was, I don't know…unsettling."

"Ugh," she growled. "I am going to kill them. What do you mean unsettling?"

"Yeah, the waitress was running low and convinced me to buy it."

"Aw man, I'm sorry," Andie said. "I should have snapped you out of it. I just didn't want to ruin it for you. And now I'm kind of curious." She leaned in like she wanted to hear more.

I tried a smile but didn't really succeed. "It was…scary. Not like anything I've ever experienced before."

Andie snorted. "Well, welcome to the cheap end of the Memory spectrum," she said, like I was some kind of Memory snob or something.

I knew it wasn't Andie's fault, but something about that stung.

"Well, I better get back to work."

"Sure, have a good shift," I said.

She turned to leave, then turned back. "Hey listen, do you want to hang out later? Just you and me? I know you get off at three and I work until five, but if you want to after that?"

"Yeah, sounds good," I said.

"Later," she said, blowing me a kiss and heading out of the break room.

After my shift I didn't feel like going home, so I headed down to the games room, which was really just a big room with some tables and a bunch of board games and puzzles and stuff. Bea and Ruthie were in there fighting over who was cheating at Monopoly. Knowing them, my bet was that both were trying to cheat, but they also both knew all the cheating tricks, so no one was getting away with any of it. I wasn't surprised everyone else had left them to it. Bea and Ruthie could really conjure up a spat when they wanted to, and neither one was much good at keeping their opinions to themselves.

Honestly, the people here were nothing if not entertaining and the time passed quickly until Andie was done with her shift.

As we headed up the walk at Andie's house, the sound of kids laughing and running around reached us and I couldn't help but think about how much life there seemed to be in the house, and I wasn't even inside yet. Lately my house had been so quiet.

"I hope you're hungry," Andie said, opening the door. "I told Mom you were coming."

"Nova!" Mrs. Simmons said, coming straight over and engulfing me in a giant hug that lasted several seconds. Long enough for me to wonder when she was ever going to let go. We weren't really huggers in my family.

"I'm so happy to see you!"

"Uh, thanks," I said. "It's nice to be here."

"Come!" she said. "Sit down—tell us everything!"

Which of course made me immediately nervous, because I never knew what that was supposed to mean. Was I supposed to catalog everything I'd done since the last time I'd seen her? Or was that just what people said?

It turned out I didn't really have to worry about it because the table was far too chaotic for anyone to have a real conversation, which I kind of loved. So much food was passed around the huge table while Andie's three little brothers competed for their parents' attention.

"How are your parents doing?" Mrs. Simmons asked.

"They're fine," I said. "Busy."

She beamed. "They have such important jobs."

I nodded and tried to crack a smile. But for some reason a lump formed in my throat. I tried to swallow it down with another bite of food, but that just made it worse as I remembered back to when my parents didn't have such important jobs.

"More! More!" Andie's smallest brother, Jerry, said, thankfully turning the attention away from me, letting me find my composure.

When dinner was done, Andie and I headed to her room.

"Well, that was exhausting," Andie said, closing the door.

I smiled. "I think it was nice. Your family is so full of life."

Andie rolled her eyes. "Yeah, so much so that no one can actually have a real conversation."

"At least they try," I said, my voice getting quiet, making the moment a little weird. I cleared my throat. "Anyway, that food was amazing," I said, flopping on her bed as my phone dinged with a text. I sat up when I realized it was from Kade.

Any chance you might be up for that something I was talking about that first night at the club?

I couldn't help but smile. I'd had a good time when we went for coffee, but I wasn't sure Kade felt the same. There was a lot we didn't really have in common. Well, one thing in particular, but it was kind of a big one, especially considering his past combined with my parental situation.

I'm a little scared, lol. But sure, why not? I typed back.

Why not, indeed? ☺ How about Friday around nine? Meet me back where we parted ways that night.

Sounds good, meet you there.

By now I was grinning like a goofball. I put my phone down and looked up. Andie was of course staring at me with an amused expression on her face. "Who are ya texting?" she asked in kind of a singsong voice.

"Uh…no one," I replied.

And I don't even know why I said that, it was clear that it was someone, obviously, but my first instinct was to always keep everything to myself.

But Andie just rolled her eyes and simply said, "Spill."

"Um, I sorta met this guy," I started.

Andie got this look on her face and jumped onto the bed in front of me, crossing her legs, leaning her chin on her hands. Apparently I had her full attention.

I couldn't help but smile at her reaction. No words, just a full-on stare to let me know I needed to continue. "It was that night at Visto. The guy who thought I was someone else."

She grabbed my arm. "The cute one?"

I nodded. "He came up to me again outside the club. Kind of rescued me, really."

Andie released her grip and tilted her head, questioning.

"There was this guy there. He was kinda creepy. No big deal."

"What do you mean it was no big deal?" she said, jerking back a bit.

"It was fine, honestly," I said, trying to sound reassuring. "Really."

Her eyes were narrowed, but she relaxed a little.

"So anyway," I said, wanting to get to the good part, "he pretended he knew me so I had an excuse to get away and we just sorta walked for a while. But I don't know, the whole thing's kind of strange."

"I like strange," Andie said, her eyes going wide now, the creep guy thankfully forgotten.

I chuckled. "Get this. He doesn't like EM."

Andie leaned back at that one and gave me a face. "What does that even mean?"

"He just…doesn't like it. And I keep finding myself wanting to tell him he's wrong, but he's allowed to have his own opinion, right?"

"I guess, but that's super weird." Andie looked like she was searching for a way to reconcile what she was hearing. "Especially since, you know, the not insignificant fact that your parents like, invented it," she said.

"Yes, I am aware," I said, sighing. "But I…sorta didn't tell him that part yet."

Now it was Andie's turn to smile. "Well, this should be interesting," she said, raising an eyebrow like she couldn't wait to see how it all played out.

9

"Nova, can you hang back a minute?" Ms. Reiner asked as the class filed out after biology. I stopped and backtracked over to her desk, grabbing a rogue piece of crumpled paper off the floor and tossing it into the recycle bin.

Ms. Reiner looked surprised. "Thank you. Most people would have walked past it, deciding it wasn't their job."

I shrugged. "I was headed in that direction anyway." The rule at work was to never pass by a mess without addressing it, and I guess it was sticking.

"Well, I appreciate it," she said, smiling. "So what I wanted to talk about was your last exam. I have to say, I'm a little surprised. Did you not have enough time to study? I understand that you have an after-school job and I wanted to make sure you're not spreading yourself too thin."

"It's not the job," I said. "I studied a lot. I..." I sighed. "Honestly I just don't understand any of this stuff."

Ms. Reiner nodded. "That's the part I'm surprised about. I know you're a bright student based on the rest of your marks. I guess it's fascinating to me that you have parents that are renowned scientists, and yet you struggle with basic biology."

I backed a few steps away from Ms. Reiner's desk and leaned on one of the desks in the front row. "I know. And I try, honestly I do. It's just that…ever since I was little my parents were always talking about this stuff with each other, and as a kid I never knew what they were talking about, so I think I started fading the conversations out."

"Okay," she said. "Perhaps you could use your parents as a resource. Do you think they would be able to help you out with homework?"

I shook my head. "They're pretty busy."

"Of course," she said with a little smile. "Perhaps some of your peers then?"

"Uh…I don't think that's an option." I decided she didn't need to know that I didn't have any friends in the class, even though there were dozens of students. Honestly, I wasn't sure if I even knew a single name.

I let out a long breath. "I know I should be able to understand this stuff—it should be in my DNA or something, but no matter how hard I try, I can't make any of it stick. It's like my mind is programmed to drown this stuff out."

Ms. Reiner lifted her eyebrows. "Even when you're reading it on your own?"

I nodded. "I start reading a sentence and my brain literally won't register it. I think there's something wrong with me, like my brain is totally scattered," I said, slouching into myself.

She leaned back in her chair and folded her hands together.

"First of all, thank you for being so honest. It's not often that students tell me what they are really feeling or what stresses they're under these days. It's a cultural shift I've seen over the past while. Everyone seems much more concerned with putting up a false front, never admitting that anything could be wrong."

I sat a bit straighter, crossing my arms over myself. I realized she was right. Everyone was always making sure everything looked good on the outside. Never mind what was happening on the inside.

"And I don't think there's anything wrong with you. I think it might be that this material simply doesn't interest you. I'm not sure how your parents will feel about it, but maybe you could consider taking a different science next term, or perhaps finding another elective altogether."

"Yeah, maybe," I said. My parents would never know what classes I was taking anyway. It's not like they ever checked.

It had been a long day and the talk with Ms. Reiner had left me feeling like kind of a failure, and all I wanted to do was binge-watch some mindless TV. Of course, when I walked in the house, I realized that I couldn't even do that. The place was a disaster. There wasn't a single clean surface to sit on, not even the floor.

I headed to my room, putting my bag in my closet like I always did, and pondered just hanging out in my room, but now that I had TV on my mind, that was all I wanted to do.

Which meant the same thing that it always meant. Cleaning.

I thought of the single piece of paper I'd picked up in Ms. Reiner's class, and how she had been so appreciative.

"Fat chance of that happening here," I muttered under my breath as I piled old flyers and take-out containers into the recycle bin. I hung up approximately twelve million jackets in the hall closet and put the dirty dishes into the dishwasher, heading back to the living room to finally watch my show.

And, as luck would have it, Mom and Dad burst through the door just as I was getting comfortable.

"Oh, Nova! Good!" Mom said, looking a little startled that I was there.

I glanced around, waiting to see if they'd notice the difference in the living room but, as always, they were completely oblivious.

"We have exciting news." She looked at Dad and gave him a conspiratorial smile. "We booked the cabin for a couple nights! We leave day after tomorrow. We wanted to go over the weekend, but they were all booked up."

My first reaction was total deflation, and honestly I didn't even know why. Life was just different now. A quaint little family getaway didn't really feel like something we did anymore.

"What about the Memory release?" I asked.

"Oh don't worry about that," she said. "We've been way too busy lately and we just wanted to do something fun. Like we used to."

I nodded, all the reasons I really didn't want to go swirling in my head—I'd have to take time off work, I wasn't exactly caught up with homework at the moment and who knows where a few days off school would put me, but I also couldn't bring myself to disappoint them, so I ended up asking Genie for the rest of the week off and Wednesday morning we got up at the frigging crack of dawn and hit the highway.

In the summers I was always by the water, building sand castles until my feet and hands were wrinkled and Mom made me stop before it got too dark. My parents used to rent a cottage for a few weeks every August, not answering phone calls or allowing any kind of work, not even work conversation. Whatever I wanted to do was what we did. If I wanted ice cream, we had ice cream. If I wanted a boat ride, we rented a paddleboat for the day. If I wanted to hang out on the beach and read, we read—though now that I think about it, I wonder how many of the activities were "suggestions" from my parents that I was led to believe were my ideas. Not that it mattered. For those three weeks every summer, I had my parents to myself.

And here we were—in the same cottage at the same lake.

But things were different. Mom and Dad had definitely brought work, and lots of it. Mom was pulling out her laptop and Dad was unpacking a bunch of Enhanced Memories. Apparently beta testing didn't take a vacation.

"Are we going to go down to the beach?" I asked.

Mom looked up, then looked around the cottage like she had forgotten where we were. "Oh, yes, of course, honey. Just let us get unpacked and we can head down for a few minutes."

"A few minutes?"

Mom sighed. "I'm sorry, we just have to do a little work while we're here. Nothing big. And I promise it's going to get better once the next rollout is finished."

I nodded.

Dad started opening the little boxes that contained the Memories, anxiously making sure each of them had survived the three-hour car ride. Which was a bit ridiculous since they were metal disks that couldn't really get wrecked unless maybe a car ran over them or something, not to mention they were packed in little boxes designed to fit them perfectly, nestled in soft padding—but he was checking anyway.

"I'm going to go for a walk then while you get...unpacked."

"Have fun, honey," Mom said, giving me a little wave without even looking up from the computer.

Outside the air was colder than it had ever been when we used to come, although the trees were amazing with all their new blossoms. I stuffed my hands in my pockets and wondered how we were going to get a good beach day out of this.

My fears were confirmed when I got to the sand and the breeze felt even colder. There was exactly one other person there, sitting on my favorite rock, which I'd been hoping would be free, but since it was the only rock on the beach large enough to sit on, it wasn't much of a surprise that the spot was already taken.

She looked up from her phone directly at me. I knew her. Well, not really, but she'd been coming here with her family for years too—almost as long as we'd been coming. So many times as a kid I'd wanted to go up to her and her summer crew, but I'd always been too shy. Or scared, or whatever. How could I just go up to the group of them and what? Start talking? That would never work, because they were always laughing and chattering away, so in order to do that I'd have to totally interrupt, which was just so rude. I'd thought about going up and maybe waiting until there was a lull in the conversation, of course, but that seemed even worse. Then I'd just be standing there awkwardly and they'd probably all think I was eavesdropping, or worse, maybe they'd all stop talking and stare at me, waiting to see if I'd say something interesting, but of course I never really had anything interesting to say.

So I never approached them.

I smiled back at the girl and gave her a little wave. She waved back and tilted her head, maybe…curious? I thought about going up to her, but suddenly I felt exactly like I did all the other summers. Like I had nothing to say. And like it was too late now. We'd spent all that time essentially ignoring each other. Were we just going to pretend we hadn't?

I looked at my shoes. When I looked up again, she was coming toward me, smiling.

"Hey," she said. "I'm Daisy. You must be new around here."

I tilted my head, confused. Did she really not have any idea who I was?

"Uh…not really. My parents and I have been coming here for years—but yeah, nice to meet you."

"Really?" she asked, and gave me a look like she wasn't quite sure she believed me. "Huh. I thought I knew everybody." Then she shrugged. "Well, either way, welcome and all that."

She started walking away. "Yeah, thanks," I said, even though I was sure I'd been coming here longer than her and it should probably be me welcoming *her* back or something. I put my hands back in my pockets and hurried in the opposite direction, all the way back to the cabin. Moments when I remembered her from before kept invading my mind, like the time she was playing tag and nearly ran into me. She'd even said sorry on her way by. Or the time she smiled at me at the ice-cream place. I never tried to be the center of attention or anything, but it still stung that I was so utterly forgettable.

When I got back Mom and Dad were both using Memories. Maybe they had forgotten about me too. I sighed and picked up one of the books I brought for beach reading.

Which was pretty much how the rest of the cottage stay went. Me sitting indoors and reading, and my parents working, taking a few minutes here and there for a quick "hike," which basically consisted of a power walk ten minutes out and ten minutes back. We tried a paddleboat ride on the last day when the sun finally came out, but it was so cold we lasted only half an hour.

I slept the entire drive home.

"Nova!" Genie said when I got to work Friday afternoon. "How was the trip?"

I shrugged. "It was okay, I guess."

"Just okay?"

"Yeah. I mean, there was nothing wrong or anything, it's just…everything was different, I guess."

Genie nodded like she knew what I meant. Or at least understood.

"I remember what it was like to be your age," she said. "It's hard. It seems like everything is always changing. It's like you don't get to be who you used to be anymore."

I nodded. "I guess so," I said.

"It sounds like it might be more than that though," Genie said, the concern showing in her eyes.

I sighed. "My parents are so busy. And even when they're around they're not, you know?".

Genie tilted her head, confused.

"They're always testing Memories. It's like I don't get one second of their time."

Genie made a little noise and nodded. "That's not ideal, for sure," she said, putting her arm around me and squeezing a little. "But it's all just temporary, right?"

"Yeah, I thought that too, but that was forever ago."

Genie nodded, letting go of the embrace. "Your parents are very important people. And I know from experience that you're an incredibly independent person. I think they know they don't really have to worry about you." She forced a smile. "You're probably the only thing they don't have to worry about these days with all the other things they have going on. I'm sure if you found a little time to sit down with them and talk about it, they'd make more of an effort. I find that when I take a few minutes to chat with the residents, or with the staff, a little communication goes a long way toward solving problems."

I nodded and tried a smile, which didn't really work. I shouldn't have said anything.

"I know it's hard but, what they're doing, your parents… it's important work, and unfortunately that's going to mean some sacrifices on your part. The way I see people turning around here, being able to retrieve Memories…well, I only wish it had come sooner."

"Why sooner?"

"For the last few years of her life, my mother didn't remember me." She pulled in a long, slow breath. "And that's hard. When your own mother doesn't even know who you are."

"I'm sorry," I said, not knowing what else to say.

Not having my parents around as much as I wanted was annoying, but to have them gone like *that*...I couldn't imagine.

I should be grateful. My parents were good people—and were using those good hearts to help people beyond anything I could ever do. I had to stop all this thinking about myself and realize that this was so much bigger than me.

Down the hall, Mrs. Henderson's cane slipped and she was struggling to find her balance. She'd just switched from a walker to a cane yesterday, which of course was good news, but was apparently taking a little getting used to.

"Sorry, hon, I better help her," Genie said, jumping up and hurrying down the hall.

10

I didn't want to be the one who showed up first, so I found a shadowy place where I could watch our meeting spot and wait for Kade to get there, and maybe steal a minute or two to observe and try to figure him out a little more. But when he got there he just scrolled through his phone, calm as could be.

I made my way over to him, trying to look as un-nervous as he did.

"Hey," he said, his face lighting up when he saw me.

"Hey," I said back, smiling and hoping it was a normal smile.

"Are you ready?" he asked, a charming twinkle of mischief in his eyes.

"Uh, sure," I said, distracted by how ridiculous I was being.

"Come on," he said, starting to jog toward a chain-link fence near the end of the block.

Inside the fence was a huge building with a worn sign that said Schuster Ice Rink.

Kade stopped, his fingers weaving into the holes in the fence and his eyes lighting up.

"Um…what's the plan here?" I asked, afraid and excited about what his answer might be.

"Do you wanna go in?" His grin was huge, almost unsettlingly so.

"I don't know…"

"Come on. You don't know how long places like this are going to be around."

"True," I said, "but what's the plan? I don't want to break any locks or cause any damage or anything."

"We won't have to," he said, starting to climb.

I had never scaled a chain-link fence before and I wasn't sure I had the strength to do it. My first instinct was to say no—it seemed so dangerous, and not just the height, but shouldn't I be worried about tetanus or something?

Of course Kade was already up and over and I didn't want to look like a coward, so I put one foot on the fence and started to climb. It was actually easier than I thought to get to the top, but once I got up there, I had no idea what to do. Kade was already way ahead of me and on the ground on the other side.

"Climb a little higher and swing one leg over," he whisper-yelled.

"Easier said than done," I mumbled, then looked down.

Definitely a mistake.

I closed my eyes and breathed.

"You're doing great," Kade said.

And that was what did it. Even though I knew he meant well, there was nothing that got me more motivated than someone giving me a condescending, coddling little push. Like I was a child or something.

I took a deep breath, opened my eyes and climbed one more step, my leg swinging over, the momentum carrying the rest of me, and then one, two, three steps down and one last leap to the ground. Which was quite a bit more of a jump than I had anticipated. I stumbled back a step and landed right on my butt.

But Kade didn't even laugh. He just held out his hand and helped me up as if nothing at all was out of the ordinary.

"Come on," he said as I brushed myself off, my face burning.

He started to slow jog toward the building looking in every direction.

This was the first moment it occurred to me that there could be someone there. Like a security guard or something. I mean, the place didn't seem all that secure, it wasn't like there was razor wire at the top of the fence or anything, but it wouldn't be out of the question to have some security.

"Are you sure we should be doing this?" I whispered as I caught up to Kade.

He shrugged. "I mean, we just scaled a fence and are trespassing, so it's not like this is something we're supposed to be doing," he said, "but honestly, I doubt anyone would even care that much."

"Do you think there's security?"

"No. I don't think they could even afford security, to be

honest. This place looks like it's halfway to falling over. I bet it will close down completely in the next few months."

He was right. The place was kind of a disaster. The only way I could tell it was still in operation was the gentle hum of some generator somewhere, which I assumed kept the ice frozen.

"Here," Kade said, ducking into a shadow close to the building.

There was a window within reach and Kade grabbed an empty five-gallon cooking oil pail from the pile of random recyclables that was spilling out of a nearby dumpster. I couldn't help but wonder if maybe the place couldn't even afford pickup anymore. He set it on the ground, climbed up and started wrestling with the window frame.

"It's tight, like swollen or something, but it's not locked."

I started looking around to see what else might be hanging around that could be handy. I didn't find anything in the recycling dumpster but there was also a pile of old construction waste—the place really was a mess—that had a piece of sturdy metal about three feet long and was potentially narrow enough to jimmy under the sill for leverage.

"Try this." I handed him the metal.

I was still whispering even though if there had been anyone around they would have definitely heard us by now. Kade was trying to be careful, but he was no ninja when it came to the sneaking-around part. More like a clumsy elephant. Which was funny, not to mention adorable, since he was the one who seemed to be much more familiar with breaking and entering than I was. I guess he knew how to pick his targets.

With one last heave using the leverage of the metal, the

window finally loosened its grip and slowly but steadily slid open.

Kade scrambled inside and whispered my name.

"It's all good. Get in here."

I stepped onto the pail and heaved my way ungracefully halfway through the window with my arms and torso on the inside and legs still dangling outside. I was very aware of how my butt seemed to be pointed right at the sky. I continued to wriggle until Kade eventually took pity on me—still, to his credit, not laughing—and helped pull me through. I could only imagine how heavy I was, all my weight on him as I finally got my legs through.

The place was dark. Like really dark.

Kade fumbled around and grabbed my hand, pulling me deeper into the building. His hands were warm and soft and I inhaled the moment, my mind trying to tell me this was a bad idea, but my body thinking it was so, so good.

As we explored, Kade opened a few doors here and there. I had no idea what we were looking for but he seemed to be on a mission.

"Yes!" he finally said. "What size?"

"What size what?"

"What size shoe do you wear?"

It took a moment for my eyes to adjust and realize that we were in the place where the skates were rented out.

"You mean we're actually going to skate?" I asked, trying not to sound as alarmed as I was.

"Um, you thought we were going to break into a skating rink and do what? Bowl?"

"I mean…I thought that maybe the breaking-in part would

be enough of an adventure or something. Actually strapping blades to our feet seems slightly…dangerous."

"Nova," he said, letting go of my hand for a second. I was pretty glad it was so dark and he couldn't see my automatic reaction to reach for him again, nearly grabbing his arm before I realized what a freak I was being. "It's not the breaking and entering I'm into. It's the experiences."

"So you've done this sort of thing before?" I asked.

"Yeah. Lots of times." He said it like it was no big deal.

It did not seem like no big deal to me. But being around Kade made me feel like I could be braver than I was. I let out a slow breath. "Eight," I said.

He grabbed a pair of skates off the shelf and set them down on a bench. My eyes were starting to adjust and I sat without much trouble, grabbing the skates.

"You have to tie them tight," Kade said, correctly guessing that I had never done this before.

The blades gleamed up at me. They just looked so…sharp.

I picked one up carefully, keeping the blade pointed away, obsessively thinking about what would happen if this thing, this heavy boot with a freaking blade on it, fell on me. I swear it could chop a toe right off.

My hands shook as I set it gently on the floor and wriggled my foot in. Tying the skates was no easy feat either—it seemed like there was about a mile of lace on each skate. Kade finished way before me and came over to help. He began pulling the laces on my skates even tighter than I had been tugging. I kinda felt like a little kid with someone kneeling in front of me, helping me, but Kade had them tied and ready to go so much faster than I ever could have.

"Okay, so…will you do me a favor?" he asked as he helped me stand.

I wondered if it was a bad sign that I wasn't even close to the ice yet and I was already wobbly.

"Sure," I said. I guess I should have asked what the favor was, but the fact was that I had already committed a crime with this guy, and I doubted whatever he would ask could be any worse than that.

His face got serious suddenly. "So I kind of have this thing that I do."

"Okay," I said, tentative.

"I have this social media video channel," he said. "And I film the stunts that I do."

"Is this considered a stunt?"

He shrugged. "I think so. I mean, we're in an arena after hours."

"Right. So…do you think it's a good idea to post a video of yourself breaking the law? Seems kinda…risky."

"Totally," he said, then grinned. "That's why I wear this."

He fished something out of his jacket pocket and pulled it over his head. It was a lightweight spandex-type material that covered not only the top of his head, but his entire face too, including a sort of mesh over his eyes. And of course I'd seen hats like that before, usually for Halloween, but Kade's had the face of a joyful puppy on it, making it impossible to do anything but laugh.

"I can't decide if that's the cutest or most disturbing thing I've ever seen."

"We'll go with cutest," he said. I could tell he was grinning even through the mask.

He pulled on a pair of thin gloves. "Can't be too careful," he said.

"You're really that worried about being recognized?" I asked, thinking he was going a little overboard.

He shrugged. "The less people know about me, and what I look like, the better."

I raised my eyebrows but didn't press any further. "Well, I don't want to be on film either," I said, wondering how concerned I should be.

"No, definitely not," Kade said. "You totally don't have to. You'll be the one holding the camera so you shouldn't get on film, but…" he said, fishing something out from his other pocket, "in case there are reflections or something, ta da!"

He held up another hat/mask, this one with the face of an adorable kitten.

I couldn't decide if the guy was ridiculous or genius. Even if we got caught, it would be impossible to be mean to someone in a cute animal mask.

At least I hoped.

Kade handed me his phone, hit the record button, and grabbed my hand, gently pulling me. I tried to keep the recording as smooth as possible as we wobbled our way down the dark hall, which was no easy feat considering I kept bumping into everything, including Kade and the walls. Eventually I discovered it was actually easier to see where I was going if I watched through the screen on the phone. Kade's camera was amazing, picking up so much more light than my eyes could.

By the time we made it to the actual ice surface, my ankles feeling like Jell-O, we were laughing so hard from all the stumbling, though I think Kade was only stumbling because he was working so hard to keep me vertical.

I couldn't remember the last time I'd had so much fun in real life. I would bet that Kade could make almost any situation fun though. It was like he radiated it.

In the darkness, Kade fumbled with the latch on the gate for a bit, but it finally swung open. The air was crisp and cold, even fresher than outside. Kade took a step onto the ice surface, still holding my hand.

"No way," I said, letting go. "If I go out there with this—" I gestured to his phone "—there is no way it's leaving this place in one piece."

He chuckled. "It's fine. It has one of those 'you can run over it with your car' cases on it."

I shook my head. "I'll film from here for a while."

Honestly, I was still getting used to walking on the damned skates. I couldn't imagine purposely going on actual ice with them.

"Fine," he said, "but you're not leaving until you come out here for at least ten minutes."

"Once we're done filming," I promised, though I secretly hoped he'd forget.

As much as I wanted to be that person who pushed themselves to do the scary things, it was more of a lifestyle aspiration than it was an actual desire. I could imagine what it would feel like to be out there gliding along on skates, and that was enough for me. Besides, if I was that into knowing, I could easily find an EM to get the experience safely.

Of course Kade looked like he had done this a million times, gliding with no problem whatsoever.

"Hey, Real Memory Makers," he said to the camera. "This is Real K coming at you from an amazing real-life arena. The location is, as always, going to remain undisclosed. We don't want all you Real K followers to know how easy it was to sneak into this place now, do we?"

Kade raced around the skating rink, doing a few tricks, nothing too daring—it probably paled in comparison to what Enhanced Memories could download into your brain—but there was something so real about it. Making in-the-moment decisions about which way he wanted to go or what trick he wanted to do next. It struck me then how he was *creating* this memory instead of being led by it. Enhanced Memories definitely felt real, but it wasn't this kind of real. An EM led the user, almost like a mental string being pulled into the emotions the person who'd made it had been feeling. It suddenly felt a little...manipulative.

Kade finished his stint on the ice and was skating back to me, still grinning wildly, like he was having the time of his life. He took the phone from my hand and stopped the recording as we took our masks off.

"Your turn," he said, his eyes practically sparkling.

"I really don't think I'd be any good at—"

"And that's exactly why you should do it," Kade said, taking both my hands this time and pulling me the last couple steps toward the ice.

He held on tight as I took my first tentative step onto the surface and I would have fallen instantly if he hadn't steadied me. I guess the good news was that in order not to fall I'd stepped out with my other foot so now I was fully on the ice.

Although that might have also been the bad news.

"There you go," Kade said, smiling, like it was totally normal that I was clinging to him like my life depended on it.

"I'm gonna fall," I said, and even my voice was shaking.

"I've got you," he said and skated backward a bit, pulling me with him so that I was gliding a little. "You've got this."

I thought I knew what it would be like to skate, like it would kind of be like doing a moonwalk only going forward, but this was nothing like that. This was more like how I imagined flying would be. If you could fly at the snail speed we were skating, that is. I was still terrified of falling, but the sensation was like nothing I'd ever experienced, and to my surprise a slow smile crept across my face. "I'm not so sure about that," I said, but a wild laugh escaped anyway.

He made a murmuring sound. "I like that," he said.

"What?" I asked. I'd been focused on watching my feet, but I risked a glance up. And his expression was…strange, like he was figuring something out.

"I like that you feel it all. Like obviously you're scared to death right now, at least judging from the claw marks in my hands," he said.

I risked one more glance up, but thankfully he was grinning. I nearly lost my balance again and dug in even harder.

"But you're feeling the joy of it too. You let yourself be in the moment. You feel it all."

I wasn't quite sure how someone was *not* supposed to feel it all, but I gave him a crooked smile anyway.

He smiled back. "There you go," he said, and loosened his grip on my hands.

I grabbed onto him even harder. "Don't let go."

"Ah, I've got you so hooked on me already that you can't let go," he teased. "Everything is going according to plan."

I let go of one hand and gave him a playful swat on the chest, which of course nearly took both of us down. He quickly grabbed my hand again and steadied us. I laughed, and then like I often did I stopped, letting it fade into a smile. As I looked up he looked into my eyes. It was an intense look. A look that said he was thinking about doing something but wasn't sure if he should. His gaze flickered to my lips and my heart nearly stopped.

And that's when it happened.

My feet came out from under me and I went down. Hard.

The moment had stolen all the concentration it had been taking to stay up and in less than a second I could feel the cold—not to mention the pain—on my butt.

And I had taken Kade down with me. We looked at each other for a pause then burst into laughter, and I didn't even care how wild it sounded. With all the nervous energy and tension and all the other things that had been zipping around in my mind in the split second before the fall, it was good to let it all out, and it was like I couldn't stop no matter how hard I tried.

Eventually Kade helped me up again and we hobbled our way to the gate, where he helped me back onto solid ground—as solid as ground could be under two thin blades of metal—and we headed back to change into our shoes.

"Thank you for this," I said as I eased the skates off.

Something about being out of the skates was both a relief and a disappointment, like coming home from vacation.

We snuck back out of the arena undetected and I let Kade

walk me home, no longer worried whether I should trust him. We talked about travel and even though I didn't have any good stories, he told me about the time when he was little and got to visit his father's family home in India and then a year later, the place his mother grew up in Britain. And even though I wanted to hear about every second of the trips, I changed the subject to music pretty quickly, making sure to steer the conversation away from my parents.

As we neared my house, we said good-night uneventfully before I headed off to bed.

But I wasn't able to fall asleep.

Instead, I kept replaying the "almost" moment on the ice over and over in my head, wondering what might have happened if I hadn't fallen.

11

I woke to a text from Kade. My heart jumped, hoping maybe he was going to ask to meet again, but it was…well, I wasn't sure what it was. Regret, maybe?

Hey Nova, thanks for hanging out with me last night. I'm sure it's obvious, but please don't tell anybody about me and what I do, okay? I could be in a lot of danger if my identity gets revealed.

If his identity gets revealed?

It seemed like such a strange way to word it.

Don't worry, I never would, I texted back, mostly to try to ease his fear. I wanted to say so much more, but texting was never really my strong suit. People always seemed to read my tone wrong and I didn't want to risk that with Kade.

I didn't really understand what the big deal was, I guess. It was cool what he did.

I looked up Real K's video channel, hoping it would help me figure him out.

I was shocked to see how popular his channel was. He had over 400,000 subscribers. He hadn't released his newest video—the one from last night—but there were dozens of others. Almost all the comments praised him for being so brave and true to his promise to make real memories. Oddly though, there were a few comments that warned him.

Stop doing this man, you're going to get hurt, one said.

Another warned about *the dangers of the Memory people coming after him*, which didn't even make any sense.

I shut the app down when Andie knocked on the door. Mom and Dad were gone, no doubt at work.

"Spill," she said before she even sat down.

I rolled my eyes—mostly to stop the ridiculous grin that I knew I wouldn't be able to hide.

"There's nothing to spill," I said. "He's nice."

She stared at me. "He's nice," she said. "That's all you got?"

I shrugged.

"Well, what did you do?" she asked.

I was about to tell her everything—the skating rink, the almost kiss...and then I remembered Kade's text. "We just um, walked around for a while."

"You just walked around?"

I nodded, glancing at my phone, then realizing if I suddenly got too interested in it, she'd get suspicious.

"Well, do you think you'll see him again?"

I finally let the grin loose. "I hope so," I said. I had to give her something, after all.

"I knew it," she said. "You really like this guy."

"I do," I said, cringing a little in embarrassment. I knew there wasn't really anything to be embarrassed about, but I hadn't really crushed on anyone like this before.

Andie beamed at me like a proud parent. Or, you know, a proud best friend or whatever.

"Can we…I don't know, change the subject or something?"

She probably sensed that she wasn't going to get anything else out of me—or more likely, probably thought there wasn't anything interesting *to* get out of me, so she did, mercifully, let it go. "It's so quiet in here," she said, looking around. "Must be nice to have the house to yourself so much," she said. "And the bathroom. There are always like a million people fighting over the bathroom in my house."

I shrugged. "Yeah, it's good, I guess."

Andie raised her eyebrows. "You guess?"

"Maybe I'm just not used to it or something. My parents have always worked, but lately it's like they're working all the time. And even when they are here I never see them."

"Why not?"

"They're always 'beta testing,'" I said, using air quotes.

Andie grinned. "You don't think it's legit?"

"No, it is. I just don't see why my parents have to do it all themselves."

"Well, EM is kind of their baby."

I nodded. Indeed it was. Their new baby now that their old one had grown up.

"At least they're not all over your ass all the time like mine are. They worry way too much. You're so lucky your parents trust you. I can barely leave the house without mine grilling me about where I'm going and telling me what time I have to be back."

"I think it's nice that they worry," I said.

She let out a huff. "Yeah, so nice that I have to be home by one thirty, all worried that I need time for my schoolwork."

"Yeah, I guess," I said. It didn't seem like my parents were necessarily all that worried about my schoolwork lately, or anything else about me for that matter. "Anyway," I said, not wanting to think about it anymore. I honestly just wanted to get away from all my thoughts, even for a few minutes. "Wanna do a Memory?"

Andie perked up. "Ooh, yeah. How could I pass up a free ride on the Memory train?"

There were always Memories all over the house. Honestly, it was a problem. Every available surface had some Memory or another on it. Andie grabbed one off the side table without even having to get up.

She opened the box and held the disk up. A moment later the hologram began to play.

"Ooh, looks like a hike," she said, squinting. "Maybe Machu Picchu?"

"Oh yeah, that one's good," I said, having already sampled it the other day.

Andie put the disk in her EM device and I looked around for a Memory I hadn't tried yet. It took me a while to find one, but in the kitchen by the fridge there was a box I hadn't noticed before.

I flipped open the lid and lifted the disk out.

The image began to play.

But it just looked like someone walking. And they were sort of hazy, like they were stuck in a fog or something, which of course made me curious. I brought the disk out to the living room where I could sit near Andie so she knew where I was if she got finished first.

I pushed Play on my EM device.

Inside the Memory, I landed on a beach. It was gorgeous, though the temperature was a little cool for my liking, especially considering I was wearing a bikini. I wanted to cover myself immediately—bikinis were not really my comfort zone, but that was the way with Memories. You couldn't choose what someone was wearing when they made a memory.

To my right, a giant blow-up ball—the kind a whole person could fit inside—was sitting on the beach not far away.

"Next!" someone yelled from over by the ball.

I looked around, realizing I was at the front of a lineup, so I headed over to the voice.

"Welcome," the man said, giving me a hundred-watt smile. "Have you ever been in one of these balls before?"

I shook my head.

"Well, it's perfectly safe. All you have to do is get in and walk."

"Okay, walk where?" I asked.

"Anywhere you want. The material this baby is made out of is some of the strongest plastic on earth. And it's one hundred percent buoyant."

"Buoyant?"

He grinned even wider. "Most people prefer to head out on the ocean for the first part of their excursion."

I looked at the ball and then out to the water. Sure enough, a few of the same balls were already out there, floating away.

"Interesting…" I said as he led me inside and sealed the door up.

"Have fun," he said. At least that's what I think he said. The whole thing was pretty muffled from inside the ball.

The floor was rounded and I wasn't quite sure how I was supposed to walk without having it tip over every which way, but I didn't have much time to think about it since Memories plowed ahead whether I knew what to do or not.

The first few steps were pretty tentative, but it was actually a lot more stable than I thought it would be.

My ball crept toward the water, hitting the sand that was wet from the waves, then all of a sudden I couldn't feel the resistance of the ground under my feet anymore. The ball bobbed with the waves and I kept walking, farther and farther out, letting out a giddy yelp when a yellow-orange fish swam right under me.

The sensation of being on water was strange and exhilarating. I thought it would be a bit like zip lining—as if you were flying—but it really wasn't. With that you could feel the wind in your hair, but with this it was like you were in your own little cocoon, warm and immune from the elements around you. Which was maybe the strangest part of the whole thing.

I mean, walking on water! That was super cool, but it was almost as interesting to be inside that bubble thing, to experience the world in a whole different way. Like nothing could touch you. There was a sense of invincibility.

I walked for a long time, heading farther and farther out to sea until the people on the beach looked like little bugs zooming around. Eventually I turned back and headed to shore. I had the urge to stay longer, but the Memory was only as long as the Memory was, and this person had chosen to head back in, so that was what I had to do too.

On the way back in, I started to run, or rather the Memory made me run, which was even more fun than the walking. The ball bounced lightly on the surface of the water, until I got going a little too fast and my feet, or the ball—one of them—got ahead of the other and I started going sideways and before I knew it I was bouncing around inside there like a rag doll, landing on my shoulder, my knees...my head.

It was ridiculous, and a bit embarrassing, and so much fun that I couldn't stop laughing.

All too soon, the Memory was over and I came back to the real world, blinking.

The first thing I saw was Andie, looking slightly terrified.

The second thing I saw was Mom and Dad standing there. Dad's jaw was clenched, and Mom had this wariness about her, rubbing her hands together like she wasn't quite sure what might happen next.

"What is going on here?" Dad asked, his teeth barely unclenching.

"Um, hi, Mom, Dad. You know Andie."

Andie gave them a sheepish wave and I couldn't help but wonder how long they had been standing there staring at each other before I came out of the Memory.

"What is going on here?" Dad repeated.

"Nothing," I said, trying to figure out what they were so

mad about. It seemed impossible that Andie would have done something offensive. "Andie and I were just hanging out."

Andie was putting the Memory disk she had used back in its box, snapping the lid shut. Mortifyingly, Dad stomped over and grabbed the box right out of her hand.

"I didn't realize you were having a friend over," Mom said.

"Sorry, I didn't think to ask. I guess I didn't think it was a big deal."

Dad stepped over to me and held his hand out. At first I had no idea why he was standing there and I just sat for a second staring at his hand. Then I realized he wanted the Memory disk. I ejected it from my machine, put it in the box, and handed it over.

"These are company property," he said, his voice softening a little now. "They are not to be played with."

Played with? I hadn't really "played" with anything since I was about ten.

"Um, okay. Sorry. You never said anything, so I guess I thought—"

"Well, you thought wrong," Dad said, looking around and collecting the rest of the tiny boxes that were littered around the room. Once he was satisfied he got them all, he turned to me. "I'm sorry if I seem abrupt. These are just…well, it's our responsibility to keep them safe."

I nodded. "Okay."

It was a miracle I got a word out at all.

"Why don't you two go to your room, Nova? I'll bring a snack up."

"Uh, sure," I said.

I wasn't sure if Andie would even want to stay after the

display she had just witnessed, but thankfully she followed me up the stairs.

Once the door was shut, she turned to me. "What was that all about?" she whispered.

"I have no idea," I whispered back. "I've never seen them like this. I mean, I guess I never really asked if I could use the disks, but they leave them lying around all over the house."

"Well, news flash," she said. "I think they care."

"No kidding. But why? They never said anything about them being secret or anything."

Andie shrugged. "I guess they could get in trouble if one of them got wrecked or something?"

"Maybe. But how would a Memory disk get messed up? It's not like we were stomping on it."

"I have no idea," she said, shaking her head. "But honestly, that Memory was so good. I can kind of see why they'd want to keep them to themselves."

My forehead crinkled. I didn't think it was that they wanted to keep them to themselves. There must be some company policy or something.

A soft knock came at the door. I rolled my eyes, then went to the door to open it for my mom.

"Here we go," she said, bringing in a plate of cookies.

I kid you not.

Cookies. Like we were five or something.

"Looks great," Andie said. "Thanks so much, Mrs. Reynolds."

"You're very welcome," Mom said.

And Andie being Andie jumped right up from the bed and grabbed a cookie off the plate. "These look amazing."

And then Mom said something, but she suddenly sounded far away. A flash of something zipped through my mind. I was speeding through the air, but it was dark. Bright lights everywhere. Laughing. Screaming, but in a good way. A searing pain stabbed behind my eye. I squinted, pressing my palm on my forehead.

And just as quickly, it was gone.

"And I'm sorry about that downstairs," Mom continued. "We were…caught a little off guard, I guess. We hadn't really told Nova that the Memories we do beta testing on weren't supposed to be circulated outside of me and her father."

I shook the weirdness out of my head. "I'm sorry, Mom—I honestly didn't know."

Mom forced a smile. "It's fine. Don't worry about it. Just… leave them for us to test from now on, okay?"

"Yeah, of course," I said, and leaned in to hug her.

I guess I wanted to shake off the tension and make sure everything was right again, but I guess Mom didn't catch what I was trying to do and awkwardly shoved the plate of cookies in my hand. She smiled again and backed out, closing the door behind her and that was the end of it.

Until a few days later when a construction crew came in and started work on the spare room, which my parents decided to turn into a "Memory Room."

And I don't know why it bothered me so much—they were probably finally getting around to organizing everything— but it all made me feel even further away from them than I had been.

And it seemed like the distance was growing.

12

Sorry if my last message was a bit much...I guess I get a little paranoid sometimes, Kade's message the next day said.

No worries, I texted back, trying to play the cool girl. Which was entirely ridiculous, but there I was anyway. Kade was unique, interesting, fun...basically all the things I wasn't. I mean, I would love to follow him on his escapades, but he probably had about twelve people waiting to go on those adventures with him at any given time. I just happened to be there for the last one.

Still, he was the one who texted me. I took a deep breath and started typing.

I don't have much to offer in the way of adventure, but...do you want to hang out again? We could maybe grab another coffee or something?

I stared at my phone as the little dots popped up, signaling that he was typing. Then they disappeared. But then popped up again. He was stalling. Not sure what to say. I almost had myself convinced that he was going to say no, when finally a reply came.

How could I resist?

I could almost see the flirty smirk on his face. At least I was telling myself it was flirty.

You can't ☺ Free this afternoon?

Wouldn't miss it.

Cool. Meet at the coffee shop in an hour?

I'll be there with bells on.

I kind of loved the way he talked. Like who used the term *with bells on* anymore? Although knowing what little I did about Kade, maybe he meant it literally. The thought of him jingling along as he walked put an instant smile on my face.

Kade was already at the coffee place by the time I arrived.

"Hey," I said, sitting down with an Iced Cappuccino.

After our last coffee date, I decided to take a page out of Kade's book and order something new. I took a sip, expecting it to be sweet, but it was decidedly not.

"Hey," he said back, with a million-watt smile.

"So I went to your video page," I said, after forcing myself to swallow the incredible bitterness. "Your subscriber numbers are huge."

He shrugged, still smiling. "They're pretty good, I guess. I just wish there were more people who actually thought the same way out there. Most of the people who watch are only interested because it's popular right now. They're all jumping on the bandwagon."

I nodded. "Which is basically all people do anymore."

"Unfortunately, yeah."

"But why does it matter if people think the same way you do? I mean, EM is pretty harmless." I hadn't really thought about how cavalierly I'd said it, it just kind of popped out. I shook my head. "Sorry, I didn't mean..." I let out a breath. "That came out harsher than I meant it."

Kade opened his mouth to say something, then stopped. The moments ticked by like days and I started to wish the floor would open up and swallow me.

"I...I guess I don't think it's harmless." He shrugged, lightening the mood.

He was good at that, I realized. Taking something I said that was kind of assholey and not making me feel like an asshole about it.

I nodded like I was agreeing with him, but then opened my damn mouth again. "I just...I mean, I get that it was bad for you, but I really think that's a pretty unique situation. Most people don't have any issues with it."

"Yet," he said. "And to be honest, I actually think a lot more people do have issues with it, they just either don't admit it, or don't realize it's a problem yet, but for a lot of people it is." He tilted his head. "You know how when new tech comes out and it's meant to be something good. The purpose of it is to make your life easier, or more fun?"

"Sure."

"And then sometimes it sort of takes on a life of its own. Like with social media. It started out as this amazing communication tool and people had so much fun with it, but then some people started to use it in ways that even the developers hadn't thought of. And others became obsessed with how many likes they were getting or whatever, and it started to contribute to all kinds of mental health issues like mass anxiety and depression. But at the same time it was still this amazing tool that people depended on, so it was hard to do anything about it. I guess I'm seeing EM starting to go the same way."

I squinted at him. I could sort of see what he was saying, but EM was so much more than all that. "Says the guy who has the huge social media channel."

He laughed. "I know. Like I said, it's a tool. And it depends how people use it."

I nodded. "For a lot of people, Enhanced Memory's a lifesaver though." I thought of Andie being more comfortable being herself, and all the residents at Golden Acres.

Kade shrugged one shoulder. "Maybe," he said, sounding less than convinced. But he cracked a smile. "Or maybe we both worry too much."

I risked meeting his gaze. "You think?" I said sarcastically.

"Maybe just a little," he said, flashing me a wink.

Which was adorable and reminded me a bit of Clyde. Like maybe Kade was an old soul, which was something people told me I was all the time. It made me wonder how people could be so different, yet so much the same all at once.

"This is going to sound completely weird," Kade said, "but I can't figure you out. And like, it's not like I go around desperately wanting to 'figure everyone out,'" he continued. "But for some reason, I keep trying to figure you out. It's like we have a lot of things we think completely opposite about, but you're easy to talk to. More than most people."

"I was thinking the exact same thing," I said, and he was easy to talk to. In fact, I found myself wanting to talk to him about everything.

"Of course you were," he said, his grin getting wider. "We wouldn't be us if you weren't."

Us.

I liked the sound of that. Except that it scared me too, and as with everything else Kade-related, I didn't know why.

We looked at each other until the silence became too long. Finally, Kade spoke. "So anyway, should we be planning our next escapade, or what? Life is too short not to live, right?"

"Too short not to live," I said, liking the sound of it. "Did you make that up? I feel like I've heard it before."

He tilted his head. "Well, I made it up, but not just now off the top of my head. It's what my video channel is called, actually."

"I like it," I said, remembering seeing it now. "Tell me more about your site. I guess I'm intrigued like everybody else."

He smiled. "Yeah, people seem curious. Like they can't quite believe I do the things I do. But like, don't you remember not that long ago people used to do this stuff all the time? Like it wasn't even weird."

"Yeah, I remember. But aren't you worried about getting hurt?"

"I don't know. I don't really remember people getting hurt that much doing stuff. Not stuff like skating or going on boats and things like that."

"But people did get hurt sometimes." I pulled my chunky sweater tighter around me.

He tilted his head. "I suppose, but not as much as the Enhanced Memory people try to say. They make it sound like everything is dangerous."

"A lot of things *are* dangerous."

"Sure, you could get hurt doing a lot of things. You could get hurt walking down the street. But does that mean you shouldn't do it?"

I shrugged. "But that's different. People need to get places."

"Ah, but do they though?" he asked. "And for how much longer? It seems like half the things people used to do have been replaced by EM, and it's more and more every day. So where is it going to end? People already leave their houses less and less. It's not inconceivable that eventually people might not leave their houses at all."

"Now you're being silly."

"Am I? Look how much the world has changed in the past couple years. What if it keeps going at this pace? What's left for them to take away?"

"They're not really taking anything away," I said. "They're giving people things. Experiences. Ways to improve their lives."

Kade was about to say something else, then stopped himself. Smiled. "I'm sorry. You obviously have a different history with Enhanced Memory than I have. I guess most people are going to have a different perspective than a recovering addict."

"That's something I'm a little confused about still," I said. "I mean, I get if you don't want to talk about it, but...I'm just having a hard time figuring out how someone can become addicted. I mean, I get that EM can make you feel happy, but it's not like a regular addiction. It's just entertainment." It didn't seem believable that a company as big as Experion—or my parents, for that matter—would put something out in the world without making sure it was safe.

"Gambling is entertainment, phones are entertainment, and people have definitely had addiction issues with those things," he said. "Do you really not think it could be a problem?" he asked, inviting me to look around the coffee shop.

I sighed. Yeah, there were a few people using EM, and even one couple who were both doing EM instead of keeping each other company, but still, what was the harm in that? In fact, they all looked pretty happy. "I don't see what the big deal is. They're having fun."

"And that's exactly my point," he said. "It starts out harmless, which is what a lot of people would say about any drug. It's no big deal, right? You hear it all the time."

"I guess." I crossed my arms.

He leaned back in his chair. "I mean, I can't presume to know exactly how it all works, but I know that once I started I couldn't stop. And I know if I did a Memory today, I'd be right back in it. Hard-core. And that's what an addiction is. You can't stop and it takes over your life."

I shifted in my seat. I couldn't really argue with the fact that EM could kind of take over your life. Even with myself, there were plenty of times I put off doing things so I could get lost in a Memory instead, but that was just procrastinating.

"I guess I can kind of see what you mean, but I still think EM does far more good than harm. People are making positive changes in their lives...like getting off actual drugs," I said, trying to drive the point home.

Kade nodded at that. "For a lot of people it can help, sure. At least in the short-term. But we're still in the early stages. It hasn't been around long enough to know the damage it can really do."

"Or the good it can really do," I countered.

He sighed. "Well, I'm afraid I have to disagree with you on that. I guess I just have a lot more experience with it."

"No," I said. "I don't think you do."

He furrowed his brow, looking like he didn't believe me. And in that moment, I knew I had to get it out in the open. "My parents sort of, um, work for Experion Enterprises," I said, spitting it out before I changed my mind.

Kade's expression went dead. My heart began to beat faster, regretting my words immediately.

A lifetime later, he spoke. "That's...interesting."

"I'm sorry. I thought I should let you know before this goes any further." As I said it, I realized how ridiculous I sounded. "Not that this is, you know, a 'this,'" I said, along with air quotes, which looked monumentally dorky. I closed my eyes and shook my head, trying to shake off the embarrassment. "Sorry, this is all so weird."

I could practically see the gears spinning in his mind as he stared at me, making me squirm. Finally he opened his mouth to speak, and I could only hope he was going to let me off the hook—to lighten everything up again, but he simply said, "I have to go."

As I watched him walk away, something tugged at me. Like maybe I was a little too adamant in defending EM. Like maybe *I* didn't even believe some of the stuff I was spewing. Like maybe some of what he had to say sounded just a little too possible.

Like maybe I had just ruined it all.

Two hours later I was sitting on Andie's bed, a little jittery from the two large coffees I'd consumed. I picked up one of the college catalogs sitting on her nightstand. "What's with all the school info?"

Andie groaned. "My dad got those for me," she said, "to help me 'make some decisions about my future.'" She finished with an almost violent eye roll.

I laughed. "Have you gone through any of them?"

"Hell no. I told you, that is all going to be obsolete by the time we get there."

"Uh, the end of high school is pretty rapidly approaching," I said. "You sure you don't want to at least start college?"

She gave me a look that implied I had lost my mind. "Why on earth would anyone do that if they didn't have to? I'm serious, there is absolutely no point."

I tossed the catalog back on the pile. "Okay then. But like… what if something happens with EM?"

"What do you mean?"

I shrugged. "Just like…maybe it gets more regulated or something."

She narrowed her eyes. "Do you know something I don't?

Have your parents said something?" Her voice was starting to sound a little panicked.

"No, nothing. I don't know, it's just that the tech is moving kind of fast. We don't know everything about it yet."

"Good lord, you're starting to sound like Real K."

I stiffened. "The uh...video guy?"

"Yeah, have you ever seen his stuff?" she asked, her voice brightening.

"I have," I said, slowly. "I'm kind of surprised you watch him though."

"I know! I don't know what it is about him, but I am obsessed right now."

"But he's against EM, isn't he?" I asked, not letting on that I already knew the answer.

"So much. But that's what makes him so interesting, I think. He's like this anomaly living in this whole other world—practically the dark ages—and I mean, it's not a world I want to live in, but it's fascinating to visit. He's this guy just walking around out there with all these memories, real ones. And I hate to admit it because I'm sure it's all a marketing ploy, but all the secrecy about who he is and the supposed danger he could be in and all that completely sucks me in."

I couldn't help but think that marketing ploys didn't really jibe with what I knew about Kade.

Andie scrolled through her phone and gasped. Like actually. Out loud. "I haven't seen this one."

She flopped on the bed beside me and started the video.

A jolt went through my stomach. It was a very familiar video.

"Any idea who he is?" I asked, pretending not to be as interested in her answer as I actually was.

She shook her head. "Nobody knows. That's the appeal, you know? Plus it takes one hell of a set of 'you know whats' to do the shit he's pulling off. Have you seen the one where he skydives? Like actually jumps out of a plane? I mean, who on earth would do that in this day and age?"

My mouth dropped open. I knew Kade had done some stunts, but I didn't realize he would take it that far. Didn't you have to take a safety course or something for that sort of thing? Was I really trying to be friends—or whatever it was we were—with someone who was ready to risk everything for a video channel?

But I knew it wasn't just for the channel. Kade wanted the experiences. He'd told me that himself. The good, the bad, and the ugly.

"That's a little scary."

"Still, what I wouldn't give to have his memories," Andie said. "I bet they'd go for thousands."

I tilted my head. "So...is that because they're authentic? Genie was telling me that true extracted Memories are worth way more than synthetic ones."

She nodded. "People say they're worth it though. Like the difference between...a watered-down grape drink—you know, the kind made with crystals—and real grape juice, like with all the nuances and depth of flavor and everything. Well, you know better than anyone. Those ones we used at your house were fantastic."

I sensed that everyone had known there was something special about the Memories my parents had except me.

"So if they're that good, then…why doesn't everybody use the extracted Memories?" I asked.

"They are SO expensive," Andie said, her eyes widening to hammer home her point.

"Okay, but what I don't understand is why they're so expensive. Like, why doesn't everyone with cool authentic memories have them extracted and duplicate and sell them?"

"Ah, because that's not possible. You can't duplicate them. You'd have to copy them—essentially synthesize them so they'd be the watered-down kind. Not original anymore."

I thought about that for a second. "Okay so, why doesn't someone like uh, Real K here…" I said, pointing at her phone, "why wouldn't he get all his memories extracted and like, make a shit ton of money?"

Andie leaned back. "God no," she said. "That would be tragic."

"Why?" I said, scrunching my forehead.

"Because then he wouldn't have them anymore."

"What do you mean?"

"Nova," she said, leaning in, "once a memory is extracted from someone's mind, it's gone. Like forever gone."

"Are you serious?"

Andie gave me a pointed look and a single nod. "I think that's why your parents were so pissed the other day."

"How do you know this?"

"Work. Genie was trying to teach me everything about Enhanced Memory a while back, but honestly, I'm so much better at interacting with the residents. All that science-y crap is just not my thing."

I was starting to get uneasy. "Well, where do the authentic Memories come from? Desperate people willing to sell them at any cost?"

She nodded. "Sometimes, yeah. Like with Experion, but sometimes it's worse. I've heard there are people out there who will go to the lengths of actually taking people. Like stealing their memories. You know, the black market."

I stopped breathing for a second. That couldn't possibly be what Kade was so afraid about, could it? "*That* was what Ami was talking about at the club the other day?"

"Yeah. Wait, what did *you* think she was talking about?"

"I don't know…weed?"

She snorted.

"Okay, but a black market Memory scene? That's all just ridiculous conspiracy theory stuff, right? People don't actually believe that."

But Andie just shrugged, which did not make me feel any better at all.

13

It was a quiet day at work and I found myself wandering, looking for something to do. It was quiet everywhere. I mean, Golden Acres never really got all that loud, but this seemed especially hushed. I headed farther down the hall toward the door marked Private. I had always wondered what was behind that door. I'd seen staff take patients in and out, but had never really had a reason to go in. I suppose I could have asked someone what was in there, but it never really bothered me that much, so I never did.

Suddenly I was curious though.

Like so curious that I took my master key and slid it into the door. I couldn't stop thinking about how Andie seemed to know so much more about Enhanced Memory than I did—even given who my parents were—and that she had gotten that knowledge at work. I honestly don't know what I was thinking, and there was a tiny niggling in the back of my head going "You shouldn't be in here," but sometimes I wasn't that good at listening to that voice. The door was clearly marked, and I couldn't pretend I hadn't seen it, but I went in anyway.

I mean, had I thought I could lose my job I definitely would have stayed out, but everyone there was so amazing and I'd never seen anyone get in trouble for anything, so in I strode.

Never mind that the actual residents were locked out from going in there, but I wasn't too concerned.

Maybe I should have been.

Because when I wandered down the hall and peeked through an observation window, my stomach tightened when I spotted Clyde strapped into a machine.

And on the machine in big block letters were the words *Memory Extractor.*

I froze, unable to look away, even when Genie caught me staring from the other side of the glass where she was running the machine that was taking Clyde's memories from him. I wanted to tear my gaze from his face, which was normally so relaxed and happy, but in that moment was distorted into something tense and severe. I stumbled back to the wall behind me, grateful to have something for support.

A moment later I apparently regained my ability to walk and hurried out, my world wobbling slightly as I headed to the waiting room to sit. It was quiet. Really quiet. I guess all the residents had moved to their rooms for the night.

Obviously I'd seen hundreds of people using Enhanced Memories, but I'd never seen the opposite side of the process— the part where memories were extracted. Most of the people at Golden Acres were in at least the beginning stages of memory loss and I knew we were preserving their memories somehow, but I guess I hadn't really put it all together. Maybe I hadn't wanted to put it all together, but the conversation with Andie came rushing back to me. How memories were gone from a person's mind forever once they were extracted. Wasn't that taking even more of the residents' memories? Making them deteriorate faster?

"Hey," Genie said, finding me a few minutes later as I tried to reconcile what I had seen.

I looked up at her. "I'm really sorry. I shouldn't have been in there."

"No, you shouldn't have, but that's not what I'm concerned about right now." She searched my face. "Are you okay?"

"I just...I guess I don't understand. It doesn't make sense to be taking memories from people who hardly have any left."

Genie sighed and sat in the chair across from me. "We're not taking them. We're trying to save them."

"But then they're gone forever," I said.

Genie nodded. "But these residents are in a place where their minds are sabotaging them out of their own lives. Can you imagine how scary that is? What we're doing with the extractions is essentially saving the most precious memories that they have left, giving them the opportunity to preserve them while they still have the chance, before they degrade even further."

"But it can't be the same as having real memories. Once they're extracted, they're just...gone?"

"They're gone from their natural memories, yes, but that's why it's a good thing. These patients' natural memories are slowly being stolen from them through their disease. This is the best way we know of right now to preserve them. They're able to relive their memories over and over again forever."

"But how do they even remember that the memories once existed?"

"We go through a lengthy scheduling process for when we'll present them with their Memories—before any memories are extracted. And the patients are fully aware of the risks before any extractions take place. This is one of the uses that Enhanced Memory was originally designed for. This is more of the good that your parents helped bring to the world." She sighed.

Somehow that realization didn't make me feel any better.

"I should have warned you what was in that room. I guess I didn't think you'd go in without asking," she said, her lips pursing. "But, curiosity is a powerful thing," she continued, her face softening. "And I get that it's a little jarring, especially if you're not expecting it."

"I shouldn't have been snooping around. I'm really sorry. It just…didn't look like a pleasant experience."

Genie nodded. "I know, and I've been told it is a little uncomfortable, but the patients assure me it's well worth it. And it's fine that you saw it. If it was really a big deal, the door would have a dedicated lock. It's not like it's a secret or anything. Most of the patients come to this facility because of the memory extractions. And hey, maybe you were meant to work here. To see the incredible tech your parents helped put into the world."

I nodded. "Yeah, maybe."

Still, as my shift went on, I couldn't get the vision of Clyde strapped to that chair out of my head.

I tried to shift my mood by thinking positive thoughts. Tried to convince myself the memories the residents were losing would now be accessible forever and how it was a miracle this kind of technology even existed, but of course I couldn't stop thinking about Kade.

"Got a story for an old man?" Clyde asked when I went to his room with his tray of food.

Clyde wasn't generally one of the residents who stayed in their room for meals—he loved people and usually wanted to be around them as much as he could—but today he'd requested it.

"Of course," I said, setting down his tray. "But are you feeling alright?"

"Good as gold," he said, with his signature wink.

"You don't usually pass up a chance to pester the ladies," I said. "I thought I'd better come and check up on you." I gave him a wink of my own.

He chuckled a little. "I think Bea and Ruthie will survive one day without me," he said.

I grinned. "But seriously, everything's good?"

He nodded. "Yeah, maybe a little tired. It's nothing—just feeling a little off."

He did seem off. Like slightly gloomy or something. And of course everyone gets a little gloomy once in a while, but I had honestly never seen it in Clyde before.

"Doesn't seem like you to be in your room."

"I'm not feeling that social, I suppose. No big deal. I'm sure I'll be right back out there in no time." Thankfully he grinned again.

That was something, at least.

"Now how about that story?" he asked.

I smiled. I wasn't much of a storyteller, but Clyde was a good audience. He would listen to anything with a smile on his face, like it was pure joy to just be alive in the world.

Today his smile was less bright, but it was still there.

"Well," I started, knowing Clyde was also good at doling out advice when he decided he had something to contribute. Maybe I could get a little help while I was at this storytelling gig. "There once was this girl, and she met this guy."

Clyde shimmied into his chair a little, getting comfortable.

"And one day they had this really great time together. Went to a skating rink, actually."

"Sounds like the good old days," Clyde said.

I smiled. "Exactly. And they really hit it off and seemed to like each other." God, I hoped that was true. I had never been good at reading those kinds of situations. "But then she kind of messed it up."

"What did she do?"

I shrugged. "Just…argued with him, I guess. They have this one thing that they disagree on. At least she thinks they disagree."

"Sounds complicated."

"It is." I cleared my throat. "Um, I mean it was."

"Right. Was," he said, his eyes twinkling.

"Anyway, then she didn't know what to do. She wanted to apologize, but she didn't really know what she was apologizing for, so she was afraid it might sound…I don't know, forced or something."

He leaned back. "Ugh, been there."

"But then it seemed even worse for her to do nothing. To let it go. And maybe let him go in the process."

Clyde was waiting for me to continue, but must have known I needed a little push. "So...what did she do?"

"Nothing yet," I said. "That's the problem. This, er, friend of mine asked me what she should do, but I really didn't have a clue what to tell her."

Clyde smiled. "So, I'm gonna go out on a limb here and guess that this *friend*—" he raised his eyebrows and looked at me "—is a little quiet, and a little shy, and maybe has a hard time saying what she means."

I shrugged, looking at my hands. "Maybe."

He leaned back and sighed. "Well, it seems there are only two things she could do."

I was nodding. "Either apologize or let him go."

"Well, I was going to say, either talk to him, you know that whole pesky communication thing, or yeah, let him go."

"Communication," I said, expressionless. "What if she was never very good at that?"

"Oh nobody's good at that," Clyde said, laughing a little. "It's what gets us all in trouble more times than we care to admit, but what I've learned in my...shall we say extensive years of experience—" he grinned "—is that we only get better at it by practicing. It's not one of those things we can learn from books or watching tutorials."

"I guess I just don't know what to say."

He nodded. "Well, the thing is if you take choice number two and let him go, well, you'll never know what might have happened."

"I'll never know," I repeated, my mind turning the idea over. "So…I would be avoiding the whole thing."

"That's right."

I sighed.

"You just decided you have to talk to him, didn't you?"

I glanced at Clyde. Obviously we were done pretending. "Yeah, I guess I did."

He nodded, knowing that's exactly what I was going to do the whole time. "Good for you," he said. "Good for you."

I left Clyde to his supper and, for the entire rest of my shift, thought about what I was even supposed to say.

I pulled out my phone.

Sorry I freaked you out. I hope we can still be friends.

I cringed as I sent it. The word *friends* never sounded so insufficient. There was more of a connection between us than that. Why wasn't there a word for that place where you're more than friends but not quite…anything else yet? I stared at my phone for a good three minutes, but got annoyed that I was being the "girl who waits by the phone," so I cut my break short and went back to work. A few minutes later I was taking some garbage out to the dumpster when my phone buzzed.

I hated that I dropped the bags and stopped to check it, but that's exactly what I did. So much for being the independent person I liked to think I was.

My heart jolted into my throat. Kade.

I took a breath before I could bring myself to look.

Hey. I'm sorry too. I hope I didn't ruin this.

The thump in my chest accelerated. *This.*

I quickly started typing back. Maybe I've been biased about everything. Can we hang out again sometime? I'd like to know more.

I held my breath, waiting for the text bubble to pop up. It did and I slowly let the air out, closing my eyes, trying to breathe calmly even though my insides were about ready to flip to the outside. Why did this feel so important?

I do want to talk but I don't think I can meet. It's too risky.

I let out a growl of frustration. At this rate I was never going to get any answers.

Why is it risky?

Because of EM. Because of who you are.

I typed quickly, desperately. I don't understand. I'm no one. Nothing.

You're not nothing. Listen, I don't even know if it's safe to text. I'll find a way to get in touch with you.

Kade, come on, this is silly.

But apparently that was the end of the conversation. I mean,

I guess it was a good thing that he was at least talking to me, and he didn't seem to be mad. Just scared.

A prickle crept up my neck. But why was I a part of that fear?

14

I couldn't help it.

The Memory Room was finally complete and I wanted to see it. My parents hadn't even shown it to me when it was finished. Maybe it was still because of the weird episode when Andie and I had been using their Memories without their "permission" even though I didn't know I needed it. And what? Now I was banned from even looking at the Memories? But it wasn't like they put a lock on the door, so I decided I could go in and take a peek. I guess I wanted to make sure everything was fine. Normal.

Maybe there was a part of me that wanted to find a way to prove to Kade he was overreacting.

Still, I waited until they were out of the house to check it out. I didn't want to break any of the eggshells I seemed to be walking on lately. And maybe that's why I opened the door so slowly, peeking in, but then I shook my head. This was my house. I was allowed to move around in it.

I straightened up and flipped on the light, thinking I had some idea of what the room was going to look like, but what I saw was kind of shocking. I knew my parents had a lot of Memories, but I had not been prepared for this.

The room was nearly empty except for a pair of chairs and row upon row of tiny drawers lining the entire wall in front of me. Glancing to the right, that wall was completely lined with drawers too. And yeah, there had always been tons of Memories lying around, but...didn't they have to return them to Experion once they tested them?

Surely most of these had to be empty.

I began to pull them open, choosing drawers at random, making my way through the rows. As I moved around the room, the knot in my stomach squeezed tighter and tighter. I'd opened a dozen random drawers all around the room and every one of them had a tiny Memory disk set gently in the center on soft fabric like a jewelry box. I pulled more drawers. All full.

As I turned to start checking the next wall, movement caught my eye.

"What are you doing in here?" Dad asked.

"Oh, I didn't hear you come in. I, uh, just wanted to see what the new Memory Room was like."

Dad nodded, but the look on his face wasn't exactly warm. "Fine. Just, leave the drawers closed, please. Those disks are very valuable."

I started to nod. "Right. But, can I ask...why do you have so many of them?"

Dad looked confused. "We test them. You know that."

"Yeah, but don't they need to be returned to Experion or something? Like, aren't these one of a kind?"

"Some of them belong to Experion, yes," he said.

I noticed that he didn't really answer the question.

"Okay, but if these are all beta testing disks, don't they have to go back to Experion to get synthesized or whatever?"

Dad let out a long breath and rubbed his eyebrow for a second—like he had a headache coming on. "Nova, this is our work. It's really none of your concern."

"I know, and I get that you need to do the testing and everything, but..." I turned to motion to the room, then sighed, turning back to him. "You and Mom, you're just always so busy now with all these ridiculous Memories."

"Ridiculous Memories?" he said. "You mean the ridiculous Memories you just had to sneak around and use even though they most certainly did not belong to you. My god, it's why we had to build this room in the first place!"

My mouth dropped open. I had no idea how it had happened, but clearly I'd completely shattered those eggshells I was always careful of, and somehow gotten the argument turned around to me. "But—" my arms dropped to my sides "—maybe I miss you guys." The words came out in barely a whisper.

He let out an exasperated breath. "Miss us? What about you. You're busy too, Nova. That new job, all the extracurricular things you're involved in now. If it wasn't for all this extra stress that you put us under, we wouldn't have to spend so much time catching up on work, and maybe we could return some of these Memories!"

What was he talking about? The stress that I put him under? I hardly ever asked for anything. They didn't give me rides anymore. Was he talking about before? Had I really been that much of an inconvenience? I mean, they used to make sure I had the things I needed—rides, a clean house...their time. But it had been a while since I'd asked for any of it. I knew they were busy. Maybe even too busy for me. But to blame me for why they had so many Memories in the house? That made no sense.

And neither did the way he was being so defensive about it. But it wasn't like he was in any mood to discuss it.

"Whatever," I mumbled and squeezed past him out of the room. Frankly, I wasn't feeling all that welcome even being in the same place as him in that moment, so I went outside, not even sure where I was going.

I walked for a long time, heading into the big park near the edge of our subdivision, trying to figure out what was going on with my parents. That Memory Room couldn't be normal. There had to be hundreds of drawers. And there was something disturbingly shrine-like about it too. Especially considering how the rest of the house was a total mess, but you wouldn't find a speck of dust in that room if you had a magnifying glass.

I walked for a while longer, but it was starting to get late. I wasn't super thrilled about going home, and I also knew that with everything swirling in my head—my parents, the unsettling Memory Room, Kade—my chances of sleep were not that great, but I couldn't stay in the park forever. Which for some reason upset me. I felt like a stranger in my own life. In my own house. Everything just seemed different now, and I was scared it would never be the same again.

I thought of Andie—her family would let me come over, but...Andie's place was for Andie, not me.

Tears started to well up, but I didn't want anyone in the park coming up to check on me, so I started to run—just out for an evening jog, nothing to see here. Maybe if I ran off some extra energy I'd have a better chance at sleep, so I ran all the way home—my lungs burning, but my raggedy emotions smoothing out a little. I found a little more focus—my whirling thoughts slowing slightly.

I stayed outside a minute to catch my breath then headed inside, where thankfully, the house was dark.

My thoughts started speeding again almost the instant I got to my room. So many things were up in the air. I tried to lie down. Even closed my eyes for a few seconds, but I knew sleep was not going to be something that visited me anytime soon.

To say I was groggy the next day would be an understatement, but I managed to power through the first part of the morning okay. On my break I couldn't stop the thoughts from pouring into my mind again. Why was Dad being so weirdly defensive about the Memories? And why was Kade being so paranoid. It felt like I was living in some kind of conspiracy theory bizarro world.

I pulled out my phone.

Can we talk? I'd love to meet in person, but I get it if you're more comfortable over the phone.

I watched the phone until the screen went black and sighed. Was he going to make me wait until my next break to get a reply, or worse, was he serious about not texting anymore? I closed my eyes and leaned my head back, just for a second, trying my best to relax.

The next thing I knew my phone buzzed in my hand and I had no idea how much time had passed. Shit, the last thing I needed was to be caught sleeping on the job. A quick glance at my phone told me that only two minutes had gone by. I let out a breath of relief.

Thank you, Kade.

I opened his text.

No, in person is better. But we have to be careful about it.

Okay, well I'm off at two today.

Victoria Park after dark?

I couldn't help but think a secluded park after dark was a bit over-the-top, even for this situation, but I wasn't about to argue.

I'll be there at eight.

See you then.

15

I was becoming obsessed with everything I might not know about Enhanced Memories. Everything in my life seemed to revolve around them lately and I wanted to pick Genie's brain, but I didn't know how to bring it up without making her suspicious. I decided medical curiosity was the way to approach it.

"Do you need any help with any extractions or anything today?" I asked.

She looked at me strangely. "It's not really something that needs a lot of hands on deck," she said. "And you seemed a little spooked about it when you saw it in action."

"I know, but I was hoping to learn about it. It's fascinating to think that we're actually saving people from losing their memories. I just think I need to start thinking about my future, and I thought, well, maybe my future could be sort of like yours. I want to help people. Plus who else has an opportunity like this? To be in a facility that does these extractions and have the chance to learn from someone who is so passionate about their work."

"I don't know," she said, squinting a little. "It didn't go so well the last time you were in there."

"I know, and I'm sorry. I was caught off guard, but I'm starting to see how much the Memory preservation can help the people here. I'd like to be a part of that."

Her expression softened. "I guess a little experience couldn't hurt."

"Really? Thanks!" I said, probably a little too excited.

"But you're only there to observe," Genie said, looking at me like she was searching for some kind of answer she wasn't sure she wanted to find.

The last thing I wanted to do was mislead Genie, but I had to find out more about EM, specifically the authentic Memories, a procedure I actually had access to.

"Get your work done and meet me at the lab at one."

I nodded and rushed off. I was determined to finish all my work early. If Genie could depend on me to still get it all done, she'd be much more likely to allow me to sit in on more extractions.

It wasn't as fun, cleaning as quickly as I could while trying not to get into deep conversation with the residents, when usually that was my favorite part. The people at Golden Acres had so much to say. I never really understood why more people didn't come to visit. Nobody had better stories than someone in their later years. Plus they had done it all before Enhanced Memories.

These were the realest stories you could find.

But I was on a mission, and while I tried to be as nice as possible, I had to tell a few folks that I was in a bit of a hurry and we'd have to chat a little later. It broke my heart to see the flash of disappointment on their faces before Diana said, "Oh yes, of course, dear," or when Maybelle said, "Oh darn it, I wanted to tell you the story about the time I was a movie extra, but no worries—it'll keep for tomorrow."

Unfortunately, I knew it might not actually keep until tomorrow because her memories were pretty hit and miss, and I would have loved to hear that story.

As I finally headed toward the extraction area, I passed by Clyde's room.

"Still in here?" I asked.

He looked up, somewhat confused. Then his eyes brightened. "Oh hi, um—" he looked down at his hands "—Nova! Hi, Nova." He shot me a sheepish smile.

I chuckled a little. "Hey, Clyde, how are you holding up?"

"Still here," he said. "Better than the alternative." I was happy to see his signature wink was still making an appearance.

"I suppose it is," I said, grinning.

Then I noticed something. There was a blank spot on his wall above his easy chair. He loved the picture that hung there.

"Getting the photo reframed or something?" I asked.

"Photo?" he said, turning to look where I was pointing.

He looked more confused than ever.

"Oh, uh, I liked that picture of Jenny," I said.

"Jenny?" His eyes were searching then, looking down at his hands, then back at me.

There was a hint of fear in his eyes.

"You know what, Clyde," I said, a knot growing in my stomach. "It's all good. Forget I said anything. I think I got mixed up. See you soon."

His face brightened again as if his worry was forgotten as easily as everything else. "Yeah, see you around, Nova."

Genie was in the hallway and pulled me a little distance away from Clyde's room. She'd caught some of our conversation.

"That's what we were working on the other day in the extraction room. We took out the memories of his daughter for safekeeping."

That knot in my stomach tightened. "And now what, they're all gone?"

"I'm afraid so. We were hoping he might retain a little something, but it seems like everything was wiped."

I let out a long, slow breath. "How can this be the best thing for him?"

She straightened up. I hadn't meant to sound like I was attacking her or the process or whatever, but she immediately went on the defensive. "He knew exactly what he was signing up for, Nova. It was Clyde's decision. He was starting to get a little blurry on most of the memories with his daughter—she died when she was twelve, you know."

"I'm sorry." I looked at the floor. "I knew she died, but I didn't know it was as a kid."

Genie nodded. "He wanted to do everything possible to hold on to her."

Obviously I could understand wanting to keep your loved

ones close for as long as possible, but this seemed like it was doing the opposite.

"But how does he even know how long he would have had memories of Jenny? The real ones?"

Genie tilted her head. "Well, he didn't, not really. He just knew he was likely to lose them someday. And with the way his other memories were going, it was probably going to be sooner rather than later."

I nodded. The whole thing was so…sad.

"What happened to Jenny's picture?"

Genie sighed. "We had to take it down. It was upsetting him because he didn't know why there was this picture of a girl by his bed. He said it was creepy."

My shoulders slumped. "And I almost made it worse by reminding him of what he lost."

"Don't worry, hon," Genie said, squeezing my arm. "That's why we do what we do here. So the most important things are never lost."

I nodded.

We made our way to the door marked Private.

"Are you sure you still want to do this?" Genie asked.

I nodded. "Yeah, I think I just…need to understand it all a little better." I was about to see my first full memory extraction, which would definitely help. And hopefully ease my mind from the niggling little thoughts about how it didn't quite sit right. I couldn't help but think maybe Kade was getting to me, making me suspicious of something that was actually kind of a miracle.

Genie got straight to it, looping the strings of a medical mask behind her ears. "My job in there is to care for the patient. Give them a sense of familiarity and help them stay calm while the procedure is going on. You'll stay on the other side of this glass to observe, okay? The patient can't see you. It's like one of those mirror things they have in interrogation rooms."

"Really? Why the secrecy?"

"It's not a secret—it's for medical observation—but we find the patients are more comfortable with fewer people, so if they don't see anyone behind the glass, they have an easier time pretending no one else is there besides me and the computer tech."

I nodded. "Okay."

As much as I didn't want to intrude if a patient didn't want an extra audience, I needed to know exactly how the extractions worked.

"And they've given you total permission to do this, right?"

"Of course. We don't touch anyone without signed consent and a vigorous psychological evaluation to determine that they are of sound mind when they sign off."

"Okay, cool," I said as she left.

It was a relief they were so thorough with the consent, but I wondered if every extraction in every facility was as thorough.

The lights flickered on in the procedure room and Genie stood back while the technician got a few machines humming to life. I blinked, my eyes taking a minute to adjust. The room looked so stark, so clinical when it was empty like that. Just a chair, which basically looked like a higher-tech version of an electric chair, not that I'd seen any of those in real life, only in movies, but still, the scene struck me as sad somehow.

We were, after all, about to pull out someone's memories.

Genie went through a door at the side of the room and wheeled Mae in.

"Here we go, Mae," she said, helping her out of the wheel-chair and into the procedure chair, then sitting beside her, holding her hand.

Normally Mae was pretty vibrant and independent and didn't need help getting around, but today she seemed a bit out of it. I realized she must have been given some kind of drug or sedative. Which made me wonder if patients some-times got cold feet and wanted to back out. But there was no reason not to let them back out, right? So it must have more to do with the procedure itself. I hoped it wasn't painful, al-though I supposed lots of medical procedures were painful but ended up being worth it in the long run. I reminded my-self again that this procedure was what these people wanted. It was their choice.

The technician flicked a few more switches on various ma-chines, then busied herself with attaching electrodes to Mae's temples, neck, and chest, even though Mae was by now sound asleep. She moved Mae's head around as needed to get all the electrodes in place, which looked strange, like she was work-ing on a rag doll. Mae looked so lifeless, and suddenly pale too.

"These monitor the patient's vitals during the procedure," Genie said, I assumed for my benefit.

After the electrodes had been put in place, the tech put a clip on Mae's finger, then finished by clicking together straps around Mae's arms and legs, locking her in place on the chair.

"Okay, is everything ready to go?" Genie asked the tech-nician, who was clicking away behind a bank of computer monitors.

"Good to go here," the tech said. "Everything looks normal."

I couldn't help but notice how *not* normal everything looked from this side of the glass. Then again, the technician had probably sat in on dozens of these procedures, if not hundreds. I supposed eventually a person would get used to the whole thing.

Although I wasn't sure if I ever could.

"Lowering the extractor," the technician said, clicking away at her keyboard.

A machine began to descend from the ceiling, lowering down over Mae's head like an oversized square helmet. Genie got up and stepped away from Mae.

I couldn't imagine how it must feel in there, not being able to move. No wonder they needed to sedate the patients first.

"The machine is essentially a computer that we plug the patient into," Genie explained. "We are then able to pinpoint the memory area—the hippocampus—and hopefully download only those memories that the patient wishes to have extracted."

I wasn't sure how much I loved the use of the word *hopefully* in that sentence, but my thought was cut off as the machine started making a buzzing noise and Mae's body lurched a little.

The technician clicked furiously on one of the four keyboards she had in front of her. "Activating the memory sector," she said, an extremely clinical tone to her voice.

I suppose it helped to disengage from the humanness of it all. To pretend that she was simply running computer programs and diagnostics and whatnot, instead of actually digging around in someone's mind and extracting bits of it.

"Extraction of sector five memories beginning now."

Memories? I thought they extracted one memory at a time. Although now that I thought about it, I wasn't sure how any of it worked. Sure, the EM disks housed only one Memory each, but it made sense that all memories would be stored in a specific part of the brain.

I thought back to Clyde and how he seemed to have lost a part of himself. The part that wanted to always be around people, to make them laugh and put them at ease. I realized that he was probably still recovering, but I suddenly worried that they could have somehow taken that from him, if it was part of a whole "sector," like the technician said. Now that I thought about it, there were lots of people whose personalities had changed seemingly overnight at Golden Acres, but I'd always chalked that up to their disease, their memory loss. My chest felt heavy as I continued to watch.

The technician turned to a different keyboard and set of monitors on the right side of the desk.

"Extraction beginning in three…two…one…"

Mae's body seized, as if being hit by an electrical pulse, and I was even more alarmed at how much like an electric chair the contraption was. I realized instantly why the restraints were there, the muscles and tendons through Mae's body showing as they strained beneath them. I instinctively reached for her, my hands touching the glass helplessly. I had to look away. I don't know how Genie and the technician could sit there and watch it, Genie monitoring Mae closely while the technician's eyes flicked from monitor to monitor, clicking a few strokes into a keyboard every so often.

And then there was a flurry of typing, as the technician

began to speak again. "And procedure complete in three…
two…one."

Then Mae's body relaxed, as if she were back in a peaceful
slumber. Like nothing had even happened. She looked exactly
the same as she had before it started, but something in *me* had
changed. Now what I noticed was how limp…how frail her
body looked all hooked up to the machines.

"Extraction complete," the technician said. "Everything
looks good." She continued to check screen after screen. "The
Memories are intact and secure in storage."

Both Genie and the technician looked relieved.

I hadn't even thought about the possibility that something
could go wrong with the Memories. That there was a chance
they could be lost, but something told me with the relief that
was plastered all over their faces, that it was not only possible, but was something that happened more regularly than
they would like.

"Excellent," Genie said, leaning in close to Mae.

The technician typed a bit more and the machine retracted
back toward the ceiling.

Genie turned to me and started to speak. At least she turned
in the general direction of me. With the mirrored glass she
couldn't see exactly where I was standing and she talked to
the space about two feet to my left.

"That's the main procedure," she explained. "All that's left
now is to wait a few minutes for the patient to wake up and
do some testing. See if any implants need to be done."

Implants?

But before I could wonder for long, she added, "Oh, and

there's a button with an intercom to the right of the glass if you have any questions."

I looked over and saw a button with several holes above it, like a speaker.

I pressed the button. "Uh, what do you mean *implants*?"

A look crossed her face, like she had forgotten I was a regular person and not a medical professional, like she was not used to explaining the basics.

"Oh right. Well, we'll test the patient to make sure she retains enough memory to get on fine, and if need be we'll implant any necessary Memories."

I wanted to ask another question. I wanted to ask a thousand more questions, but Mae was starting to stir and Genie needed to tend to her.

As Mae's eyes fluttered open, there was nothing but fear in them.

"It's okay, Mae," Genie soothed, stroking her hand. "You're safe. The memory procedure went very well." She smiled down at Mae, who seemed to be calming a little.

Genie certainly knew what she was doing. It wasn't really my business to be questioning her, it's just that…well, there were so many questions to be asked and no one else to answer them for me.

Still, I promised myself I would wait until the time was right. And it certainly wasn't when poor Mae was sitting there all skittish like a cat who'd had a pail of water dumped on her.

Genie smiled, still looking into Mae's eyes. "Recognition seems to be there."

I knew she was talking about the fact that Mae seemed to recognize her and that it was a good sign. Which stirred even more questions in my mind. Were there instances when the patient didn't recognize Genie afterward?

"How are you feeling, honey?" Genie asked.

Mae started to speak. "The cardboard daffodil regurgitated a sweater calf on three o'clock."

Genie nodded and patted Mae's hand as if what Mae had said made perfect sense.

"Vocabulary seems to be off," the technician said.

"Okay, Mae," Genie said, never taking her eyes off Mae's. "We have to do a little fixing up in there. It'll be just a minute longer."

Mae looked confused, but Genie stroked her hair as she lowered a breathing mask down over her face and in a moment Mae was fast asleep again.

I guess Genie realized I'd have questions since she answered some of them before I could even ask.

"The patient is having some issues with language," she explained through the glass. "Sometimes that happens and we have to go back in and implant some standardized Memories."

"Standardized Memories?" I asked, forgetting she couldn't hear me.

I was about to press the intercom button, but Genie was already giving orders to the technician. "Standard English," she said, flipping the page on the chart on the table beside Mae. "Apparently she spoke a bit of Norwegian, but I don't think that will be necessary for today," she said.

There were two chairs set up near the glass and I sat, my mind spinning.

Standardized Memories.

Memories that you could just implant into someone on a

whim, I thought, blinking, trying to process. So like...patient loses their motor skills...oh no worries, we'll stick some standardized ones back in. What did that do for a patient's personality? I couldn't understand how this was all just...fine with everybody.

The dull throb behind my eyes I'd been feeling more lately started to pulse as the technician lowered the machine again.

But I couldn't watch any longer. I checked my phone. My shift had been over twenty minutes ago and I decided I'd seen enough.

I burst out of the Private door and nearly ran smack into Andie, who was on her way to the TV room with a tray of tea for some of the residents. I threw my hands up and stopped short of knocking it right out of her hands.

"Hey," she said, beaming like it was a lovely miracle we'd missed the nearly inevitable crash.

"Hey, Andie, sorry," I said, a little out of breath.

"First one?" she asked.

"First one?" I repeated, then looked back as the Private door finished shutting. "Oh, uh, yeah. Have you ever sat in on one of those?"

"Oh sure," she said, "a few times." She started on her way again as if it was no big deal.

"Don't you find it...a little disturbing?"

Andie set the tray on the table where Bea and Ruthie were having one of their famous arguments. Today it was about how the weatherman was most certainly hotter than the anchorman, except that Ruthie thought it was obviously the opposite.

"Are you oblivious, lady?" Bea was saying, her tone increasing in its severity by the second.

"What are you talking about? Don't you think this guy looks a whole lot smarter? I mean, what the hell am I going to do with someone who is clearly all brawn and a little short on the library materials upstairs?" Ruthie tapped her temple with her index finger, trying to drive her point home.

"More like what I wouldn't do," Bea argued back.

"Ladies," Andie piped in. "No need to argue. Have some tea and enjoy your eye candy in peace." She beamed her high-watt smile their way.

"Thanks, Andie," Bea said, then continued mumbling something about pecs and quivering thighs.

Andie snorted a slight laugh then backed away. "Those women are going to be the end of me."

I smiled. Though I couldn't help but wonder how long Bea and Ruthie would even still be Bea and Ruthie.

"Sorry, what were you saying?" Andie asked.

"I just…I don't know what to think about what I saw in there." I motioned toward the Private door.

Andie nodded. "It can be a little surprising the first time around, but these poor people are terrified of losing everything. Their memories are all they have left."

"But that's the exact thing they're taking away!" I couldn't keep the slight screech that always came out when I got worked up out of my voice.

Andie shook her head. "You know that's temporary. This is the solution to memory permanence."

"I know but…" I sighed. "I guess I didn't know about how sometimes standardized Memories have to be implanted after the fact. Like how sometimes they take away too much or whatever it is."

"Oh," Andie said knowingly. "You had one of those. Yeah, I don't really like that either, but—" she tilted her head "—well, it's not an exact science yet. The only way to extract the memories is to take them in chunks."

"Chunks?" I said. "That doesn't even sound in the same ballpark as exact."

"I know, but it's how it works. The patients know this."

I closed my eyes. "They know that they might have such huge chunks removed from their memories that they could lose their language skills?"

Andie guided me into one of the family meeting rooms. "Get yourself together," she said. "Yes, they know all that. They also know that it's as simple as pie to stick those language skills right on back in there if need be."

"And that works every time?"

She glanced away. "Not every time, no. But almost all the time. To the residents, the ones who have already lost so much, the risk is more than worth it."

I needed to calm down. Getting worked up in front of my friend—a friend who had nothing to do with any of this besides helping follow through with residents' wishes—would not get me anywhere.

"I'm sorry. Listen, I think watching Mae like that just... got under my skin a little."

"I'd say," Andie said, lifting her perfect eyebrows. "Are you going to be okay?"

I nodded. "Yeah. I guess. I haven't been sleeping well."

"Well, maybe you should go home and try to rest awhile?"

"Yeah, good idea," I said, motioning like I was about to head toward the staff room. I turned back. "Can I ask you something?"

"Anything."

"This Memory implant thing, like with Mae and her language issues? It's different than EM somehow, right?"

"I think so. From what I understand, the Enhanced Memories like the ones most people use are only temporary. The Memories don't stick forever, right?"

"I guess," I said. "But...I don't know. I feel like I retain a lot of them." A thought struck me then. "Do you think the authentic Memories, like the ones my parents bring home from work, last longer than the mainstream ones? I feel like that Memory I did at the club is already kind of starting to fade."

Andie shrugged. "That would make sense, I guess."

"So what about the implanted Memories, like the language ones they put back into Mae?"

Andie tilted her head. "I think they last forever. At least that's what Genie told me." She paused for a second. "Well, as far as they know right now, anyway."

"So like, if someone were to lose all their memories—like say amnesia or something, could they, like, put all their memories back in for them?"

Andie looked at me like I had grown a second head. "Well, I suppose, if they had those memories stored somewhere, but of course they wouldn't have that. A person doesn't know ahead of time if they're going to get amnesia."

"Okay, makes sense," I said, nodding. "So like I wonder if you could implant other Memories, like the standardized ones or...maybe even someone else's into that person. I mean, it would be sad that they lost everything, but…at least they'd have a second chance at life, right?"

Andie was quiet, like she was thinking it through. Eventually she made a face like she conceded the possibility. "I suppose in that kind of worst-case scenario it could be possible. But I've definitely never heard of anything like that before." She looked at me pointedly. "You sure do have one hell of an imagination, girl," she said, shooting me an approving smile as she headed back out to work.

I smiled back, but it faded the second she had her back turned.

16

The park was already deserted except for a lone figure on the swings, the chains squeaking a bit as he rocked.

"Hey," I said, settling myself into the swing beside his.

He jumped a bit, startled by my arrival. He'd been deep in his own thoughts. "Hi," he said, his face suddenly brightening.

A wave of relief washed over me.

"Thanks for agreeing to meet," I said, as if it were some covert operation.

Which I guess it kind of was.

He smiled and looked at his feet, swinging them out, gaining a bit of momentum. The chains squeaked faster.

"I probably shouldn't be here," he said.

I looked away. *Of course he thinks he shouldn't be here. He thinks I'm unsafe, whatever that means.* And I don't know where it came from but I was suddenly fighting off tears. It seemed like life was…so hard. Everyone else seemed to sail along, EM-ing their way through everything, and all the shit had kind of been falling on me, even though I did nothing to ask for it. Not to mention I didn't even know what I was doing. It's not like anyone had taught me the bus schedule, or how to take care of the house. Some days it seemed like this was it. That I was pretty much on my own for good now.

I knew I was being ridiculous and dramatic, which wasn't really my style, so I fought those tears hard, willing them to reabsorb into the backs of my eyes. I pulled in a long, shaky breath and cleared my throat.

I could sense Kade look up at me then, and I think he raised his hand to reach for me, but I was not about to look at him with the wateriness that was threatening to gush forth.

"Nova," he said, his tone serious. "You don't understand. I mean that I shouldn't…but I can't seem to stay away."

His swing stopped dead.

I had been concentrating so hard on keeping my emotions at bay that I didn't really understand what he was getting at. "Stay away from what?" I asked, wiping my eyes and trying to compose myself with one last sniff, risking a glance his way.

He paused for a moment. A long moment, looking into my eyes, so intensely that I nearly had to look away. Finally he seemed to set himself, like he was pulling up something from inside. "Don't you realize by now? I can't stay away from you."

"Oh," I said, blinking.

He turned his swing to face me more. "It's like you don't have anyone protecting you. Looking out for you." He shook his head like he wanted to say more, but didn't know how to say it, then sighed. "Or at least that's what it was at first. But then…I don't know. Then I got to know you and you're so… real." He smiled. "And curious about life in a way that no one else seems to be anymore." He shook his head. "Sorry, that probably doesn't make any sense."

I shook my head. "Don't be sorry," I said, my swing unmoving as I watched this beautiful creature in front of me. "Not very many people say the things they really feel anymore."

"I didn't want to say it," he said. "But I've made that whole pact with myself to live a real life." He chuckled a bit, like maybe he was regretting it now. He pushed off and began to swing again. "And," he continued, his face gaining some of his Kade-ness again, "the good, the bad, and the ugly and all that." He grinned.

I grinned back.

His swing slowed. Stopped.

"So…it's good then?"

I never thought I'd see an expression like that on someone I liked. A look of, what was it? Hopefulness? Mixed with fear, maybe a little excitement. I guess I thought I'd always be the one giving that look instead of being on the receiving end of it. I certainly never imagined I'd be both giving it and receiving it at the same time, but here we were.

"It's good then."

He gently grabbed onto the chain of my swing and pulled me closer, my feet starting to lift off the ground, making me feel light, as if by physically lifting me, he was also lifting this other weight, this baggage that had been piling on my shoulders. Like maybe I wasn't so alone after all. I leaned in the last few inches, finally getting to the moment I had been wondering, thinking, dreaming about since that night at the skating rink.

His lips were soft. Warm. Like coming home somehow, like this was the most right thing that had happened in the last...I don't know how long. I'm sure there must have been a time in my life that felt right before that moment, but if there was I couldn't remember it. Strange how memories can fly straight out of your head in big moments. Like they're scuttling away to make space for a new memory, giving it room to grow—to make itself what it needs to be, then nestling back in after the moment has been captured.

And then I thought about how if I wasn't careful I'd miss this memory-making moment because I was worrying about other things and so I let all those things go, concentrating on Kade and the way he held on so tight to that swing with one hand and on to me with the other. And how that hand was making its way from my shoulder up to my neck until he pulled me with both hands, needing me closer, and me needing him closer. I wasn't sure how much time passed before a little quiver rolled up his arm and suddenly his lips stopped kissing and started smiling.

"I didn't really think this through," he said, his lips still pressed against me. "If I don't let go soon, my arm is going to start shaking."

I started laughing and he did too. He finally let go, moving his hand to my arm, but the moment was still magical somehow, like it was cool that a moment could be broken, but somehow made even better.

We sat for a moment, faced toward each other on the swings. His thumb grazed across the edge of my elbow.

"That must have hurt," he said, brushing over the small scar there.

I shrugged. "It's no big deal. It was just a scratch."

He nodded, focused on that tiny raised bump and all I could concentrate on was trying not to sound out of breath like my blood was rushing through my body at warp speed, which it was.

Eventually we stood and he walked the two steps over to me, and I noticed again how tall he was and how protected I felt as he leaned down to kiss me once more. And the memories in my head backed up again, knowing this one wasn't done being born yet.

We stayed like that for a while, nowhere near ready to leave each other's arms. When we eventually let go and started walking again, I looked at my phone and it was way later than I expected even though it felt like only five minutes. I guess when people say time flies when you're having fun they aren't kidding.

"So," he said after we'd walked in silence for a while, each lost in our own thoughts. "Now what?"

I laughed. "I have no idea."

He took a deep breath. "I know with all that," he said, gesturing back toward the swing set, "it's pretty clear there's something here, but I honestly don't know what to do about it."

My stomach started to tighten up, squeezing the butterflies out of their pleasant little home. "Why do we have to do anything about it? Can't we spend time together and let it, like, just be or something?"

He sighed. "That's the problem. I don't know how to spend

time with you without being scared. It's like I can't stay away even when I know it's dangerous. I'm on edge right now, wondering who might be watching you."

I shook my head. "No one watches me, Kade. That's ridiculous."

"Nova," he said, like I should know better.

"I thought you were worried that people were watching you, not me."

"You are who you are."

"Because of my parents? They barely even do new research anymore. They mostly do quality testing on the product." Even though things hadn't been great with my parents lately, they were still my parents and I guess I felt the need to defend them. And yeah, something weird might be going on with them, but they weren't dangerous. "Look, I've known them my whole life. I know them better than anyone. If there was anything dangerous going on, I would know it."

He sighed. "I want to believe you but—" A car turned up the street, the headlights landing momentarily on us. "Shit," Kade said, looking around, then his gaze landed on me again. "I have to go. I've already been here way longer than I promised myself I would be."

"Kade, no one is following us. I'm just not that important—I promise," I said, pleading, panicking that he could walk away right now and talk himself out of ever seeing me again.

But Kade was already backing away, his wild eyes turning to land on me again, softening.

"I wish you weren't," he said, with an apologetic smile, "but you *are* important." He sighed, closing his eyes.

He looked at me one last time as he turned to run. "You're important to them…and you're important to me."

17

It seemed like every time I left Kade, I was conflicted. Trying to figure out who was right, him or me? I'd seen so much that was good about EM and all the things it had done for so many people, but something about it was starting to feel…off. Was that Kade's influence? Was I really that easily manipulated?

I didn't think so, but I supposed anyone who was being manipulated probably didn't realize it was happening. Still, I was sure Kade wasn't a manipulator. Sure, he had his agenda with his video channel and wanting to spread awareness about living a full life without EM, but he'd had plenty of chances to try to push me into hating EM, and he hadn't done that. He'd given me his opinion, but he'd always let me have mine too.

Everything was off these days, and as I walked into my house, things didn't get any better. Mom was just finishing a Memory, and when she saw me, she quickly tucked her EM machine beside her, down into the cushions of the couch. Her eyes darted to another EM machine on the table. Which was odd because Dad was on the other side of the room using his EM machine, so it couldn't be his.

"Oh hi, honey!" Mom said, falsely cheerful.

I decided not to pull any punches. Surely she couldn't think I was that dense. "Do you have two EM machines?"

Guilt coated Mom's expression. "I guess you caught me," she said, laughing it off. "I was using my personal EM machine."

"Did your work one break or something?"

"No," she said, her tone a little sugary. "I just like to use a different one sometimes. They log the info off the work one," she explained. "Honestly, they're so snoopy. Sometimes I just want to enjoy a Memory without someone looking over my shoulder, you know?"

"So, they put a limit on your usage or something?"

"It's a ridiculous new rule," she said, awkwardly pulling her "personal" EM machine back out of the couch. "Some people at work are doing studies. It's all silly Occupational Health and Safety stuff."

I nodded as if I agreed with her, but I couldn't help but think about Kade and how he couldn't stop when he really got into EM. "I guess it's for the best though, to find out what this stuff does to people long-term or whatever."

Mom shrugged while she ejected her EM disk from the machine. "I suppose governments always want to put restrictions on things. It's their way of trying to control people."

It was kind of a strange thing for Mom to say. She'd never been one to think the government was all out to get people or anything. She always talked about how rules and regulations were important in order to have a flourishing society.

"Or just to make sure the people are safe, I guess," I said.

"Well, of course EM is safe. We, of all people, know that." Her voice was more serious now. Almost like she'd been challenged on the subject before.

"Yeah, I guess," I said, not wanting to contradict her. Not after my last run-in with Dad. "But like, how do we know? Or how do you know?"

"Nova, your father and I invented the tech," she said, pursing her lips. "Obviously we know."

"Yeah, I know, of course, but like, how do you know there's not a threshold that someone shouldn't go over? Like what if there's a limit that someone can withstand before it's too much. Before they get addicted."

"Addicted? Where did you get that idea?" Mom crossed her arms.

"I don't know. I've heard that sometimes people can start to have a problem with it."

Mom shook her head. "You can't get addicted to Enhanced Memory, honey. It's impossible."

I bit my lip, mulling this over, but decided that wasn't really an explanation. "But...are you sure? I mean, it seems like sometimes when people do a lot of EM, they have a hard time stopping."

"That's ludicrous."

"But like, for example," I said, taking a deep breath. "Do you think you'd be able to stop if you wanted to? I mean, you and Dad have to use EM a lot." My words were picking up speed as I said them, like I needed to hurry up and get them out before I lost the nerve.

Mom's head jerked back. "That's kind of an insulting thing to say. Of course we can stop. We can stop anytime we want to. Other than the fact that it's our job to use them."

"Yeah, I know, but what about the personal Memories?" I asked, walking over to her. "Like, you could totally give me your personal EM machine and at least stop doing those Memories, right?" I held out my hand, inviting her to give me the second machine.

She straightened her shoulders. "Of course I could if I wanted to. But quite frankly I don't want to. And I seem to recall that your father and I are the adults here, and the adults make the rules, not the children. Honestly, I don't need this in my own house."

To be fair, she looked exhausted. Like she just needed some time to herself. Which of course meant pulling a new Memory out from a box on the table and inserting it into her personal EM machine, like that was the end of the conversation.

"Yeah," I said, nodding. A sting that was becoming familiar prickled behind my eyes as she pressed Play. I was still nodding. "That's what I thought," I finished under my breath.

I didn't know what to do with myself. Everything was fidgety, my hands, my feet, my heart. Even breathing didn't feel quite right. It was like I knew I had to do something, but I couldn't. I didn't control what my parents did, even if I was scared it wasn't right. Mom was right about one thing. I was the kid—stuck with them and this uneasy spiral. Not old enough to do life on my own, and too old to live in a care-free world anymore with the two of them spinning around me as I tried to huddle in the middle, keeping it all together. Had I been that oblivious before, or had everything really changed as much as it seemed?

But I couldn't just sit there and watch them with their EMs. It was too depressing. They had been such hard workers once—it was how they created Enhanced Memories, working tirelessly for years—but I realized now that besides beta testing, I hadn't really seen them work in months.

I started wandering the house, searching. I had no clue what I was looking for—just a direction maybe, some clue about what to do. If I had a bit more information, maybe everything would make sense again. Mostly I think I was looking for a way to justify why my parents had so many Memories and why they needed to use them so much. Maybe I'd find some kind of ultimatum from Experion saying they were required to test even more, or a study showing that Memory usage was harmless—something, anything to tell me I was overreacting.

I did not find any of those things.

What I did find when I turned on the screen to my dad's computer was a memo from my parents' company that he had left open.

<u>NOTICE TO EMPLOYEES</u>

IT HAS COME TO OUR ATTENTION THAT SEVERAL DISKS FROM OUR MASTER MEMORY BANK ARE CURRENTLY UN-ACCOUNTED FOR. AS SUCH, WE WILL NOW BE ISSUING A MANDATORY BAG SEARCH FOR ALL EMPLOYEES AS THEY LEAVE THE PREMISES. WE WILL CONTINUE TO MONITOR

THE SITUATION CLOSELY AND KEEP ALL STAFF INFORMED WITH UPDATES UNTIL THIS MATTER IS SOLVED.

PLEASE BE ADVISED THAT IF EXPERION ENTERPRISES PROPERTY IS FOUND TO BE IN THE POSSESSION OF A STAFF MEMBER UNAPPROVED, IT WILL BE GROUNDS FOR IMMEDIATE FIRING AND COULD RESULT IN CRIMINAL CHARGES.

MANAGEMENT
EXPERION ENTERPRISES

My stomach flipped like I'd been the one caught doing something horrifically wrong. Little did it matter that I rarely did anything I wasn't supposed to, other than snoop through my parents' stuff, I guess. I stood frozen, having a very good idea where those missing Memories could be.

I took a deep breath and started pacing as my mind raced, scrabbling for solutions. This couldn't be my parents. They weren't like that. They would never. They weren't bad people—they were kind, caring...so generous. They took care of everyone around them—always praising the employees working under them, making sure they didn't work too late or got time off when their kid was sick, making sure everyone had everything they needed. Making sure I had everything I needed.

At least they used to.

My stomach rolled then as it struck me that, even I— knowing them the way I did, and having once trusted them with all my heart—had just finished rifling through their office to dig up information. Clearly that trust was gone even before I'd seen the memo.

Didn't I already sense it? I'd known something was off with the Memory Room—Dad being so defensive about it, and how they'd completely blanked on my play, all the Memories they used that weekend at the lake...hell, all the Memories they used all the time.

I had to face it. Mom and Dad were in trouble.

But what was I supposed to do? Maybe I could contact Experion. Plead with them to go easy on my parents and maybe get them some help or something.

But even if they did get help, they'd never be allowed to stay with the company, or if they did, everything would change. People would look at them differently and always wonder if they could be trusted.

I had to find another way to help them. If my parents were really doing all this—resorting to actually stealing Memories, and from the people who signed their paychecks no less—there was only one explanation.

Addiction.

I needed to talk to Kade.

18

Can you come over tomorrow?

It was going to be a long shot, but I couldn't think of anyone else to turn to.

Nova, you know I can't come to your house, Kade texted
back.

I know you don't want to, but I wouldn't ask if it wasn't important. I think my parents are in a lot of trouble.

I'm sorry, but I can't.

I have to show you something, and I can only show you here.
I took a deep breath and finished the text. Kade, I'm really
scared. I need you.

I waited for an eternity before the little dots letting me know he was typing me back appeared.

Can you promise it will be quick and no one will be there except us?

Yes, my parents have work. After everything I knew, I couldn't believe they were still going, but I guess they still had to feed the addiction somehow. It will only take a minute.

I'll try.

I should have been relieved, but my stomach started churning more than ever. I didn't fully understand what Kade was so scared about, but I was starting to think that whatever it was, he might not be as paranoid as I used to think.

I didn't sleep at all that night and paced the house while I waited for him to get there the next day, trying to straighten up a bit, but my mind couldn't focus. My eyes darted a hundred times toward the Memory Room. I couldn't stop thinking about those little drawers, and the memo. What was I supposed to do about the memo?

Finally a knock sounded at the door, so quiet I almost didn't hear it.

It was Kade, but if I hadn't been expecting him, I might not have opened the door at all. He was covered from head to toe in black, black cap with hoodie overtop and a pair of sunglasses.

He snuck in quickly and peeked through a crack in the doorway before closing it and locking it behind him.

"I'm sorry for the mess," I said, not really knowing where to begin.

"You know I don't care about that," he said as he looked around.

He was obviously distracted, but did come over for a hug and I let the relief wash over me, relishing in the moment.

But soon he pulled back. "Okay, what was it that you needed to show me?"

I closed my eyes and took a breath. "I guess I was wondering about how you were with Memories when you were having your issues."

He tilted his head, questioning.

"Like did you collect them?"

He shrugged. "Memories were the most important thing. I tried to get my hands on as many as I could."

I nodded, starting to walk toward the Memory Room door. "I need to know what you think about this, since you have some experience in the area of, I don't know, collecting Memories, I guess."

I opened the door and stepped inside.

Kade took a couple steps in, his gaze moving all the way to the ceiling as he slowly turned. "What is all this?"

I sucked in a breath. "Uh, Memories," I said.

"These can't all be Memories," he said, moving closer to one of the walls of tiny drawers.

"They are," I said, hoping he would think it was…less disturbing than I did.

He pulled open one of the drawers. "Are these…?" He pulled another drawer, then another. "Are these all extracted Memories? Like the authentic ones?"

He carefully picked a small disk out of the drawer and immediately a hologram of someone throwing a javelin came to life.

"I guess," I said. "I didn't even know there were different kinds until a little while ago."

He tossed the disk back into its drawer and dropped his hands quickly, like the disk was full of germs or something. He turned to face me. "Nova, this collection…it's not normal."

He turned to me, a weird expression on his face. He started backing slowly away from the drawers. "I can't be in here."

"I'm sorry," I said, quickly closing the drawer he'd left open. "I just…needed someone to see. I needed to figure out what was going on with my parents."

Kade started pacing. "I have to get out of here," he said, backing out of the room. "You shouldn't have brought me into a room like this. With my history, you shouldn't have even told me a room like this existed."

I shut the Memory Room door as I followed him into the living room.

"I'm sorry, I just don't know what to do. I—I guess I wanted to know what you thought."

"A regular developer wouldn't have access to this kind of a collection," he said, still pacing. He moved the curtain in the front window and peeked out.

"Well, um, I guess they're not regular developers then. I don't know. They were in on it from the beginning. They helped create Enhanced Memories, which is why I'm so worried. My parents have been doing this longer than anyone."

He finally stopped moving and looked at me. But the moment he did I kind of wished he'd start pacing again, because the look he gave me was chilling.

"Your parents invented Enhanced Memories?" His voice rose at the end of the sentence.

"Not by themselves," I said, suddenly defensive.

Honestly I wasn't even sure if that was true or not.

"You've brought me—the guy who is trying to do everything possible to stay safe from EM—to the house of the people who invented it?"

"No one knows you're Real K," I said, taking a step toward him.

His eyes got wide and he startled, kind of ducking, and looking frantically at the ceiling. "Jesus, Nova, don't say that out loud. They could be listening."

I don't know what he thought it was going to do, but he pulled his hood over his head again, as if to hide.

"Kade, what are you talking about?"

His eyes opened wide again. "Stop saying my name!" he yelled, then started going from doorway to doorway. "Is there a back way out of here?"

I shook my head. "Ka— Sorry, I won't say your name. Can't you stop for a second and tell me what is going on? Why are you freaking out? I know something is going on, but I can't figure it all out." Tears sprang to my eyes and I fought hard to keep them from falling. Kade's face softened for a second.

"Look, I'm sorry. For all of this. For who you are. This must be terrible for you." He looked around again, finally spotting the back door past the kitchen. "Especially if they're going downhill like you say." He looked at me, so serious.

Searching. "I have something I need to show you too, but I can't do it here. I can't even be here. I'm scared, Nova, I'm sorry." He seemed like he wanted to say more, but his fear of…whatever it was, was too much. "Meet me tomorrow after work at the place we met the other night."

He turned and hurried to the back door, unlocked it and poked his head out to look around. When he decided it was clear, he stepped out, closed the door behind him, and ran.

19

Everything seemed to be falling apart all around me, but doing my job was the one small thing I could control.

As I made my way into Mae's room, I was surprised to see her sitting in her chair by the window.

"How're ya doing, Mae?" I asked, knocking lightly.

She turned and beamed a radiant smile my way. "Hi."

"Looks like a nice day out there," I said as she turned back to the window.

She nodded. "Life up the blanket making turnips read seven."

"Sorry?" I asked, certain I had heard her wrong.

She turned back to me, smiling as brightly as before. "Brown laundry upends and cords sunshine it many such."

"Ah," I said, nodding as if I had any sense of what she was saying.

Unfortunately, I did have a good sense of what was going on. Her language was clearly going again.

"Bustling sleep and windows noising with medicine goats?" She was looking at me with questioning in her eyes now, like I hadn't responded the way she thought I was supposed to.

It was weird, like she wasn't hearing the words that were coming out of her mouth. She acted as if she was making perfect sense and like I was the one who was confused. I hated that I was the one who had taken the smile off her face.

"Oh hey," Genie said, peeking her head in. "I need to borrow Nova for a second, Mae," she said, smiling.

Mae still looked confused, but managed a nod.

"What's going on with her?" I whispered once we got to the hall.

Genie shook her head, solemn. "It's unfortunate, but this happens sometimes. Her brain didn't take to the language download too well."

"Why haven't you gotten her back in there to download it again?"

Genie let out a long sigh. "It's complicated. But the simple explanation is that her brain is too delicate right now. It's trying to re-form synapses and neural pathways—it's going through too much change. We can try again in a few weeks, but from past experience, it's not likely it will take a second time. Her brain has undergone too much stress."

"So like, she has brain damage?"

"In a sense, I suppose so, yes."

"And everyone just thinks this is okay to keep doing this to these people?" My voice started to rise a little, and Genie motioned for me to speak lower.

"Like I told you before, the residents here know the risks to what they're doing. They go through intense screening and have decided that keeping the memories of their loved ones is worth the risk. It's a quality of life issue. I know it can be hard to understand when you're young and your memories seem like they'll be there forever, but unfortunately, that's just not the case for a lot of people."

I squeezed my eyes shut and rubbed my forehead. "It keeps getting worse and worse."

"What does, hon?"

"Enhanced Memory. It's like, ruining lives all over the place."

"Nova, you know that's not true. The vast majority of the residents here are happy with the opportunity they get to—"

I couldn't take it anymore. "I'm not just talking about the residents in here. I'm talking about what's going on out there," I said, making a sweeping gesture with my arm. "Everything's going wrong out there and it's like people refuse to see it."

"What are you talking about, Nova? Enhanced Memory is a godsend. It's a miracle."

I let out a frustrated groan. "Like I said, maybe people don't see it," I said. I wanted to tell her that I wasn't sure that everyone had the information they needed to make an informed decision. That maybe all the people out there in the world didn't really know what they were getting into, but of course I had no real proof. "Look, I'm sorry, I just...I don't know. I better get back to work."

"Yeah, maybe that's a good idea," Genie said, giving me a look like she was worried.

I needed to get out of my head. I needed to lighten

my mood. I needed a little of the Clyde optimism he was known for.

I knocked quietly at his door, surprised and thankful he was in his room. I was feeling selfish, I guess, and wanted some time with him all to myself.

"Hey, Nova," he said, his eyes bright.

I let out the breath I'd been holding. I hadn't even realized I had been worried until that moment. The last time I'd seen Clyde he hadn't been quite himself, but his smile announced that the light had returned.

"You're looking like you're having another rough day, kid," he said, and even he looked worried.

Which made me feel guilty about always coming to him with my problems. It wasn't his job to make some kid feel better, although I did suspect he enjoyed sharing his wisdom—especially with someone who really wanted to hear it.

"I guess you could say I've been going through a rough patch, yeah."

He raised an eyebrow. "More boy trouble?"

"No. Well, yeah," I said, chuckling a little. "But that's the least of my worries lately."

Clyde shifted in his chair. "Yeah, there seems to be a lot of that going around lately. It's like the world itself has lots of worries these days."

I tilted my head. As I thought about it, Enhanced Memory and all the complications I'd suddenly discovered about it came to mind. "Yeah, that does feel kind of true."

I didn't want to get into a big discussion about the whole EM thing with Clyde though. I'd come here hoping to feel better, not worse.

Clyde stared off into space for a bit, just thinking about it all. "I guess things are always moving forward. I've seen a lot of big changes in my day, but somehow lately, things feel different. Like there's a weird energy in the world."

"A weird energy?"

Clyde nodded. "I don't really know how to explain it. It's like a...disconnection, I suppose. Like people forgot how to be."

That was an interesting idea to mull over. And certainly not the lighthearted kind of thought I'd come in here seeking. But I couldn't argue with him. "A loneliness," I added. "But I don't know how to change that. I was supposed to go to this party a while back, but it seemed so much easier not to go, so...what does that mean? That we're starting to like the loneliness?"

Clyde sighed. "Maybe we're just more comfortable with the loneliness than we are with the uncertainty of putting ourselves out there. The uncertainty of the unknown."

The idea filled me with unease. If that was the case, how would things ever get...less lonely?

"It's funny," he continued. "People used to do everything they could to interact with each other. They would plan these huge, extravagant events, or create entire leagues of team sports and things like that...and I think it was simply about being around one another. Having people to talk to and an event like that would give them lots of things to talk about."

"I remember," I said. "I used to play softball when I was little." A tiny smile crept across my face as I remembered high-fiving my teammates after a big hit. "Once I even hit a home run. I mean, I was like seven, so it wasn't a real home run, just a normal hit and the fielders fumbled the ball a couple times so I was able to make it all the way around the bases, but it was so exciting. My first home run."

Clyde's smile was huge, as if it had been him running those bases that day. "Exactly." He looked at nothing as he continued to smile, but then his expression started to fade. "There doesn't seem to be a whole lot of that going on anymore. It's sad to think about people not having those kinds of moments anymore."

"Just Enhanced Memory," I said.

Clyde tilted his head. "Yes, and that's an amazing thing, for sure. Honestly, thank goodness for it, since my memory isn't what it used to be, but those are just moments, aren't they? A great experience, sure…but then what? What about hanging out and yakking with the guys after a game? Or sitting around playing cards and telling stories about the experiences? That's the stuff that builds relationships."

My stomach tightened, realizing he was right. I had no desire to go to parties or make new friends, and my parents didn't seem to have any desire to have much of a relationship with me anymore. And yeah, it felt like maybe I was building a relationship with Kade, but…maybe that was because we were having real experiences.

After a long pause, Clyde let out a humorless chuckle. "If you ask me, the way the world seems to be going, it feels a lot more dangerous for kids not to be out there playing like that. And for the adults not to be out there enjoying watching them. Or enjoying each other's company, for that matter."

I nodded, unable to shake the tension seeping into every part of my body. "If we would have had this discussion a couple weeks ago, I'm not sure I'd agree with you as much as I do now."

"Just another part of the change going on, maybe," Clyde said. "I hadn't really started thinking about the way everything has changed until lately either. But something just feels off these days."

I didn't have the heart to tell him I might have an idea what was off about him. He already had this sense that we were losing our relationships—maybe the most important thing in the human experience, and now he'd lost the memories of an entire member of his family. No wonder he felt a little bit off—even if he didn't consciously realize what he was missing. There had to be some kind of emotional fallout to all this.

Memory loss was devastating, of course, but...what if what we were doing was making it even worse?

An alarm sounded on his phone. "Ah, we're going to have to cut this short, kid," he said, sitting up a bit straighter. "It's time for the old Memory machine."

My heart drooped. Even though Clyde was feeling the general lowness of the world, he didn't directly recognize what might be causing it.

And unfortunately, I was becoming more and more certain I did.

As I walked home, a girl approached from the opposite direction on the sidewalk and I forced a smile. It was a habit I'd picked up when we used to live in a smaller town. Everybody smiled at everybody.

"Hey...it's you," she said, her face brightening with recognition.

"Sorry?" I asked, having no idea who she was.

"Oh," she said, looking slightly disappointed. "Sorry, I thought you were someone else."

"Okay," I said, though something niggled in my brain.

I was used to it and I'd always chalked people recognizing me up to having "one of those faces," but it had been happening a little too much lately. Unease slithered through my chest.

"Um, well, have a good day."

I nodded. "Yeah, thanks."

But the whole way home I couldn't stop thinking about her. Or about all the other strangers who thought they knew me. And another question kept popping into my thoughts. What if I didn't have one of those generic faces?

Kade had said the name Harlow that day in the club, but I had no idea what her last name was.

When I got home I pulled out my phone and headed to my room.

I was wondering if you could help me out with something. You know that Harlow girl you thought I was that first time we met? Do you know what her last name is?

Weird question, lol, he typed back, but thankfully after a pause he added, It's Beckman.

Cool, thanks.

I typed Harlow Beckman into the search bar on my phone. The results that came up were strange. There was nothing really about Harlow herself, but there were a ton of people who seemed to be wondering what happened to her.

Search result after search result. Hundreds of them.

What happened to Harlow?

I miss Harlow Beckman.

Where is Harlow Beckman now?

Why did Harlow delete all her accounts?

There were also a few news stories.

Crowd gathers at Harlow Beckman's residence hoping to catch a glimpse of the star.

Harlow Beckman reported missing by hundreds of fans. No confirmation from her team.

And a few conspiracy theories.

Harlow abducted by aliens!

Harlow Beckman is not in hiding. She's no longer with us.

No longer with us? Like dead?

But as strange as all these results were, none of them was what I was looking for. I'd hoped to find a picture or a video or something that would give me a clue as to why people kept mistaking me for her. I scrolled through page after page until finally, on page seven of the results, something looked promising.

Harlow Beckman: Real Footage.

I clicked on the link as fast as I could.

And there she was. As far as I could tell, at least. The footage was filmed from far away and was super grainy, like it had been shot in dim light or something, but there on the center of the screen was a girl. She wasn't looking into the camera—more like someone was shooting without her knowing. She was at a party. It was crowded and people kept walking past the camera but not so you could see their faces, just their torsos, like the person filming was crouched or sitting.

And then the girl in the film leaned her head back and laughed. Like really laughed.

The footage caught me off guard. I sat up straight in my bed, squinting to try to see deeper into the grainy film. I zoomed in even more, but all that did was make it even more grainy and harder to see. I zoomed back out and backed up fifteen seconds, back to the laugh.

My stomach tightened as I watched. Something was really not right about all this. Because there was something about that laugh. Something so familiar.

20

I still had an hour before Kade and I were supposed to meet and I was spinning out.

The front door shut and I pulled my sweater on and headed downstairs. Maybe if I could smooth things over with my parents and make one thing halfway normal again, everything else would make more sense too. But halfway down the stairs, I stopped. They'd walked in the door only two minutes ago and they were already both absorbed in a Memory. Dad still had his coat on.

Watching them on opposite sides of the room with their blissed-out expressions was strange. I watched as my mom's arm drooped to her side as she started "living" the Memory. I could only imagine what they were "remembering." Some sort of adrenaline-filled police chase, maybe, or perhaps some seedy love affair. Who knows, maybe they'd found a way to combine the two by now.

I was tired. The whole thing made my stomach turn.

Of course, that could have also been the sickly sweet smell of rotting fruit wafting from some corner of the house. In the past few weeks the mess had piled up again and I couldn't ignore it any longer. The entire place looked like it had been ransacked. I thought maybe once things got bad enough, Mom and Dad would finally notice.

I guess I was wrong.

I had only a few minutes before I had to leave, but I pulled one of the big garbage bags out from under the counter and started chucking. Mountains of take-out containers mingled with dirty dishes and empty cereal boxes, and clothes draped over everything, dropped haphazardly on every available surface. The stacks of unopened mail made me wonder if they were even paying the bills anymore.

I opened the fridge, then slammed it shut again, realizing in an instant that the rotting smell was only a preview of the real situation. I dropped the garbage bag.

I was so done.

I went to the living room, my eyes wandering to the room beyond that, and I became even more disgusted at how spotless everything in there was. Of course they took care of that room. It was pretty much their temple.

A shrine to their precious Memories.

It used to be a spare bedroom, just big enough for a bed and a couple bookshelves. But that was before they found Andie and me using the Memories. The room was dim and had a revered atmosphere to it. A place of worship dedicated to the mind.

I wandered in and pulled open one of the drawers exposing the small disk. As I took the disk from the drawer, a tiny ballerina slowly spun to life, as if freed from an old jewelry box, only in holograph form. It likely contained an experience of being a dancer onstage. Probably the lead dancer. Why make a mediocre experience when you could make a spectacular one?

A stabbing pain shot through my head, behind my eye, along with a flash and sounds of screaming in the background. I sighed. Another headache coming on. They'd been happening for way too long. I really needed less stress in my life.

I shoved the disk back into the drawer, definitely harder than was necessary.

If it weren't for this room, and what it represented, I would still have some semblance of parental figures.

"Hey!" my father yelled from outside the doorway. "Be careful with that."

I sighed. Of course he noticed me in here. He wouldn't notice if I brought home some sketchy dude and started making out in front of him, but he noticed the moment I set foot in their precious new Memory Room.

"What are you doing in here?"

"Nothing. Just trying to find a place that isn't disgusting."

"What are you talking about?" he asked as if it was a legitimate question and didn't actually realize the state of the house/hellhole.

"It's disgusting out there," I said, motioning toward the rest of the house. "Is anyone ever going to clean? Or like, take care of shit?" The throbbing behind my eyes intensified.

"Watch your language."

"Language?" I said, amazed that was what he decided to focus on.

"You're still a child. You shouldn't talk like that."

"I'm seventeen."

"Exactly. And as long as you're living under this roof, I will not tolerate you speaking like that."

"You won't tolerate it," I said, my voice flat. "Right. So what about all the stuff I have to tolerate?" I was surprised at how calm I sounded when inside my chest was a pulsing jumble of rage and frustration, desperate to tear its way out.

"As if there is so much to tolerate as a teenager," Dad continued, opening the drawer I'd slammed shut, no doubt to make sure the precious contents were still in perfect order. As if the drawer unit wasn't made to withstand hurricane-like forces.

"Um, have you even taken a look around lately?" I hated how my voice was shaking. I took a deep breath and moved toward the kitchen, thankful he was at least following me. It was kind of a miracle I had his attention at all.

I sucked in a breath before I whipped opened the fridge, allowing the full stench of it to hit him straight on. He took a deep breath to say something, but nothing came out as he was assaulted by the putridness of it. He covered his mouth and nose, his shoulders slumping a little. Maybe he was actually resigning himself to the fact that he really hadn't been taking care of things.

But then he straightened back up.

"Please close that." He said it quietly, but could not have been more serious.

I closed the fridge with a little more force than was probably necessary, a few papers that were stuck on the door escaping their magnet prisons.

He walked back out of the room. It was my turn to follow him. I'd finally gotten his attention and I was not about to give it up.

"So are you going to take care of this?" I asked, waving my arm around the room.

My mother finally seemed to notice something was going on. Surprising, since there wasn't even a train plowing through the front door.

"What is happening?"

Dad turned to her. "Nova seems to think we're neglecting her." He said it in a way that implied an eye roll.

Mom sighed. "Nova, there are thousands of children that would love to have the life you have."

"Are you kidding me? Having to take care of everything while my parents are off in their own little worlds of fake Memories?" I wanted to throw the fact that I knew about the memo from Experion in their faces, but I honestly didn't want to hear more lies. But I couldn't just keep my mouth shut anymore either. I didn't want to be the "enabler" everyone was always talking about in those detox shows.

"We are not off in our own little worlds," my mother said. Her overly defensive tone making her sound like she didn't even believe herself.

"Right. And this place turned into a dump for no reason."

"What are you talking about?" Mom looked around the room uneasily.

I turned to Dad. "Should I demonstrate the kitchen situation for her?" I blinked, daring him to argue that this place wasn't fit for humans to live at the moment.

"No." He put his hand up quickly to stop me. "That won't be necessary."

"What is she talking about?" Mom looked at Dad questioningly.

I sighed. "The fact that you don't even know what this house has become proves my point."

Mom continued to blink at Dad like she had no idea what was going on. Which was probably the most authentic thing I'd seen out of her in days.

"Your 'beta testing' is completely out of control. And I know you're not just doing it for work anymore."

Dad looked at Mom, confused. I guess she hadn't told him about me catching her with her second EM machine.

"Sometimes we need a little break. Something to take the edge off all the stress we're under," Mom said, defensive.

"The stress you're under," I repeated. "What stress? It's like nothing matters to you anymore. You used to look forward to things. To making breakthroughs at work, to trips to the lake, to…I don't know, leaving the damn house for anything other than work! When was the last time you even thought about any of that stuff? About anything other than the next EM disk?"

Dad looked back at me and had a strange expression on his face, like he hadn't really seen me in a long time. Maybe he didn't realize how much time had passed while he was otherwise occupied. And something in that look made an idea bubble up in my mind.

I knew it was a bad idea, but it also seemed so, so good. It was wrong, of course, but it would get their attention.

I stared at my parents, both looking at me with bewildered looks on their faces. Neither one of them had really been living lately. At least not in the real world. And I was pretty sure their minds couldn't quite focus the same after what they'd put them through.

But for once I had their attention.

I took a few deep breaths, fighting the pain in my head, and decided. It was probably the worst thing I had ever considered doing, knowing what it would do to them. Correction: it was *definitely* the worst thing I had ever considered doing, but I wasn't sure I could bring myself to care anymore. In fact, that was exactly the reason I was suddenly so sure I wanted to do it.

Before I could talk myself out of it, I stormed into the Memory Room.

So many drawers, so little time.

I pulled...tentatively at first, watching the first drawer flop unceremoniously to the floor with a clunk.

I knew my parents would be right behind me and I wanted to get to as many Memories as I could. I lunged at the drawers, pulling as many as my arms would allow, barely registering Mom's screams. One drawer after the other went flying, disks spewing from them, each crash more satisfying than the last.

"Nova, stop!" Dad yelled, but it only pushed me on.

It wasn't delight I was feeling, exactly, but there was definitely a satisfaction, watching those little silver disks—so alluring, and yet so threatening—scatter into as much chaos as my life had become because of them. I felt out of control, each pull driving me further into my frustration, fueling me like some kind of chaotic fury was finally unleashing.

Dad tried to pull me away. But he couldn't keep hold of me as I wriggled out and got to another drawer, yanking it free along with a few more.

Finally he got a hold of both my arms and pulled me away.

The wreckage was fantastic as I breathed heavily, a wild, out-of-control feeling surging through me.

"What have you done?" he said, panic in his voice.

You'd think he'd be grateful—this was probably the first real memory he'd made in a very long time, but apparently not.

A couple of the drawers were sideways, the disks fallen out with holograms playing, or at least trying to play...flickering to life, then sputtering out, then fighting their way to life once more.

Mom dove to the floor, frantically trying to collect her precious Memories, acting as if I had stomped her child or something. Little matter that I *was* her actual child.

"Are you done?" Dad asked, loosening his grip on my arms a bit.

I stopped trying to pull away from him, realizing that my outburst had only proven that the Memories truly were the only things they cared about in this world.

I walked out of the room as my father joined my mother on the floor, desperate to restore the room to its pristine condition as quickly as possible. It was a pitiful display, but one that solidified exactly what I had suspected. After all that adrenaline and burst of rage, my shoulders slumped. Nothing had changed. Those little metal disks had become more important to my parents than anything else.

Including me.

"This room is off-limits from now on!" Dad yelled after me.

I couldn't bring myself to answer as I stormed out of the house wondering how everything got so messed up so fast.

It was like they weren't even my parents anymore, barely a glimmer of the people they'd once been. I fought tears as I walked, wondering if I'd ever see the real them again.

21

Kade knew something was wrong the moment he set eyes on me. I guess I wasn't hiding the tears as well as I thought. I shook my head a little, not even knowing what to say. "My parents. There…there's something wrong. They're out of control. I just…I need to figure out a way to get them the help they need so that everything can go back to normal."

His shoulders fell a little. "I'm sorry you're going through all this," he said, his eyes full of concern. But he was distracted too. Like he was trying to figure something out. "Especially after…everything else that you've been through."

I crinkled my brow. "What are you talking about?"

"I have to show you something. I should have shown you before, but…I just couldn't do it in that house. It was too risky." He sighed, apparently not knowing what else to say.

Kade fished his phone out of his pocket, scrolling through his photos and videos. He had a pained expression on his face, like he was having some kind of inner battle and both sides were losing.

"Here," he said, holding his phone to me.

The video finished loading and began to play. My own face stared up at me from the screen.

And it might have been my face, but the rest of me was different. Blond hair where mine was brown. Lots of makeup when I preferred hardly any. And more unsettling, a huge personality where mine was, well, tiny. A voice in the background of the video yelled, "Harlow!" and the girl turned.

"Harlow?" I asked, the fear that had been simmering in my guts grew to a fiery boil.

On the grainy video I'd seen before, there was definitely a resemblance and I could kind of see why people might have mistaken us, but now, seeing this, the similarity was unsettling.

Her voice was mine too, except for the fact that she could sing, belting out some song that was playing in the background, though nobody in their right mind would be listening to the version playing over the speakers when she was giving a show instead.

"Yeah," Kade said.

"That's so weird," was all I could muster up.

He watched me closely.

"You must have known her pretty well to have this footage," I said. "I could hardly find anything on the internet."

Kade nodded. "Most of it has been taken down."

I scrunched up my forehead. "I don't get how that's possible. The internet is huge. If she was as popular as you say, how do they...scrub the internet of her presence?"

"That's the scary part. That's the kind of power they have. I don't know if they do the dirty work themselves, or if they feed people Enhanced Memories that have suggestions in them—like hypnosis or something—to make them take stuff down or what, but either way, it's a huge undertaking. This is a big deal." His words were serious, like he was afraid I wasn't taking this seriously enough. "Just...you need to keep watching."

The tightness in my stomach turned into an all-out roiling. I was terrified of the next few minutes. I'd been avoiding thinking about the possibility, always pushing it away. I just...didn't want to know for sure.

Kade nodded like it would be okay. "I promise, I'm right here beside you."

"I don't think I want to see the rest of this video."

"I know, but I'm here and I'm going to stay here as long as you need me."

I wondered if he meant tonight, or like, forever, because that's about how long it felt like I might need him.

The video kept playing and Harlow was dancing with someone now and they kissed. And it looked so easy. So natural.

I thought back to the kiss that Kade and I had shared—slow and tentative, I'd been so nervous, so unsure with what I was doing. But she looked like she was having the time of her life. I couldn't take my eyes off her. Maybe it was because she looked so much like me and it was freaking me out, but also there was this...magnetism about her. Like I would have loved to be in that place with her. Everyone was paying attention to her, but in that way that sometimes happens with people—none of them fighting for her attention, and she wasn't all wrapped up in herself or pushing for their attention, it was like...I don't know, she was sending them all good vibes somehow, even though her focus wasn't on one particular person. Her focus was on everyone all at once.

And then it happened. The thing that Kade knew would happen.

The thing that punched me right in the gut and sent a sizzling jolt of pain through my head.

As Harlow laughed and did a quick turn to the camera, she put her hand up to move the hair from her eyes. The shot got in nice and close, and I saw it.

The scar on the inside of her right elbow.

I looked at Kade. He knew I'd seen it.

I pulled my own sleeve up, looking at the very same scar that Harlow possessed. I remembered how he had focused on it that night in the park.

"H-how?" was all I could say, but I already knew.

The scar was jagged and one of a kind.

"Do you remember how you got it?" Kade asked.

"Of course, I..."

It was about to roll out of my mouth like it was on the tip of my tongue, but then the memory that seemed like it had been there a moment ago floated away like a dream. I thought harder, but the more I tried the further the memory seemed to scurry away.

My hands were shaking and tears were forming and thoughts were swirling and I didn't know what to do with myself. I wanted to run, but where would I go?

Because what I wanted to run from was myself.

The world got quiet.

"The day you got this was actually a great day," Kade said after the silence got thick.

I looked in his eyes, searching. I didn't want to think about how he knew better than me how I got the scar.

"It was at a carnival. One of those traveling carnivals where they set up all the rides in a couple days and the fair is in town for a week, then what seems like an instant later it's gone again."

The carnival. Yes, something was familiar about that.

"There were a few of us there that day. Paddy and Jess and Ray," he said. "And me."

I nodded, a tear jumping from its ledge. I was afraid to make a sound. Almost as afraid as I was not to, to stop Kade before my entire world imploded.

But it was too late and so he kept going.

"We went on the roller coaster."

A flash of memory zipped through my mind, the same vision of the roller coaster that I had seen before even though I couldn't recall having ever been on a real one. The wind in my hair, the scream on my lips, the overwhelming freedom and exhilaration.

I was Harlow.

"We ate so much sugar and greasy carnival food we were ready to puke. And then you were spinning…you were always twirling, like you were in love with the world—and it loved you back too."

A small choking cry escaped my lips. It was there, just out of reach, like a dream I'd once had and the feeling he was talking about was so close I could almost touch it. I closed my eyes to grab hold, but it floated away too.

"The whole day was amazing, but then at the end, while you spun around to talk to Ray, your elbow caught on a jagged piece of metal. Hard. It was something that should have been covered over but with the hasty way they'd set up the carnival they'd missed it. Your laugh turned into this haunting scream and you knelt down grasping your arm and none of us knew what happened at first, and then your dress, that white dress you always wore, started splotching with red."

Kade closed his eyes, remembering.

"And it was terrifying at first, but then you stood, the blood soaking your dress. I'll never forget the blood. And then you started laughing like you always did. You were hurt, but you wanted to let us know you were going to be okay, and so you did what you did best, and laughed. You were always laughing that amazing laugh of yours. Even when you were hurt. It was like you made it your job to make sure everybody had a good time. And people loved you for it."

People loved me.

The phrase was strange strolling through my mind. It was so very opposite of the way I always remembered feeling.

"The cut went all the way to the bone," Kade continued, then chuckled a little. "I'm embarrassed to say I nearly fainted when I saw that bone through the blood—it was so white, much whiter than your dress—but Jess was rock solid, knowing exactly what to do. There was an ambulance set up outside the fair. I think they always do that at those things, you know for people who get dehydrated or eat something bad, but they were good with your arm too. Total experts, bandaging you up and instructing us to go straight to the hospital because you were going to need stitches."

Another flash then, of Kade trying to entertain me in the hospital. Not that I remembered all of it, but I remember thinking it was taking forever. I could almost feel the ache in my arm. I rubbed my scar.

I could only push the next few words out in a whisper. "What happened to me?"

He knew what I meant. I was done hearing about the hospital visit. I needed to know what happened after that.

Kade shrugged, looking almost ashamed. "You were still around for a while. Your cut healed, we kept on the way we always did. With the others, always looking for something new and exciting to do. Posting on social media. But then..." He paused, and it was like he was trying to find a way to say the rest but it was going to be impossible to hear no matter what words came out.

"Just say it," I eventually said, my eyes softening.

"And then one day you were...gone."

Something rose up in my chest, emotions turning to rock and settling themselves in my throat.

"Gone?"

He nodded. "You stopped answering everyone's texts. Stopped posting on all your accounts."

You. He kept saying you but that wasn't right. This Harlow person, she wasn't me. I mean, in my mind I understood that somehow I used to be Harlow, but I didn't feel like her.

"How long ago was this?"

"I don't know exactly, maybe a year or two ago?" He cleared his throat. "For a while she had talked about taking off. Leaving everything behind and starting fresh somewhere else, so at first I thought that's exactly what she had done. I was even happy for her. But then a couple months after she was gone I started to realize things weren't right. She had disappeared off the internet. All her old posts had disappeared. No one had heard from her. I got in touch with every person she'd ever had contact with that I knew of, but there was just nothing. Not a peep. And I kept having this weird thought like she had been erased."

"You didn't think she would have erased the accounts herself?"

"It didn't make sense," he said. "She loved her online family."

"And this was over a year ago?"

He nodded. "Around there, yeah."

I sucked in a deep breath. "We moved here a year ago."

He took my hand.

Tears filled my eyes. "But...I remember always being Nova. Remember being her as a kid. Except now, especially since I met you, I have these...other memories. Flashes."

Kade nodded. "I've heard flashbacks are possible after extractions."

"Was Harlow like you? Against Enhanced Memories?"

Kade shrugged. "Harlow wasn't super into EM. She tried it, but didn't really like it. Said they made her feel wrong, like living in someone else's skin."

I shivered.

"She said life wasn't any fun if you weren't making your own memories," he continued. "She was kind of ahead of her time that way, I think."

I started walking, shaking my head. "None of this feels real. I remember this whole life as Nova."

"I'm sorry, I don't know how to explain that. I only know what I've seen."

"So if I'm Harlow, how am I also Nova?"

He didn't answer. Didn't have an answer any more than I did.

So many thoughts were running through my head, one hitting me like a jolt. "With Harlow?" I couldn't help but ask. "Did we…" I let the question trail away.

He shook his head. "No, Harlow and I were just friends."

"But she sounds like a lot of fun," I said, trying to keep the pang of jealousy at bay.

It seemed so bizarre to be jealous of someone when that someone was actually you. But if you didn't remember any of it, was it even real?

He nodded. "She was adored by everybody, and I adored her too, just not in that way. We were…too close, if that makes any sense. Maybe we were too much alike to be interesting to each other. I've always been drawn to people that were more grounded than me, and Harlow was definitely not grounded, which of course was part of her appeal to everyone else. Like she was this free spirit, but because I was the same way, I knew she wasn't really free. She was always searching."

"And then you saw me that day in the club."

He let out a breath. "I suspected you were her from the start—I mean, obviously you look exactly the same, but then you acted so different. It caught me off guard. At first I thought maybe amnesia or something, but then I realized with Harlow disappearing off social media, something else must have been going on. We had both been into real memories and building these followings on social media, but she was so out there in the open about it. I thought she was reckless for being so public and showing her face on her videos. I mean, she was brave, don't get me wrong, but she also took a lot of unnecessary risk by doing that."

"Seems like it was a poor choice," I said, looking at my feet as I walked.

More thoughts started to wiggle their way in. Harlow seemed like she had it all. She was confident and friendly and made everyone want to be around her. I was the exact opposite of that.

Because they made me that way.

"This is all just—" But of course there was no way to finish that sentence. I stopped and looked at him. "It's all so unreal. My god, I'm not even real."

"Nova," he said, taking a step toward me. "You're real. You're so real. You're the most real person I've met in a long time."

"How can I be real when I have absolutely no idea who I am? Harlow…I don't know, she doesn't seem real to me at all, but then I get these flashes. Like a dream, only it's so much more than a dream, but they only last a second. But if she's what's real, what has always been real, then who the hell am I? This girl with all these memories? Memories from when I was a kid, except, I know they can't have happened. Were they made up in some lab? From some developer's imagination?"

"Nova, you're real," Kade said, but I wasn't really hearing him.

"Jesus," I said. "I'm a work of fiction."

My arms dropped to my sides, defeated. I closed my eyes and tried to breathe. It's all I could manage.

"I'm so sorry, Nova," Kade said, tentative. "I didn't want to upset you. But this," he said, holding his hands out palms up, gesturing to me, "this is what I mean. You, Nova, are so real." He was talking low, like he didn't want to spook me. "Even if you haven't always been this way, it's who you are now. And that's what matters. You are still you, no matter what your history is."

But of course it wasn't that simple.

"You knew."

He tilted his head. Questioning.

"You knew I was Harlow all along and you just…befriended me? You thought it would what? Be funny to play along? Watch the fake freak girl?"

"Nova, I was trying to protect you. I had to figure out how much danger you might be in—how your parents were involved. I was so afraid of making it worse. I thought you'd never believe me and go straight to them, and if they found out you knew they might…I don't know. They could do something even worse. I never wanted to hurt you. You have to know I wanted to tell you all along, but I didn't know how."

"You could have just said it!" I yelled.

"And would you have believed me?" he asked.

"I don't know," I yelled. "But you kept it from me! You had the video!"

"I know. I…still didn't think it would be enough. You said yourself that people have always mistaken you for someone else. You could have just explained it away. We're talking about something that no one knew was possible. I couldn't even put it together for the longest time, even knowing what I knew."

I tried to access her—Harlow—find her inside my mind, but I couldn't.

I was numb.

"I need you to send the video to me," I said.

"Are you sure?"

I nodded and he turned his attention to his phone. A moment later, my phone pinged.

Hadn't I known something was wrong...off somehow? The way I didn't even feel right in my body anymore, like I didn't quite fit, always bumping into things and tripping. Was I actually trying to relearn these things inside a new body? That was some kind of ridiculous sci-fi shit.

And I remembered flashes. Bits and pieces of being her. Harlow.

But...I felt even less like I belonged in this body. In *any* body.

Kade tried to take my hand, I guess to soothe me, but I took a step back.

"It's like all of this," I said, gesturing between us, "it's all fake. Whatever this is built on is fake. You had all this information and just kept it to yourself. And yeah, I get that you didn't know what to do with that information, but...I just...I can't be around you right now." And the words were meant to sting—I guess I was hoping someone else could feel some of this pain for me—but it was the look I gave him that was really meant to draw blood.

And it worked, he looked wounded, but only for a second.

As much as he was involved in the whole thing, he knew it wasn't his turn for it to be about him.

Which made me even angrier somehow.

He reached for me again, but I turned away. "Just...leave me alone!" I said, my voice rising.

"Nova...don't—"

But I didn't let him finish.

I was already running.

22

Of course, I didn't have anywhere to go. I couldn't go home. It was only in that moment that I honestly didn't know if it was safe to even be around my "parents" anymore. What if they suspected I knew? And what the hell did I even know, anyway? That I used to be Harlow and that what? They weren't even my real parents?

My god, they weren't even my real parents.

So who the hell was?

The contents of my stomach threatened to rise up and I concentrated on breathing. But then I realized that was weird too. Because *who* was even breathing in this body?

Stop, I said to myself, pushing the idea out of my mind. I couldn't go down that rabbit hole. The fact was that this body was breathing and I was in it. Not that I knew who "I" was, but I couldn't just stop. Someone was in this body and I owed it to her to figure out who.

I slowed to get my bearings. I had been running aimlessly, not even knowing what direction I'd been going. Up ahead I recognized a schoolyard. I wasn't that far from Andie's.

I started running again, trying to figure out what to say when I got there, but then I realized I didn't have to say anything. I'd just tell her I needed her and she would be there. Of that, at least, I was a hundred percent sure.

I was terrible at hiding what was going on inside me. The second Andie opened the door she knew something was up. And she knew it was something big.

She didn't say a word except to yell into the next room. "Ma! Nova's staying over!"

"Okay!" was her mom's reply and the relief that washed over me with that one word was immense.

No questioning. Just a simple "okay" like I was always welcome.

Andie grabbed my arm and dragged me to her room, probably not wanting anyone in her family to see me and start asking a bunch of questions. And then, in true Andie fashion she waited patiently while I broke down, finally letting the tears flow like they'd wanted to for the last who knows how long.

When I finally got to the point where I could talk again, she didn't pepper me with questions like I was worried she might, just simply said, "Tell me," the look of concern on her face letting me know I was safe.

But how do you tell your best friend that you're not the person you thought you were? That *they* thought you were?

I took a deep breath and started with my parents. I told her all the things that had been going on. With the fights, the

Memory Room, the memo from Experion and how I was afraid they were addicted.

"Are you sure that's even possible? I know your parents have been weird lately, but addiction? That seems a little extreme," Andie said.

"Anything's possible with new tech like EM," I said. "I know it seems like everything is all peachy with it, but maybe that's just what they want us to think."

"But it helps people. It's helped me," she said.

I could tell she was trying to fight the idea, like I had. EM had done so much good for people, and this bright, shiny thing was suddenly losing its luster.

She didn't want the image of it to be tarnished.

I didn't want it to either, but it was.

"They counted on people not questioning the safety of it."

She nodded, thinking. Reckoning. "I guess. It just seems... so harmless."

I nodded. "Until it's not."

"Can we take a second and think about this rationally? It sounds pretty conspiracy theory–ish to me." I could tell she still wanted to believe in EM. To see only the good.

"I know it all sounds unbelievable, but need you to believe me, Andie. I haven't told you everything yet, and the next part is going to sound even weirder, but I just need you to listen right now."

She looked a little worried, but must have decided to hear me out. "Okay, sorry. You have my undivided attention."

"Okay, thanks," I said and took a deep breath knowing Kade was the next thing to explain. "So you know Real K?"

Andie nodded. "Of course. Love him."

"Right, well…it's Kade."

I'd never seen her eyes so wide. "Shut up!"

I nodded. "I'm serious. You know that skating rink video? I filmed it."

"Oh my god," she said, giving me a little slap on the arm. "You have been holding out on me."

Which made me chuckle a little. And honestly, it was good to laugh, a relief from all the crying, I guess. But it didn't take long before we got serious again.

"So why does he do all the secrecy? What's he hiding?" she asked.

It was a question I'd asked myself a hundred times a day since the moment I found out.

And I finally knew the answer.

I took a deep breath. "That's the part I'm scared to tell you about."

She crinkled her brow. "Scared? How much worse could it get than what you've already told me?"

"Kind of a lot," I said, with a humorless chuckle. "Mostly I'm scared you're not going to believe me. It's pretty far out there."

"Worse than your parents being addicted to something I didn't even know you could get addicted to, and the fact that you're dating a dude with a secret identity?" she asked, and I knew she was trying to lighten the situation, but she had no idea.

I smiled, but then said, "Yeah. A lot worse."

Her smile faded.

"I think the thing that Kade is worried about—and the reason he keeps his identity secret—is that he's scared of people wanting his memories."

Andie tilted her head. "I don't get it. Couldn't he just keep them to himself and not worry about it?"

"In theory, sure. But do you remember when I was asking you about if a whole new set of Memories could be implanted into a person—like if they have amnesia or something?"

"Yeah," she said, her voice becoming unsure.

"Well, I know for sure that it can now, and I'm pretty sure Kade is worried it could happen to him too." The thought sent a new wave of nausea through me as thoughts of Harlow surfaced again.

All this time I'd been thinking about me, Nova, and how this was affecting only me, but suddenly I got a flash of Harlow. And how she'd been, what? Erased? I swallowed hard and sucked in air, trying to switch my focus back to Andie.

"Wait, like they would take his memories?" she asked.

I nodded. "Yeah, maybe. And maybe replace them with new ones."

"But why would they do that? Even if they took his good memories, couldn't they just leave the rest as is?"

"Maybe," I said. "Or maybe not."

I fished my phone out of my pocket and opened the text Kade sent me. I started the video and turned it toward Andie.

"You used to be a blonde?" Andie said, her eyes lighting up. "Cute!"

"Hey, guys," the voice on the video said as Harlow sang in the background. "This is my friend Harlow, the one I was telling you about." The voice faded then and the camera got in closer to Harlow, her song getting louder.

"Harlow?" Andie asked. "But that's you."

"It's not me," I said, and Andie gave me a look.

"No way," she said. "I've heard of doppelgangers, but that's kind of uncanny. Where did you get this?"

"Kade sent it to me. He used to know Harlow."

"Wait...is that the name he called you that first night at the club?" Andie asked, her mouth dropping open.

"Yeah."

The video was getting close to the part where my scar was about to appear.

At first Andie didn't notice it. She'd seen my scar a million times, sure, but it wasn't on her radar the same way it had been for me. But then, as the person filming tried to stand or something, and the camera shot jiggled, it got close on Harlow's elbow, just for a second, and Andie picked up on it. She squinted. "Wait, this totally is you. Why are you saying it's no—"

But I cut her off. "I promise you, it's not me."

It took her a second, probably trying to figure out why I was flat out lying to her, especially with such an obvious lie that could be proven wrong. Then I could almost see her thought pattern change as she started to figure it out. "Wait, amnesia. Are you saying..." She pointed to the screen, still not a hundred percent there, but getting close.

"I think I'm her, like in her body, but I don't remember any of it. Any of her."

Andie's hand moved to her face, covering her mouth. "What the hell does that mean?"

I let out a breath. "I don't know. All I know right now is

that I have all these memories—I can remember my whole life as Nova and yet…" I motioned to the phone.

Andie had an expression on her face like she was trying to work it all out but it was physically painful. "So you're thinking they implanted your Memories into Harlow's body?"

"It's the only thing that makes any sense. Not that it really makes any sense at all."

"Holy shit, that's dangerous." She looked me up and down as if double-checking to make sure I was alright. "Oh my god, your parents. Do you think they were the ones that took her?"

"No," I said immediately, horrified that she would even think that. They were my parents. But as I thought about it, about all the things they *had* done, I realized I wasn't so sure. "I don't know," I added, my voice a whisper.

Andie grabbed my hands. "I'm so sorry this is happening to you," she said. "Something like this should never happen to anybody. And it's twice as bad because we don't even understand it. I just keep thinking that I don't understand *why*."

Tears filled my eyes. "I don't understand either."

I had been trying to be strong. Trying to connect all these impossible dots in my mind, but my body had had enough. Andie moved beside me, put her arms around me, and let me cry.

We sat there for a long time, Andie handing me tissue after tissue and just holding me. Letting me know she was there for me…and it felt like she would be, no matter who "me" turned out to be. And I think half the tears were from relief that she was simply there. That no matter what happened— and I had no idea what was going to happen to me now— she would be there.

Eventually my tears ran out and I wiped my face, more exhausted than I'd ever remembered being, but I felt lighter too, like I wouldn't have to get through this all alone.

Andie moved back around to face me, cross-legged. "So... what do we do now?" Andie asked. "Call the cops or something?"

I let out a long breath. "I don't know. Do you think there's any chance anyone would believe me?"

Andie's face morphed from hopeful to pained. "No. I'm sorry, I don't think anyone would believe you right now."

I nodded. "We need more information. More proof."

"Right, okay. So...how do we do that?" she asked.

"I have absolutely no idea."

She sighed, scratching the back of her neck. "Okay, let's work through this. Who is out there that might have information?"

"My parents," I said. "And Experion, I guess."

She let out a huff. "Except if any of them realized we knew even half of this, you'd be in even more danger than you already are."

I swallowed, then nodded.

"And Kade," she said. "Kade knew." Her expression changed then. "Jesus. That asshole knew all along and he didn't tell you."

"I know," I said, frustration starting to bubble up again. "But he was looking for Harlow. He was like us. No one would believe him."

I could practically see the wheels spinning in Andie's mind as she nodded. "I guess if you think about it—here's this guy who has spent all this time worrying about his friend, and when he finds her, she's a totally different person. Imagine how much that would mess with you?"

I tilted my head. "Yeah, I think I can imagine."

Andie nodded. "Right. But then what do you even do with that? It's not like he could just tell you right then—it's not like there'd be a chance in hell you'd believe anything he said. But it's not like he could walk away either."

Her words were making me uneasy—making too much sense. And I'd completely left Kade standing there. Not knowing what to do all over again. "And he would be protective of his friend, so he sticks around. Tries to figure out what to do."

Andie nodded. "And then he spends some time with you and starts to fall for you."

My face flushed.

"So then he's confused," she continued. "And what is he supposed to do? Maybe he wants his friend back, but she's gone. And there's this other person he cares about now, and on top of it, he's scared for his life."

I swallowed the acid trying to crawl up my chest and crossed my arms around myself, clutching to the sides of my sweatshirt.

"And now he knows for sure the extremes these people will go to in order to steal memories," she said. "And he has some good ones. Really good ones." She paused, looking me in the eyes. "I honestly don't know what I would do in his place."

And suddenly I didn't either. I'd been so pissed at him for keeping this huge secret...but, did he really have any other choice?

"Shit," I said. "I have to text him."

23

In the morning, I texted Kade a million more times, but still no answer. I was definitely not a phone person, but on my way to work, I dialed his number anyway. It kicked in to voicemail after the first ring. Which was weird. Did that mean that he was already on the phone? Or that it was turned off? I could never remember that.

I'd checked his video channel a hundred times last night too, hoping he was too busy editing his next video to check his phone, but nothing new had been posted since the skating rink.

In the staff room on my break later that afternoon, I tried to formulate a plan. I dialed Kade's number again. Same thing, straight to voicemail.

I shot off another text.

Where are you? I'm starting to get really worried.

The sinking feeling in my stomach turned into a chasm the more I thought about him.

I texted Andie. He's still not answering.

Shit Nova. That's not good. We have to do something.

The flutter of worry in my chest had expanded to a heavy dread. I'd tried not to let my mind wander to the worst places, but those were the only places it wanted to go. I couldn't stop thinking about how he disguised himself on his channel and how he had been that day in my house. The fear that I had written off as paranoia seemed so real now and the idea of one more night of not hearing from him was terrifying.

I couldn't keep sitting there doing nothing. But what did I really know about Kade? He knew where I lived, where I worked, but I knew none of those things about him. In fact, I wasn't sure if he even did work, other than on his video channel. With how popular it was he probably made plenty from ads and sponsors and that might be all he needed. God, I didn't even know if he was still in school.

With fear spreading through my bones I realized that for as much as it felt like I knew him, I actually knew nothing *about* him. But that couldn't be true. I started to pace, chewing on the skin around my thumbnail. Okay, think. What did I know?

I knew he had his video channel. Maybe I could try to contact some of his fans? But then what would that do? They didn't even know who he really was. At least I knew Kade and not just Real K. I knew where I met him. Club Visto. It's where he thought he recognized me. I recalled seeing him with a few people there. I mean, it was a long shot, but what else was I supposed to do all night? I texted Andie.

Can you meet me at work after my shift? I might have an idea.

What's the plan?

I don't know for sure, but I think I need to go back to Visto.

We headed to the club as soon as I was done with my shift.

"Thanks for the moral support," I said as we neared the club. "And helping me keep my shit together."

"Always," Andie said, heading straight past the line again, getting us in even more quickly than the last time.

The club was amped up. As I approached the entrance a guy jumped in front of me out of nowhere, like a few inches in front of my face and screamed, arms outstretched. But it was a relatively friendly scream, as friendly as a scream could be, I supposed, and he had this huge, goofy grin on his face. He was out to have a good time, and he must have thought randomly jumping in front of people and whooping it up was the way to do that. I blinked, pulling in a deep breath to try and calm my jackhammering heart.

"Jesus," Andie said, watching the guy disappear, still dancing, as we stepped into the club.

Maybe it was because of the sour taste in my mouth from the last time I'd been there—with the unsettling Enhanced Memory experience and everything—but Visto seemed even more jarring this time around. Or maybe there really were more people—it was hard to tell. Everything was flashing

238 • SACHA WUNSCH

lights and booming sounds and people all up in your personal space. None of which were my favorite things.

And now that I'd arrived, I wondered if I would even recognize any of the people I'd seen with Kade, even if by some miracle they were there. Which led me to the thought that, oh my god, maybe Kade himself would be there and was like, trying to avoid me or something, which would be so mortifying.

But that couldn't be the case. We were starting something real, weren't we? That couldn't have been an act.

At least I hoped.

I surveyed the warehouse-like space. Where the hell were we supposed to even start?

I sighed. I needed to start at the start and work my way around, and hope that people would kind of, I don't know, stay in their little sectors. Even I knew that wasn't going to happen and if I was going to find anyone that could help, I was going to need luck on my side.

I motioned to Andie to follow and I started to wander, making my way around the edge of the room, moving toward the right. The dim lighting with intermittent flashes was not helping me see anyone's face clearly so I moved slowly. Really slowly, breathing deeply, using all my effort to stay centered and calm in the chaotic environment.

My low-grade anxiety was starting to rise, but I shoved it away and kept studying faces. Of course, as I did, all the faces started to blend in, all looking the same. For as many differences as people had—hair color, skin color, sizes, and features, we all did look quite a bit the same when the lighting was just right. Or just wrong in this case.

Andie tapped me on the shoulder and pointed. Ami and Mason were waving at her from across the room. She motioned that she wanted to go talk to them. "First I'm going to give them hell for leaving you last time, and then I'm going to grill them. They know everybody here, maybe they can help," she yelled over the noise.

I nodded, following her. But then in a flash, I saw someone familiar. He was tall, and something about him made me think of Kade. It wasn't Kade, not even close, but I felt like I had seen him somewhere that related to Kade. Like maybe one of his videos? But as the recognition took a second to dawn on me, the guy disappeared. My eyes darted frantically, but he was nowhere to be seen. I closed my eyes and took a deep breath, struggling to remember details.

Dark hair. Spikey. Light-colored shirt, maybe white. A kind of bounce to his gait.

I opened my eyes, scanning—slower this time, actually seeing.

There.

I tried to grab for Andie, but she was already out of my reach. I knew I should follow her, let her know where I was going, but I couldn't risk losing the guy in the crowd. I had to help Kade. And I couldn't shake the feeling that I had to help Harlow too. The way she'd just been swept away as if she were nothing. I had to…I don't know…do something for her.

The guy had made his way halfway across the room but it was definitely him. I started to move, weaving my way in his direction. I had to lean this way and that to try and keep sight of him, but thankfully he was so tall, and with the bounce to his step, he bobbed even taller as he walked.

A little opening cleared and I rushed through, slowed again by another bottleneck in the crowd, but much closer now. And then, in an instant, I was right behind him—he had stopped, getting another drink at the bar. From what I'd heard, the bar used to be the busiest place in a club, people always needing more drinks, but now with the popularity of EM, drinks had sort of fallen by the wayside. Still, I had to wriggle my way in beside the guy.

"Hey!" I yelled.

He looked down at me, alarmed. I suppose I might have sounded a tad confrontational, which was purely by accident because of the volume it required to be heard in there.

"Um, hey?" he said.

"Sorry," I said. "Um, you're friends with Kade, right?"

"Who?" he yelled, leaning down to hear me better.

"Kade!" My voice screeched from the strain.

"Oh yeah," he said, smiling and looking around. "Is he here?"

"I don't think so. Listen, I'm wondering if you've seen him around today."

"Today? No. I haven't seen him in a few days. But that's Kade, you know?"

Unfortunately I didn't know.

"So, you haven't heard from him?"

The guy must have sensed that I was more than a little eager to talk to Kade. He held up a finger, asking me to wait for a sec while he paid for his drink, then motioned me to come with him. He ducked into a nearby hallway, which was by no means quiet, but was slightly less booming. I realized Andie was no longer behind me. I thought she would have followed, but she must not have seen me turn around.

"So you must not know Kade very well then," he said.

I shrugged. "Why?"

He tilted his head. "Well, this is kind of his thing. He's not one for staying in one place for long. He likes to go on these—" he looked away, trying to find the word "—excursions, he calls them. You know, making memories and all that." The guy kind of rolled his eyes like he didn't really understand the point of it all.

"So he just disappears? And doesn't let anyone know where he's going?"

"That's kind of the point, I think. To get away from all this." He motioned to the bar. "I mean, I'll never understand it, but to each their own, I guess." He gave me a huge grin. "Anyway, have fun!" he said and was off, back out of the hall and into the crowd.

"Jesus, Kade," I mumbled to myself, leaning my head back on the wall.

Something told me the guy was right. That Kade was a wanderer and didn't like to stay put for too long, but something even stronger told me there was no way he would have taken off without at least sending me a text. We were deeper into…whatever this was than that. And I knew he wouldn't drop a bomb like the Harlow thing and then just walk away to make me sort it out by myself.

A couple of girls came giggling out from a door at the end of the hall, one walking backward so they could face each other, talking loudly. I couldn't really make out what they were saying—the heavy bass of the music was too loud, vibrating my entire being—but the moment they saw me, they gave each other a strange look and both quickly hid the items they'd been holding, one shoving hers into a pocket, and the other a purse. They suddenly quieted too and fell into line side by side, sneaking their way past me not saying a word.

I knew it couldn't have anything to do with me—I was just standing there. It was more like they had been caught doing something they shouldn't and wanted to get away as quickly as possible.

One of them glanced back, her face seemingly relieved that I hadn't followed them. Which was also kind of weird. I looked back down the hall.

What was behind that door?

I started to text Andie to try to explain where I was, but someone else, a guy, came from the club side of the hallway, his step pausing momentarily when he saw me. I pretended to type something on my phone. He seemed convinced that I was harmless and continued down the hall. I strained my eyes to the right, trying to get a glimpse of what was going on, but too scared to look up in case he caught me staring.

The guy knocked on the door. But it wasn't a normal knock. It was jilted. Deliberate.

Two slow, then three a bit faster. One...two...three, four, five.

Nothing happened.

But then he knocked again in the same way, one...two... three, four, five, and the door immediately opened and he was whisked inside, quickly, like they didn't want anyone to see what was going on.

Which immediately made me want to know what was going on.

But was the knock the only thing you needed? Tap out a simple secret knock and they let you back there? And then what?

I could assume, I suppose, that something shady was going on. But there wasn't that much shady stuff that happened anymore. I guess there were still a few illegal drugs out there, but they weren't commonly used. Not since Enhanced Memories had become so easy to come by. It had basically taken away every other vice. If heroin was your thing, why not feel the same high by manipulating your mind with Memories of getting high instead?

That one had been quite a breakthrough. I remember the headlines screaming about how no one would have to die from drug overdoses anymore.

I swallowed.

The door opened again and an older guy exited, pocketing something, a huge smile on his face, looking like he'd just gotten the best news of his life. I already had my phone at the ready, pretending I was minding my own business, looking for a little quiet. He passed right by me, barely even noticing I was there.

I was more convinced by the second that something very weird was going on behind that door. But I couldn't just waltz up and knock.

Not yet.

I closed my eyes and leaned my head back on the wall. I didn't mind waiting. It wasn't like I had anything better to do. Of course my mind started doing the thing where it keeps playing the same ideas over and over again. Thoughts of Kade filled my mind, so many things good…but then potential scenarios of what happened to him crept in. I checked my phone again to make sure he hadn't suddenly replied, but of course there was nothing. I checked his video channel.

Wait.

Something was different on his page. There was a new video! My heart soared as I checked to see when he had posted it, expecting it to have been in the last couple hours. But…that couldn't be right. The timestamp said more than a month ago. But…why would he delete his recent videos? I felt a little better knowing that if changes were being made to his channel, that must mean he was making the changes. Which had to mean he was okay.

Except…then what did that mean for me? And us?

I scrolled further through his feed, realizing that there were more than just the two recent posts that had been deleted. I couldn't remember what all of them were, but I very clearly remember seeing, and watching, the video from when he went skydiving. But no matter how many times I scrolled through his list of videos, the skydiving one was no longer there.

Why would he take that one down? It was his most-watched video. It didn't make any sense. Unless…unless he wasn't the one who took it down.

I'd been so engrossed in my phone that I didn't notice another person coming up the hall toward the door. I froze as the woman passed me. She was not like anyone else I'd seen at the club—older, with long black braids and wearing a colorful, flowing caftan. She looked so poised, so put together, calm. So…out of place at this club filled with kids and early twenty-somethings. I couldn't help but think that she wasn't just there for the club atmosphere.

She reached the door and I held my breath.

There it was. One…two…three, four, five.

Like the last guy, they made her knock it out twice before they allowed her past. The guy at the door seemed annoyed with how deliberately she carried herself, not hurrying for him—or anyone else, I suspected. She smiled and looked him straight in the eyes as she glided by.

He shut the door a little more forcefully than he had when the other guy had gone in.

So that was it. Or at least I hoped. Do the knock and you're in.

Of course, what happened after that was a mystery.

But that wasn't even the most pressing mystery of the day. Or the minute, really. I looked at my phone again.

With every moment that ticked by, the cloud of dread around me grew.

I walked up the hall and knocked.

24

I knocked the requisite second time.

I knew it was a dangerous game to play. There wasn't much in this world that was off-limits anymore, but that only made sneaking into a potential black market Memory den that much more dangerous. If this conspiracy went as deep as I was afraid it might, these people would be guarding their secrets with their lives.

And as the guy pulled the door open and I spotted the gun on his hip, I realized they probably weren't against ending other people's lives to keep their secrets either. He gave me a strange look, like he wasn't sure I belonged, which of course I didn't, but I guess because I knew the knock he let me stay.

The room was dim and it took a second for my eyes to adjust. I was surprised how many people were there. Some were seated on couches, obviously in the middle of an Enhanced Memory experience, and others were chatting like it was the most natural thing in the world to be back there, like they did it all the time. I spotted the woman with the braids sitting with a man who seemed to be wearing an old-timey aviator hat, goggles and all, perched on his head. She sipped a glass of wine and waved a waitress over.

But instead of a drink tray, the server had a large square tray with a strap attached around her neck. There were several tiny boxes inside the tray and as she leaned toward the woman, she lifted a lid on one of the boxes. Enhanced Memory disks, the shiny metal ones, not the plastic disposables.

Everyone in here seemed so confident, so comfortable, and I wondered if this was what the old high-roller poker rooms must have been like back in the day. Only those who could afford it were in here, and only the finest of everything would do. The finest drinks, the finest decor, and I suppose the finest Memories.

And in this place I had no idea how I was supposed to act. I found a shadowy corner of the room and watched for a few minutes, drinking it all in. Most of the people were older than me, though the girls I'd seen giggling on their way out had to have been close to my age. Rich kids, I guess. I looked around for more. Finally I spotted a guy. He seemed younger, close to my age.

He might be my best shot.

Heart beating wildly, I strolled over and slid into the other side of the booth from him. He had three shiny EM disks lined up on the table.

"Are you doing all those tonight?" I asked, hoping he wouldn't send me away. At least not immediately.

I needed to establish a presence here. Figure out how not to stand out. Try to belong.

He looked at me a little startled, then kind of sneered.

Off to a great start.

"What business is it of yours?" he asked.

I raised my eyebrows trying to convey a look that said "What's your problem?"

"Just trying to make conversation."

He sighed. "Sorry. Bad day."

I nodded at the Enhanced Memories on the table. "So I see."

I wondered what constituted a bad day in this guy's world. He seemed like a spoiled rich brat, to be honest.

"Didn't get into the college of your dreams?" I guessed. "Or no, the girlfriend dumped you." I was trying not to be condescending, really I was, I mean, it's not like I'd ever really wanted for anything either, but this guy was on another level.

He looked at me, unamused. "Actually, I found out I'm sick. Terminal."

"Oh," I said, suddenly feeling like the biggest asshole on the planet. "I'm so sorry," I said. "I didn't…"

He started laughing then. "I'm kidding," he said. "You should see the look on your face."

In an instant that look turned from terrible guilt to seething.

"Yeah, my girlfriend dumped me," he said, shrugging.

He picked up one of the Enhanced Memory disks and it came alive. The hologram that popped up was like nothing I'd ever seen before—basically a porn show.

"Jesus," I said, looking around. "Put that thing away."

He laughed at me again. "You got something against sex?" he asked.

The truth was I'd never really gotten that far in my love life. I made a face and he set the disk down.

"No, I don't have anything against sex. I just..." I was about to say that I didn't believe in Enhanced Memory sex because it couldn't possibly live up to the real thing, but then I remembered where I was. A frigging black market Memory den. "I guess I don't think it needs to be advertised."

"Ah, a little prudish, are we?" An amused smile played at his lips.

I rolled my eyes and tried to not shift in my seat to show how uncomfortable I was with the whole thing.

"So what else you got there?" I asked, glancing at the disks.

I didn't particularly want to know, but I was desperate to change the subject.

"Oh, more of the same sort of thing," he said. "I guess I thought I would be lashing out at her if I did these or something."

I shrugged. "I guess that makes sense. Especially these premium Memories."

He nodded. "Just like the real thing."

"The real thing," I said, and nodded too, as if I had any idea what the hell I was talking about.

Honestly, I just wanted to keep him talking. If he went into an Enhanced Memory coma right now I'd be stuck on my own again. It felt safer sitting with someone else than wandering around by myself.

A waitress brought a bottle of champagne to the table.

"Thanks," the guy said, as if he were expecting it.

The server set a second glass in front of me.

"Oh that's okay," I said, trying to wave it away.

"Why not have some?" the guy said. "It's not like we have to pay for it in here."

I tilted my head as if in agreement and tried not to look too shocked. Yup, like a high-roller room. "I suppose, if you don't mind me intruding."

He finally grinned. "It's not an intrusion. And actually a distraction might be the thing I need."

I wasn't sure how I loved being called a distraction, but even with the questionable EM disks he did seem harmless enough. Although for a moment I wondered why I thought so. I felt pulled to give him the benefit of the doubt. I had this weird sense that I might be feeling something—a trusting—that was left over from Harlow.

"I'm Jayce," he said and reached his hand across the table.

I shook it. "Nova."

It quickly flashed through my mind that maybe I should have used a fake name, but I hadn't really prepared for that. Hadn't really prepared for anything. Besides, I'd probably forget a fake name anyway and screw the whole thing up.

"So what brings you in here tonight, Nova?" he asked, pouring the champagne. "What's your guilty pleasure?"

He meant Enhanced Memories, and of course I didn't have anything prepared to answer that either, so I quickly grabbed the champagne and took a sip. I'd never had champagne before and tried not to act surprised that the bubbles sparkled all up my nose. I suppressed a cough and swallowed the sweetly sour fizz.

"I don't know what I'm in the mood for, to be honest," I said, hoping that would placate him.

He raised an eyebrow. "You could try one of mine."

I rolled my eyes again. I guessed that was kind of Jayce's deal. He was that guy that good-naturedly made fun of everyone until they got used to him. I'd definitely seen his type before.

"Thanks but I'll pass," I said. "I was thinking something more…I don't know, dangerous."

He tilted his head in appreciation. "I almost bought one of those," he said. "A new one that hasn't been seen before."

I furrowed my brow, not understanding what he was getting at.

He leaned in close, conspiratorially. "I heard they got a skydive in."

I gasped. Like literally gasped. Not, of course, for the reasons that Jayce likely assumed, but because my thoughts immediately flew to Kade, suddenly terrified that he could be in even more trouble than I feared.

I cleared my throat. "Are you serious?"

He nodded, then his face turned solemn. "A little above my budget though," he said, looking disappointed.

I had no idea how much a black market Memory was, but something as rare as a legitimate skydive? People would be willing to pay serious dollars for something like that.

"I bet," I said, trying to look awed instead of the way I actually felt, which was that I could throw up at any moment. I tilted my head as if I'd just thought of something. "Do they ever say where the Memories come from?"

Jayce looked at me a little strangely.

"I mean, a skydive is pretty rare. I wonder where it came from." I shrugged, to let him know I didn't think it was a big deal. Just curious.

He didn't take too long think about it. "Someone sells their memories, I guess."

I nodded. "Yeah. Yeah, you're probably right," I agreed, wishing I believed it.

Someone slid up to our table then. The woman selling Enhanced Memories. "Did I hear you talking about the sky-dive? Care to make a purchase?" Her smile was so gleam-ing it nearly hurt my eyes. Like she'd practiced that smile for hours until she'd gotten that exact mix of "I'm sexy but still sweet and I'll do anything for you." Something in that smile made me think of this documentary I saw once on instant hypnosis. It terrified me at the time, the way they made it seem like it could be true, but I'd shaken it off as impossible anyway. Now I wondered.

I blinked the thought out of my head. "Um, you know, I'm still thinking about what I want," I said, flashing her a smile of my own, one that I hoped said "I'm just an innocent, lovely person, no need to worry about me."

"Okay, but don't wait too long or they'll start to wonder if you're a cop or something," she said, looking over at the guy at the door, who was paying way too much attention to our table.

Then she tilted her head back and laughed like it was the funniest thing in the world. I couldn't help but think that maybe she'd done a few too many Memories herself and wasn't quite right anymore.

"Oh sure, yeah, no problem," I said, filling the silence

until she wandered off to the next table, flashing the practiced smile again.

I turned to Jayce, who was flipping one of his Memory disks over in his hands, making the video start, a seductive moan coming in a short burst, then stopping as he flipped it down since the videos only played if you were holding them just the right way.

"How *did* you find out about this place, anyway?" he asked, absently.

"Friends," I said, hoping that would placate him.

"People aren't supposed to give the code out," he said.

I shrugged. "People are unreliable, I guess." I crossed my arms. "And how did you find out about it?"

A grin played across his face. "My parents have a membership. They get sent the new secret knock every week."

I nodded. "And are you named on that membership that belongs to your parents?" I asked, raising an eyebrow.

He chuckled. "Touché."

I risked another glance toward the guy at the door. The good news was he wasn't paying any attention to me anymore. The bad news was that he was paying attention to someone else.

And the *very* bad news was that it was someone I knew. Sort of.

What was her name again? Ugh, more details that wanted to escape me. She worked with my parents, that much I knew for sure—I'd seen her at one of the release events at Experion. I looked away, terrified that she would spot me, though she probably wouldn't remember me anyway. Those Experion events were held in the huge auditorium at their headquarters, with hundreds of people in attendance. Marjorie, that was it. Her name was Marjorie.

I let about half a minute pass then glanced again. Marjorie was walking away, heading through a door with a sign that said Management.

But what was someone who worked at a legit Enhanced Memory company doing here?

Seeing her only worsened my fears that this was dangerous. Also I felt like I was wearing out my welcome. But I didn't know how the hell I was going to get out of there. Something told me that no one got out without buying a Memory. Of course, Jayce did have those three all lined up in front of him.

"Do you want to get out of here?" I asked. "My place isn't that far away. Maybe we could, I don't know, make a real memory or something." I tried to paint a suggestive look on my face.

His eyes widened. "Are you serious?" Jayce asked, sitting extremely upright.

"Listen, you're sweet, and I kinda feel bad that you got dumped." I shrugged.

Jayce quickly gathered up his Enhanced Memories and shoved the disks in his pocket.

As we got up I glanced at the door. The security guy was looking our way. I plucked one of Jayce's disks out of his pocket and held it up, letting the raunchy video play as we neared the bouncer, hoping he'd believe it was mine.

Jayce looked a little startled, but as soon as I winked (taking a cue from my favorite elderly friend) and said, "For a little inspiration," he grinned and watched along with me as we walked.

I shot the doorman a smile as we waltzed out the door and back into the club.

Now all I had to do was get rid of Jayce and I was home free.

Unfortunately, he was watching me very closely. Probably worried about his precious Memory.

"Ready?" he asked.

"Um, sure," I said, my mind scrambling. "I just have to sneak to the bathroom for a sec," I said as we passed one of the facilities.

I handed him back his Memory disk, unhooked my arm from his, and pushed through the door before he could protest, quickly taking in my surroundings.

The window was high, but thankfully there was one. Of course, the bathroom was also packed and there was no way I would ever get out undetected. But if there was one thing I knew, it was that there was something about women in bathrooms. They became friendlier. More helpful.

I picked out the most badass-looking girl I could find and went up to her.

"I'm so sorry, but could you watch the door for a sec to make sure that guy doesn't come in?"

She looked mildly alarmed. "What's going on?"

I looked back toward the door. "There's just this guy out there. He's not a bad guy, he's just a little...overeager. Can you make sure he doesn't see that I'm sneaking out?" I pointed to the window.

The girl's face morphed into a look of knowing, like maybe she'd been in a similar boat before. She nodded once. "We got this." She turned to another girl in the room. "Aubrey, watch the door."

The girl, Aubrey, tilted her head and sort of shrugged in agreement like this was a request she got all the time. The original girl turned back to me. "Come on." She motioned me toward the window and bent down to give me a little boost.

Public bathrooms, man. Truly the most helpful women in the world.

I boosted up and quickly unlocked the window, sliding the pane of glass open. I glanced back down. "Thanks so much!" I said and heaved myself through the opening.

"Don't mention it!" she yelled as I eased myself toward the ground and dropped the last couple feet.

I felt a little bad for Jayce. I mean, he was no stand-up gentleman or anything, but I didn't really think he was horrible either. He would get over being stood up by some random girl at the club. Besides, I had more important things to worry about right now.

Like what the hell had happened to the guy that really mattered to me.

I pulled out my phone. There were five messages from Andie, each one growing more frenzied. I sent a quick text back letting her know I was okay but had to leave—she was so going to kill me—but I took off at a run anyway, heading to the only place I could think of where I might find some answers.

Home.

25

The whole time I ran I was trying not to cry. My house was the last place I thought I'd be running *toward* after all that had happened, but it was the only place I might find some answers. Seeing Marjorie at the black market den made me realize this went way deeper than any of us had realized. Which made it so much more dangerous. Of course, it did explain some things about my parents and how I...became me.

Christ, *became*.

Not born, but manufactured in a way. And then the tears came but I kept running, trying to sort it all out in my head, but of course it was all too complicated—especially for my mind right then.

Because I also couldn't stop thinking about Kade—and how he was just fine until he met me. Or was it found me? I wiped another wave of tears. He was better than fine. He had this huge platform that even if it had only had a slight chance of changing people's minds, there was still a chance.

I ran for several minutes then slowed—along with my tears—as I reached my neighborhood. It was so quiet at night. All the little families tucked safely into their beds. It had a different feel here than the rest of the city. Like the place was untouchable. Like the outside world couldn't infiltrate. It was almost like there was something...manufactured about the whole area.

I walked the final block slowly. I had been desperate to get here as fast as I could, but now I was having second thoughts. I headed up the walk, trying to formulate a plan. With any luck my parents would either be sleeping or in the middle of an Enhanced Memory session. After our last encounter I had no idea what I was supposed to say to them, or how I might feel when I saw them, or...how they would react to me.

Thankfully the house was dark. Like really dark, and kind of creepy. A beam of moonlight sliced through the living room, distorting the proportions, the walls looming far above me, closing in. For it being my own house, I felt utterly out of place. I closed my eyes and tried to compose myself.

The room was empty. Perfect. Maybe they were out. Or maybe they were in bed.

I went straight for the Memory Room and turned on the light.

I had no idea what I was looking for. The tiny drawers had no markings on them or any indication of what was inside. All I knew was that I needed more information, so I started opening drawers randomly, pulling out disks and letting the little holograms play so I could figure out what was on each disk. After I closed a drawer back up again, I almost instantly forgot which drawer I'd already seen inside.

And there were hundreds of them.

I sighed, restarting at the bottom left corner, deciding to work my way up a row at a time.

The first drawer contained a Memory where the recipient received some kind of philanthropic award. The next was a shopping spree knowing you had an unlimited amount to spend. Drawer number three showcased a person solving a ten-year cold case murder.

It quickly became clear the Memories weren't categorized or in any sort of order. Which made no sense. There was no way my parents had every one of these drawers memorized. There had to be a list or directory somewhere.

I looked around the room but it was basically empty. No clutter on the chairs and nothing besides the drawers and a single painting on the wall. Still, I kept searching, behind the door, under the chairs in case something was taped to them, and even considered pulling up the carpet though I knew that was probably a long shot.

I stood for a while, my hands on my hips, then went to leave, hoping to find a clue in the rest of the house, flicking off the light as I went. But before I stepped out of the Memory Room I noticed something. A key.

It wasn't obvious, just sort of a shimmer on one of the drawers about three quarters of the way up near the middle. But it wasn't exactly the middle—no, it was more random than that.

I flicked the light back on hoping to get a better look, but the moment the room was illuminated, the shimmer vanished. I turned the light off again.

The shimmer showed only when the lights were off, painted on with some sort of glow-in-the-dark material. I pulled out the drawer and grabbed the disk from inside. A holograph of someone literally unrolling a scroll that contained a list.

It had to be the contents of what was inside each drawer and my heart started to beat a little faster. But my excitement fell away the moment I realized what this actually was.

It was a Memory that had to be downloaded.

I flipped the disk over in my hands like Jayce had done back at the black market den.

The stairs squeaked, my heart nearly clawing through my chest. Someone was on the fifth step from the bottom, the one I always avoided when I was trying to be quiet. I peeked my head around the door and watched my father set an Enhanced Memory disk on the side table then disappear into the kitchen. He must have been on his way down to return the disk—and probably get another—but decided to go for some water or something.

I had to move and fast. I snuck out of the Memory Room and headed for the front door, but he was already coming out. I only had time to grab the doorknob, open it a crack, and close it again as if I had just walked into the house.

I had never seen my father move so fast. He lunged for the side table that he set his disk down on and pulled open the drawer, grabbing a gun and aiming at me before I had any idea what was going on.

I heard the click of the gun cocking before I finally had the sense to yell, "Dad!" and fling my hands up in surrender.

"Wha…?" he asked, sounding confused and a bit groggy, which had become pretty common lately.

"Jesus, Dad, why do you have a gun?"

The arm holding the gun wavered a little, almost like he was about to lower it, but then he straightened his shoulders, the arm holding firm.

I reached back with a shaky hand and flicked on the light. "Dad, it's me, Nova."

He blinked, grabbing the gun with both hands, startled, his eyes needing to adjust. But his eyes were different somehow. Filled with confusion and...a vacancy that made me wonder if he had been doing EM nonstop since our last encounter. Which wouldn't be all that surprising, I supposed. I shimmied to the left a couple steps in case the damned thing went off, giving him a moment to figure out what the hell was going on.

"Dad? It's just me."

"But it's the middle of the night," he said, his head tilted like he was still trying to clear the fog from his mind.

He looked terrible, with dark circles under his eyes—eyes that couldn't quite seem to focus, although they were trying.

"It's late, I guess, like ten. But it's not the middle of the night."

The gun stayed pointed directly at me. "It's not?" I got the sense the confusion was starting to fade, but only by a little.

"Yes, Dad. It's me, Nova," I repeated, hoping his head was clearing.

I had to remember that he didn't know I knew about Harlow, and all that implied about him and Mom. Yes, we'd had a terrible fight, but that was the extent of it. I couldn't let on that I knew things were much, much worse. Certainly not with a gun pointed at me.

"Nova," he said, relief creeping into his voice.

He pulled the gun down slightly so that it was aimed at my leg. I had seen my father confused before, but I'd never witnessed this level of anxiety. Like he wasn't sure if he could believe his own mind.

"Hey, Dad? Could you put the gun back in the drawer?"

He looked at the gun then, like he had almost forgotten it was there, then looked back up at me, surprised. "Oh. Oh yes." He cleared his throat and shook the final bits of fog out of his head. "Sorry uh, I wasn't expecting you to come home this late."

My face turned pink, the gravity of the situation hitting me. That could have gone so, so much worse. When the hell did they get a gun? "Um, I guess I didn't realize..." I said, drifting off and motioning toward the drawer that the gun was safely tucked back into.

He looked at the drawer and then to me again, finally focusing on my face. "Oh, well, um," he said, putting his hands in the pockets of his housecoat like he needed something to do with them, jacked up from adrenaline.

He started to pace, and I don't know if it was the way we had left things last time, or if he was alarmed at what had just happened, but he looked really uncomfortable. Like standing in the same room as me made him twitchy.

Or maybe it was something else altogether, because I had seen that same behavior before. At Golden Acres.

I'd seen visits from families to their loved ones when their memories were already starting to fade and they recognized a face, or a voice, and something told them they knew who the person in front of them was but couldn't quite place them.

There were varying degrees of how much they remembered and at the start they would only forget a name for a few seconds, but it always threw them off, like they were trying to work out how they could have forgotten who their own wife was.

It always put an awkwardness on the whole visit.

"Dad?" I asked, trying to make my voice as nonthreatening as possible. "Do you want to sit down for a minute?"

He looked at the couch. "Oh, uh, yes. Good idea."

He sat and I chose the chair across from him. I didn't want to spook him even more by getting too close. I'd seen Genie do the same thing a hundred times at Golden Acres.

I had so many questions, not the least of which was how in the hell it took Dad so long to figure out it was me. Unfortunately I was terrified I might know the answer to that. What if the constant use of Enhanced Memories was actually degrading his brain, fueling this new anger, this new violent streak? Whatever was going on was most definitely centered around EM in some way. But I had come here for information to help Kade. Still, I needed to be careful, putting some distance between him and the gun.

I took a deep breath. "What do you know about Harlow Beckman?"

His eyes snapped up to mine then, fear chasing away the sadness. "No. We don't say that name." He closed his eyes and tilted his head at a strange angle, almost like a twitch of pain. "I mean we don't know that name." He looked off into nothingness again.

"You don't know it or you don't say it?"

He was fiddling with his hands, nerves making him tap and rub them together in strange patterns.

"Dad," I said loudly, but he didn't respond. "Dad!"

Still nothing. Just the hands and a weird head twitch every so often. He seemed to be working himself into a kind of frenzy. I'd never seen him like this, but I did know there was one thing that always calmed him down.

I approached him with caution and grabbed his elbow, helping him up. "Come on, Dad, let's get you settled." I led him toward the Memory Room and as we neared he started to calm down a bit. He walked into the room and it was like a blanket of calm floated over him as he ran one hand along the drawers.

"I'll go get you a glass of water," I said, but he wasn't paying attention anymore.

I looked away. The way he treated those Memories with such gentleness, such love. How was someone supposed to compete with that?

My father didn't care about having a glass of water, but I needed something to do. An excuse not to watch him in there, so I headed to the kitchen anyway. I leaned on the counter with no idea of what my next step was. I reminded myself that even though he still felt like my father, I really had no idea who that man in the next room was. I clutched the edge of the counter, realizing I didn't really know who I was.

But I couldn't go there. Not now. Not knowing that Kade was in danger and I might be the only person in the world who knew it. I needed to get to him. But where would they take him? It had to be somewhere that would have extraction machines. Someplace that produced the authentic EMs. I glanced through the doorway and at the side table where Dad had set the Memory disk down before he grabbed the gun.

Jesus.

If there was anyone who would definitely have an extraction machine—probably many—it would be Experion Enterprises.

Where my parents were still on the payroll.

And where Marjorie, the woman I'd seen at the black market den, was also on the payroll.

Experion was not the upstanding company everyone thought it was.

I didn't even want to think about what that meant about my parents. Right now the only thing that mattered was that they had access.

Their keycards. I needed one of their keycards.

I started searching frantically, shoving take-out containers and stacks of papers around the counter. I closed my eyes and took a deep breath. If I was a keycard, where would I be?

My dad usually wore his around his neck on a lanyard, taking it off as he entered the house. Keys. It might be with the keys. Of course, my parents weren't all that good at putting their keys in the correct place anymore, but I had to check.

Dad was still in the Memory Room, which had a perfect view of the front closet where he'd installed the key rack for easy access when putting his coat away. He was distracted trying to choose a Memory, but I couldn't risk him seeing me. I had no good excuse to be in that closet—I kept my coats upstairs—and he was already paranoid about everything.

I went back to the kitchen and actually grabbed the glass of water I'd promised and went back toward the Memory

Room. Thankfully Dad was finally choosing one, lifting it gently out of its box.

"All set?" I asked, and he actually looked at me and smiled now.

I handed him the water. "Oh yes, thank you," he said. "I think I'm going to head to bed."

"Okay. I'm right behind you."

Knowing the kind of danger Kade could be in made everything seem like it took a thousand times longer. But finally we made our way upstairs, Dad heading to his bedroom to use another Memory.

I flicked on the light in my room as if I was actually going to get ready for bed, waited for his door to close, then grabbed my bag that I'd left behind on my last unplanned departure, and snuck back down the hall as quickly as possible without making any noise. Careful not to step on the fifth step, I made my way down and eased the front closet open. The keys were way in the back and hard to see, but I nearly did a little jump when I saw it.

The keycard was there.

26

I felt exposed on the sidewalk, the streetlamps spotlighting me, so I moved into the shadows. The road heading toward the Experion complex was lined with poplars, and I stayed inside the tree line. But it was quiet and no cars passed in the few minutes it took me to get there.

There was a huge gate for cars to drive through, but it was manned by a twenty-four-hour security guard. The keycard would work to get me past the gate, but the guard would definitely know something was up. Even if he didn't know my parents personally, my Dad's picture was right there on the card.

My only hope was finding another way in.

My head still throbbed and I couldn't get the image of Harlow's roller coaster out of my mind. I moved away from the gate, farther into the trees, still making my way around the complex, hoping for some kind of brainwave to hit me and show me a way in. The fence was a basic chain-link that I could probably climb over, especially after my experience at the skating rink, but I had no idea what kind of security was there.

Once I reached the back, I crouched to survey the situation.

The fence looked straightforward, no barbed wire at the top or anything, just a fence maybe fifteen feet high to climb over.

I stepped out of the shadows and took a step, but a flash of light sent me diving for the ground. I peeked up to see someone a few dozen yards away carrying a flashlight and making their way down the fence.

Security.

I lay as flat and as still as possible as the guard passed by, though she didn't seem to be paying much attention to what was beyond the fence, her flashlight beam sweeping across only the area inside the complex.

The moment she was out of sight around the back corner I rushed the fence and climbed as carefully as I could, trying not to make it sway too much or make any noise. If anything terrible was going to happen, it was pretty likely to be in that moment, but I had to try. I had to think about Kade.

I made it up and over without incident until my pant leg caught as I tried to swing my leg around to go down the other side. I had too much momentum going, already letting go with my other leg to descend, and ended up flipping upside down, hanging there by the tear in my jeans. Which promptly began to rip, and I couldn't help but think this was why people didn't do this kind of stuff in real life anymore.

I latched onto the chain-link for dear life and tried to free my jeans, flinging my leg around, making way more noise than I would have liked. The cloth finally came free and, not knowing how much time I had before the guard came around again, I swung around upright and clambered down the rest of the way as fast as I could, my heart hammering.

It took a second to get my bearings after the unexpected blood rush to the head, but in a few seconds I was running. I didn't really know where, just generally toward the buildings and into the shadows where hopefully the guard's flashlight couldn't reach me.

Flattening myself against a building, I took a moment to catch my breath just as the guard circled back to the south end of the complex. Way too close for comfort.

Still, I was in.

I stayed motionless and concentrated on nothing but controlling my breathing, which took some effort considering the adrenaline and the sprint to the shadows, but the guard passed right by, oblivious to my intrusion.

There were several buildings in the complex and I didn't have a clue what any of them were used for. I closed my eyes and wished for a little luck, heading for the door of the building I was leaning on, and quickly swiped my newly acquired keycard. The little light turned green and I was in within seconds.

I stood for a minute, allowing my eyes to adjust to the darkness. The place seemed to be some sort of administrative building where the day-to-day running of operations probably occurred. Definitely not what I was after. I didn't need the executive offices—I needed to find where the real work was done.

The labs, the research facilities, the medical chambers.

I opened the door a crack, peeking back outside. Everywhere was thick with shadows and I made my way into them, not seeing the guard's flashlight, but moving slowly and quietly just in case.

The next building was larger. I snuck up to the door and looked in the direction of the fence for a flashlight beam, but there was nothing. I held the keycard up to the panel, the light turned green, and I eased my way in.

This building wasn't as dark as the last. It was dim, and I didn't see any people, but things seemed to be happening at least. Beyond the small utility room where I stood, a wall of glass showed a huge room—an entire warehouse—lined with banks upon banks of computers, little lights on the machines blinking like information was moving around—being stored, retrieved, sent out...who knows.

Memories took a lot of computing power with all the tiny details and everything, but I'd had no sense of how big the operation might be. This server room took up the entire building.

The moment I took in the enormity of the room I realized that even once I found Kade the world might still be in trouble. Enhanced Memories were being made here, right in my own backyard. And we were spreading them around the world.

The thought made me queasy, thinking about my parents. Trying to understand what their intentions had been. They must have thought they were doing so much good. But... how much did they know about what was really going on with Experion? A lump formed in my throat thinking about them. I had all these memories from when I was a kid, our family trips, weekends at the lake, running and laughing and playing. Was any of that even real?

I shook the thought out of my head. I could think about all that later. For now I had to focus on Kade.

I went through the same motions, sneaking out of one building and heading to the next two buildings, finding additional offices and then some labs, though they were small. No one was around. Finally I came to the final building in the complex. I closed my eyes and sent a little wish for luck out to the Universe, putting the keycard to the panel. The light turned green like all the others.

I snuck into the outer room, which was dim like the rest of the buildings. Assuming this building was the same as all the rest—empty except for equipment—I probably wasn't being as careful as I should have been.

I rounded a corner, not even bothering to peek around it first or try to be quiet or anything, taking a few steps up a short hallway. Up ahead a few more steps was an actual person—a security guard.

I couldn't stop the gasp from escaping my lips, adding to the noise I had already made, but strangely, he didn't turn around.

And then I saw it. A discarded box set haphazardly aside on the desk beside him. A tiny box exactly like all the boxes back at my parents' house. I knew the man's slump well—his head tilted back with his hands flopped unceremoniously to his sides. He looked like my parents looked all those times in the living room.

He was in the middle of an Enhanced Memory.

I supposed it would be kind of hard to resist all the authentic Memories that must be stored there. I thought about how freeing it would be to be sitting right there with him…escaping. Nausea rippled through my stomach as I pushed the thought away, focusing back on the guard.

He was pretty terrible at his job, but that was definitely a good thing for me. I only wished I knew how long the Memory was going to last.

Still, at least I wasn't caught.

Yet.

A lineup of screens in front of the guard showed various locations around the building. I'd been looking for cameras in all the other buildings, and thank goodness hadn't spotted any, but realized I had been careless. It wasn't impossible that I could have missed them. Not to mention they might have been monitoring the people coming and going using keycards and wondered why on earth my father was roaming around all over the place.

There was one good thing about stumbling upon this guard though. It must mean there was something worth guarding in this building, more valuable than the others.

I tried to formulate my best plan of action. I could attempt to do something about the security system, which might risk rousing the guard, or I could go take a look around as quickly as possible to see if I could find Kade.

I decided on somewhere in the middle.

The power supply was directly under his feet, so it would be easier to quickly unplug the monitors at the back of each screen. The only problem was I'd have to be directly in front of him for several seconds in order to do it. But at least I wouldn't need to touch him and risk alerting him.

I quickly ran around to the front of the desk and started

wiggling the cords, keeping one eye on the guard. The cord solution actually worked better than I thought since I could wiggle them loose but still leave the end of the cord balancing in the hole, which made it seem like they were still plugged in. With any luck this guy would struggle to figure it out and hopefully make a bunch of noise and alert me to get out of there before being discovered.

I hoped whatever was in this building was worth the risk. If I were to get caught now, not only would I be screwed—along with any chance of understanding what had happened to me...to Harlow—but Kade would too.

Another bolt of pain shot through my head behind my eye. I had to stop thinking about Harlow when I was right in the middle of, you know, illegally trespassing and whatnot, since stress was what seemed to trigger the shooting pains and phantom screams in my head.

I started through the final building. The first room had a sign on the door that said Lab A. There were three others in the same hallway: Lab B, Lab C, and Lab D. I had to use the keycard to get into the first lab, but once I did it was clear that this room, like all the others, was deserted. Of people, anyway. What was in there was a single extraction machine, just like the one we had at Golden Acres.

Checking the next three labs I found the exact same thing. Extraction machines, but no people to be found anywhere.

Shit. I breathed heavy for a few seconds, fighting tears.

Kade wasn't there.

27

But he had to be here somewhere, he just had to, didn't he? I snuck out of the final building, thoughts pouring into my head. What if I had it all wrong? What if Experion didn't have anything to do with this at all? But it was the only thing that made sense. I'd seen Marjorie at the black market den and she was high up in the company. Someone here had to know something.

But there was nowhere else to look for Kade. I'd checked every building.

Well, except one. But he couldn't be in there—it was too small. Really, it was more of a shed. There was no way it was any kind of medical facility. But maybe…what if it was just a place to keep people locked up?

Either way, I had to check. If I didn't, I'd always wonder.

I moved to the shed and started to fish out my dad's key-card until I realized there was no scanner on the door. There was no keypad, no nothing to indicate it was even a secure entrance. Or an entrance at all, for that matter.

The building was small and unassuming. If you were looking from any side, you'd never think anything was strange, but a quick circle around it told me that there was no way in. No door at all.

Which of course didn't make any sense.

I rounded the shed again, but the only thing I could find was a small water tap on the south side. It was attached to the shed but low to the ground. Not something you would immediately notice. I crouched and studied it, then worked up the nerve to twist it to the right. It looked old and a bit rusty, and I expected it to squeak and be hard to turn, but it was only made to look old. In reality it was new and well maintained and turned as smoothly as if it were brand-new out of the box.

As I finished turning it, a vacuum-like sound came from the east side of the building. I quickly went around to discover a hidden door had popped open. I waited a moment, making sure no one noticed, and that there was no one inside about to ambush me, but all remained still. I crept up to the door and stepped inside.

The door immediately shut behind me.

Everything was so pitch-black it was impossible to get a sense of my surroundings. I willed my eyes to adjust, and fished around in my bag for my phone, but before I got it out, the entire room started moving.

The whole thing was an elevator.

I finally found my phone and pulled it out, tapping the screen to illuminate it. But there really wasn't much to illuminate. This elevator had no buttons, not even an emergency stop. As it started to move, a low, blue light turned on, as if powered by the movement itself.

I had no choice but to go where it took me.

And hope there was no one on the other end.

The descent seemed to take forever—I couldn't even imagine how far underground I must have traveled—before the elevator finally came to an abrupt halt. I hid off to the side in case there was someone outside, though what good it would have done, I wasn't sure—an elevator doesn't just arrive with no one inside—but I was running on pure instinct, my heart pounding so hard the only thing drowning it out was my jagged, panicked breath. I realized only at the last second that if this had been the place that Harlow was kept, someone might recognize me.

The doors opened with a quiet "ding."

The hall was empty. I let out a whoosh of air and closed my eyes, sending the Universe a silent thank-you. The hall was also very long—endless almost—and it was bright, though I suspected it seemed so bright only because the elevator had been so dark.

Something about the place seemed familiar, a little déjà vu tingling through me. A flash, a jarring snippet of a hallway just like this, bolted through my mind. I grabbed the wall for support as the pain swept through. *Focus*, I told myself. Right now the only thing I could do was find Kade. I desperately wanted to know Harlow's story, but I also knew I couldn't change the past.

Thankfully I didn't see any obvious security personnel, but

there was activity in the distance. I headed toward the nearest wing, the first branch off the main hall on the right.

As I peeked around the corner, it was as if I was looking down almost the same hallway I was already in, also seemingly endless. I knew it couldn't be, of course, but the sheer size of this place was making me more nervous by the second.

Be smart and move quickly.

I headed down the hallway.

I was about to come up to a door on the left. The good news—and the bad news—was that the doors each had a window, which would allow me to peek in. Of course, that also meant that it was possible for whoever was inside to spot me too.

I took a deep breath. I knew if I stopped to really think about what I was doing, I might lose my nerve, so I plowed on, slowing as I neared, getting close to risk a peek inside. I tried to calm my breathing as I stood for a second then eased in for a look.

Strangely, the room looked less like a jail cell, which was kind of what I was expecting, and more like a hospital room, complete with the adjustable bed and a bunch of machines and screens surrounding it. Besides that, the room was empty.

I moved on quickly. My luck could turn at any moment and it would be devastating to get caught now after all that had brought me here.

There was a bit of noise coming from up ahead, but it still seemed pretty far off so I continued on, coming to the next door, this time on the right. I peeked inside and the room looked exactly the same as the last, with one notable difference. There was a woman in the bed who appeared to be sleeping peacefully. There was something unsettling about the whole thing and I ducked under the window in case she chose that exact moment to open her eyes.

The rest of the hall was much the same, my dread increasing with each window I peeked into. Most of the rooms were occupied with people in a gentle slumber, but it struck me as strange that there were no workers. If these people were patients, then…wouldn't they need nurses and doctors? Then again, this wasn't a hospital. So what were these people even here for?

So many thoughts swirled in my mind, and none of them good. Had they all had their memories taken away? Were they here by their own choice? I thought of Harlow again, a tickle prickling behind my eyes. I shook my head. Now was not the time. I had to keep going.

I tried the door at the next room, where a guy not much older than me was resting. As I slipped into his room he remained still. He looked so alive, so healthy, as if he'd been rejuvenating for weeks. Even his skin was practically glowing.

At first I was worried he might wake up as I came in, and I had a story at the ready that I was lost—which was pretty flimsy, I admit. If someone were lost why would they wander into a room with a patient? But it was all I had. Seeing him though, so deeply asleep, his waking was the last thing on my mind.

I grabbed the chart hanging at the end of the bed.

His name was Eric Wilton, and it looked like he'd been at the medical lab for about four weeks. I didn't really know how to read a medical chart, but I figured all the things wrong with this guy had to be listed on there somehow, at least in code or something, but there was…nothing.

Other than routine data like height and weight and several readings of blood pressure and things like that, there was nothing except one small notation near the bottom. A drug that was being administered—and had been administered for the entirety of his stay so far. He was being sedated, kept asleep. I set the chart back down slowly, trying to keep my breathing steady, one question taking up all the space in my mind. If these people were here voluntarily, why would they have to be sedated?

I crept back out of the room and peeked in a few more windows with the same results. Everyone was sleeping more peacefully than I was sure I'd ever seen people sleep.

An idea was forming in my mind, but I didn't want it to be right.

I snuck into another room, quickly checking the chart of Jessica Heston. She had been there for almost three months! And the exact same drug was listed on her chart. I glanced at the drip bag hanging above her bed. More sedative.

I was getting close to the end of the hall and the quiet noises I'd heard all the way along were getting closer now. My heart started to beat faster as scraps of phrases became audible.

"…hear about that circus theater performer?"

"The acrobat, yeah. Amazing, but I'm more interested in that fighter pilot."

"Ooh yeah, or the skydiving kid—"

My heart raced. Skydiving. They had to be talking about Kade. I crept closer, desperate to hear more.

"That kid is an absolute goldmine. I can't wait to see what else comes out of him."

I crouched behind a hospital bed that had been left in the hall, conveniently in a shadowy spot.

"Totally. You should come down to Sector Four if you have time this afternoon and observe. And get there early. We're doing him and the former Xtreme Games champion who never gave up his dangerous lifestyle, so I think the gallery is going to be pretty full."

The other person made an agreeing mulling sound. "I mean, he's got great experiences, but probably not too many of those fifteen-thousand-dollar ones."

Fifteen thousand? I thought. Was that what his skydiving Memory was priced at?

"Maybe. They say they've only tapped the surface. He's only been under twice, and no one even knows what the Xtreme guy has in his head. He wasn't even on social media."

I allowed myself a long exhale. If the skydiving kid was Kade it meant that he was at least alive, and that they might not have gotten too many of his memories yet.

"They've got them going under in a couple hours again," the voice continued. "No one has these kinds of memories anymore. Not at their age."

"It's incredible how fresh they are. These kamikaze kids are out there still doing this stuff," the voice said in disbelief. "Can you imagine the danger?"

The other voice murmured something too quiet to hear.

"So many of the subjects' memories are degraded and old. People just aren't doing this stuff anymore, not since EM went mainstream."

"There's just no way to get the same kind of money out of them," the other voice agreed.

Money. All this for money. All these people trapped here, not knowing what was going on. Mike Wilton, the Xtreme Games guy, everyone else.

Harlow.

Focus, I reminded myself, closing my right eye to another shot of pain. I couldn't solve all the world's problems. Today all I had left in me was to maybe save one beautiful boy. And that would be enough. If I could just get to Kade, he could help me figure out the rest. We could worry about the rest of these people together.

And for the first time I had a real destination to search for. Sector Four. Assuming the giant "one" above the hallway I'd gone into meant Sector One, I'd have to head back to the main hallway to find Sector Four.

I had to start moving. Everything was stacked against us, but because his extraction was soon, they might have Kade awake and prepping, and with any luck, he'd be alert enough to make an escape.

28

I was about to step out of the shadows and move back toward the main hall, but caught myself just in time when I realized the voices were coming closer. I flattened against the hospital bed, holding still, praying nothing on me was sticking out where they might see.

But they turned the corner and headed back up the wing toward the main hall, chatting away like everything was normal.

Focus, I reminded myself again. I couldn't be doing things like that. I had to think before I acted. I had to watch for the dangers. Too much was at stake.

But my frustration grew enormously as the two lab techs, or whoever they were, made their way back up the hall so slowly it nearly drove me nuts. I looked down at myself. Normally I wore black—I liked to fade into the background wherever

I went—but here the black was a stark contrast to the white lab coats these two were wearing.

I couldn't very well follow behind them in that bright hallway and risk one of them turning around—so I used the time to check out the room where the techs had come from. It seemed to be some sort of staff room with lockers and a small kitchenette area. There were a few lockers that didn't have locks, and those were the ones I went straight to. In the third locker I hit the jackpot with a lab coat.

When I returned to the hallway, the gossipy techs were exiting the other end. I made my way down the hall as quickly as possible, feeling slightly more secure with the coat on.

I slowed as I came to the main hallway, my ears straining to hear any sound, but there didn't seem to be any. I risked a peek around the corner and the hall was as empty as when I'd arrived.

I moved toward Sector Four trying to look "normal." If someone were to come into the hallway behind me it might look a little shady if I was all creeping around on my toes, or ducking, or running, or one of the other million other things my body wanted to do to get there faster or more quietly.

I slowed as I neared Sector Four. There definitely seemed to be more activity there. Maybe this was where new people were brought. I hoped that didn't mean all those people in Sector One had been stripped of all their best memories.

A sense of familiarity hit me again and my stomach started to turn.

I had to get Kade out. But what about all the other people stuck here—maybe by consent, knowing exactly what they were getting into, or…maybe not. Maybe they never wanted to be here at all. Maybe they were like Harlow.

There was no one in the hall, but there were certainly people that were awake down this wing, and if I'd been prone to gambling, I'd bet there was a lot more staff down here too. But I moved forward staying close to the wall, ready to duck into a room at any moment.

I peeked cautiously into the first window where there was some talking. There were two people in the room. One with a lab coat and one in the bed. I decidedly did not like the way the person on the bed was held there with restraints. There was fear in her eyes, but something that told me she had resigned herself to her fate too. I fought the tears that started to sting the back of my eyes and moved on.

There was still no one in the hall so I moved to the next window. Another woman restrained to the bed the same way the last one had been. She was awake, staring at the ceiling, then her eyes flickered to me and blinked. There was something about her eyes, something seemed…missing in them.

I moved on quickly. Thankfully the people in the next two rooms were sleeping and looked peaceful enough. More talking floated to me from somewhere down the hall, but I couldn't make out the words.

I peeked into the next window and couldn't stop myself from letting out a tiny cry when I saw the eyes that looked back at me. They were the beautiful eyes of a boy I had kissed, and when his eyes fell on mine and went wide, a little flutter kicked up in my chest. He recognized me.

My eyes darted around the room before I entered, then I raced in as fast as I could.

"Nova?" he asked, his voice a little slurred and confusion rippling his face.

"Hi," I said, my voice almost choking. Suddenly feeling ultra-awake and unable to contain my grin, I rushed over and wrapped my arms around him.

He couldn't hug me back, of course—he had the same restraints as everybody else—but he seemed to relax a little in my arms.

Then he pulled back a little. "How did you—?"

I frantically wrestled with the restraints, wanting him out as quickly as possible. "We have to get you out of here."

I pulled his arm out of the first restraint, moving on to the one around his chest, then moved to his feet. He was able to reach the restraint on his other hand and help.

We got him free from the bed and he was trying to stand but was having a little trouble. The drugs that were still wearing off weren't helping matters.

I glanced back out to the hall. Three doors down, a wheelchair was parked outside another room.

"Wait here," I said.

"Please no. I can't be alone."

That was the moment I knew. I had risked everything to find answers, sure, but more than that, I was willing to risk it all for Kade. I turned and went to him, putting my hands on his arms. "I won't leave you, I promise." I looked him in the eyes as I said it, hoping he knew how serious I was. That we were in this together. That I never, ever wanted to leave him. "I'm just going into the hallway for one second and I'll be right back."

He glanced at the window in the door and took a breath. "Yeah. Okay, yeah," he said, with a frantic little nod.

I rushed out to the hallway and grabbed the wheelchair, Kade opening the door for me as I brought it inside his room.

"I need my stuff," he said, already trying to put his pants on.

"No," I said. "We'll be too obvious if you're wearing street clothes. I think you need to stay in what you're wearing."

"Right, yeah," he said, scratching his head, still moving clumsily. "Sorry, I'm not thinking straight."

"You've been sedated for a while, it's going to take a bit."

He nodded. "Maybe the shoes though? In case we need to make a run for it? And can we hide my clothes in the chair, just in case?"

"Yes. Good thinking." I rummaged around in the closet for his things while he got situated in the chair, tucking his clothes around him.

I put his cell in his lap and found a pair of those little paper booties. Once he slid those over the tops of his shoes you could hardly tell he was wearing any. The idea was for no one to see us, but if they did, hopefully we looked like a tech taking a patient for a treatment or whatever.

"Wait. I have to film this," he said, fiddling with his phone.

"Kade, it's more important to get you out of here."

"It's not more important. Nothing is more important than potentially letting the world know what's going on here."

He started the recording and panned the camera around the room.

"Okay," he said with a nod.

I checked the window one more time and then we were on the move.

But I didn't get far before he whispered, "I need footage of the rooms."

"Kade, that is too risky."

"Just...you do it then," he said, shoving his phone toward my hand.

I looked all around. There were some people walking in the other direction but no one was paying any attention to us.

Rather than argue and risk arousing attention, I grabbed his phone and rolled Kade a little closer to the right side of the hallway. As we neared the next room, I held the camera up, allowing it a quick glimpse of what was inside. But I kept moving. I was not going to stop for anything, no matter what Kade said.

As we moved into the main hall, I allowed a small glimmer of hope to creep into my chest.

Maybe this whole time I had thought I wouldn't really be successful, but here we were, rounding the corner into the main hall and toward the elevator.

And there was no one in sight.

We passed Sector Five on the right and Sector Two on the left.

Halfway to the elevator.

Adrenaline began to surge through me. We were going to make it!

We just had to get past the next two branches where Sector Six and One were across from each other and there should be no more chance of being spotted. And we were there...we were passing the halls. I couldn't hear any voices.

I breathed deeper, like I'd been half holding it in this whole time.

"Nova, stop," Kade said, hitting the brake on the chair, and my excitement. "We can't be seen leaving like this. With me in the chair."

"Right," I said, frustrated both that we had stopped and at the fact that I hadn't been thinking as clearly as I should have. "I guess it wouldn't make sense that I'm leaving with my lab coat either."

I hadn't noticed any cameras, but that didn't mean there weren't any. What if someone was watching?

I quickly redirected the chair toward the first hall I'd gone down. With any luck, that first room would still be empty. Peeking through the window, I breathed a sigh of relief, quickly maneuvering Kade inside, then shoved the lab coat into the small closet while Kade changed into his clothes. And I guess I wasn't thinking because I turned back around while he was still pulling his shirt on. His back was turned and I sucked in a breath, both from knowing I was invading his privacy and because he looked really, really good without his shirt on.

I quickly spun back around. Thankfully, he didn't seem to notice.

"Ready?" he said, after finally getting everything on.

I nodded. "Let's go."

I peeked out. Kade was leaning on me, still not fully functioning. No one was around. We quickly made it to the elevator, and a sense of relief as the elevator bell dinged and the doors started to open flooded through me. We were nearly out.

And then...the doors opened farther, revealing a man, his face illuminated by his phone. Kade stiffened beside me, and I froze too.

Nowhere to run. Nowhere to hide.

The man still hadn't noticed us as he pushed off the wall he'd been leaning on and turned to exit the elevator.

Then he looked up, startled. Met my gaze.

My stomach lodged itself somewhere in the vicinity of my throat, time standing still as we stood in a silent standoff.

29

Kade smiled at him like he owned the place. "Hey," he said with a nod.

The man glanced at Kade as he said it, looked back to me, then back to Kade, his expression never changing.

The seconds passed like hours as I held my breath.

The man finally gave Kade a nod, heading past us to the left, down the Sector Six hall. A moment later, we were headed back up to the surface.

"Well, we're out," Kade said, thankfully breaking the silence and the tension that was stretching its way through my body.

"That guy definitely looked suspicious."

Kade nodded. "But we made it."

"Yeah," I said as the door to the outside popped open with a little hiss.

I glanced at my phone. It had been on silent since the club

and I'd barely had time to think about it. Andie had sent so many messages. My stomach tightened. I'd left her hanging for so long.

I glanced at the newest one.

Where are you?! I'm freaking out!

I started typing. I'm safe. No. I hit the delete key. I'm fine. I'm with K.

I knew it wouldn't hold her over forever and I wanted to say more, but at least she knew I was still here and that I'd found Kade, but paranoia flooded through me. What if they were keeping tabs on my phone?

I took a moment to process what I'd done. Rescued Kade. Gotten him free. The gravity of what was really going on in that bunker hit me then too. This was so bad for the people down there. Could have been so much worse for Kade if he'd stayed much longer. My stomach rolled. I wanted to grab his hand, to steal a moment just for us, but he was already tentatively stepping outside, then quickly ducking behind the building on the side where the false tap was.

We started to move, first over the fence, then into the trees.

Once we were a safe distance we crept out of the trees so we could move faster. I glanced back toward the complex, then picked up my pace.

"We need to stop these people," Kade said as we ran. "We can't keep letting them do what they're doing."

"I know, I've been thinking about that. I think maybe my parents can help."

"No. Absolutely not. That's the last place we should go. They'll look for me there. They know we know each other."

"But where else will we find any information on what's going on at Experion?"

We ran for a minute, getting distance between us and the complex. Finally Kade spoke. "You're right. It might be the only place we'll have a chance at finding anything incriminating, but we need to get in and get out as fast as we can."

"Right," I said, keeping pace beside him. But there was something that I couldn't stop thinking about. "Kade? What was it like in there?"

He looked at me, a serious expression on his face. "You don't want to know."

"Maybe. But I need to know. For Harlow."

He slowed to a walk and I followed suit. After letting out a long breath, he finally spoke. "It was…confusing. It was like I never had complete control of myself. Of my mind. The drugs, I think."

It was an idea that seemed familiar, but I didn't know if it was because the body I was in had probably gone through the same thing, or if it was because I feared I still might not have that much control over my own mind.

"Everything was always foggy," he continued. "But there are moments I can remember. When they were hooking me up to that machine mostly." He turned to look at me. "I don't like that machine."

I nodded. I'd had the same thought when I'd watched Mae in the one at Golden Acres. I wondered then if I'd felt it when I was Harlow too. I shook my head. Harlow felt so foreign—a stranger—but at the same time, I almost thought I could feel her in there. Somewhere. Like a ghost.

"Can I just...have a sec?" I asked.

Kade nodded and I wandered into the trees for some space, not knowing what I was doing. Not knowing what I needed. Desperately wishing this would all go away. All I wanted was to go back to before.

But before when? Before I knew about Harlow? Or back to when Harlow still existed? But then...what about Nova? Even the idea of being Nova struck me as wrong now, which meant what? That I was nobody?

This can't be real, this can't be real, played over and over in my mind, but my body somehow knew differently, my instinct, my intuition—all telling me that it was perfectly real, this thing that had happened to Harlow. To Nova.

I hugged my arms around my body, realizing I was still holding on to Kade's phone. And I wanted to resist, but I didn't have the willpower. Not anymore. I'd been focused on finding Kade, but I couldn't use that as an excuse anymore. I just wanted to see her again. I wanted to know her.

Scrolling through his videos, I quickly found the one he had already shown me, but there were others there too.

I needed to feel...I don't know—I needed to feel something. It probably wouldn't help, but I needed to feel like myself again. I couldn't remember the last time I'd been... comfortable in my own skin. I guess I thought maybe everyone felt a little uncomfortable in their skin sometimes. Or all the time.

I wanted to feel something different. I couldn't sit in this wrongness for one more second. I pressed Play.

In the video, Harlow was spinning, arms open wide, head tilted back to the sky as she laughed. So I leaned back and stared at the stars beyond the tops of the trees.

And then I spun too. I tried to remember what I used to be like as Harlow. I spread my arms out wide and closed my eyes, trying to conjure up her memories. But maybe "remembering" was wrong.

I needed to "be."

I slowed down and let the movement wash over me, emptying my mind of worries, thoughts—and especially memories. The world around me got quiet, calm...expansive. Like somehow I was connected with it all—the air, the trees, the stars.

And for a moment, I felt it.

Felt what it had been like to be her. To spin because it stopped the spinning in my head. And it wasn't a memory, it was deeper than that. A knowing in my bones. In my soul.

An inkling that it all didn't matter—but not in a bad way— the world would keep spinning, good and bad, right and wrong. And the only thing that made sense was to carry the light with you, the happy, instead of searching for it.

And I smiled. And tears came to my eyes. And then I... lost it.

As fast as the sensation had come it was gone and I was Nova again. No. I wasn't Nova either.

Not Nova.

Not Harlow.

I dropped into a crouch, my hands covering my head, no longer able to stop the tears. No longer able to carry the happy. And even though I was in the middle of nature, it felt like the world—the noises, the wind, the darkness—were crowding in, taking my space like maybe I wasn't quite worthy enough to inhabit it in the first place. Which made sense, I supposed, since I wasn't even a real person. I cried, wondering if I would ever really know who I was supposed to be.

Eventually Kade pulled me up. "It'll be okay," he said softly. "We'll get through this together."

I nodded, wiping my face, knowing that giving up wasn't going to help sort anything out. I didn't know if finding answers would either, but I had to try.

I started running again, Kade just behind me. "So what's the plan when we get there?" he asked.

"I'm not entirely sure," I lied, because how could I even be thinking what I was thinking? Enhanced Memories were the entire reason we were all in this mess in the first place. But I couldn't come up with any other way.

Even though it was the last thing I thought was safe anymore, I would have to use EM. After the mini-meltdown, I seemed to have a new burst of energy—nervous energy—and it carried me all the way to my house. Once there though, I stopped, my stomach churning again.

"It's okay, I'm just as scared as you are," Kade said, and I knew it was true. He was probably even more scared than I was.

I stood at the door.

Once I stepped inside, everything would change. I stood there for a minute, just breathing, telling myself that everything had already changed.

I turned the knob.

My parents were in the living room, in the place I had come

to expect them to be. Sitting with EM machines clutched in their hands.

Eyes closed, headphones on. What used to look so normal to me looked very different now.

I went to them, my hands shaking. Pulled the EM machine out of Mom's hand and stopped it, then Dad's, as a strange detachment washed over me, like I was watching from outside myself.

They blinked at me.

"Nova?" Dad asked.

"Nova," I said, letting out a humorless laugh. "Are you sure you don't mean Harlow?"

Mom's eyes widened, then she tilted her head. She was still in her EM stupor and things didn't quite seem to be registering.

"What are you talking about?" Dad asked, but he must have known the charade had come to an end. He rubbed his forehead, the look on his face searching, like he was trying to figure something out.

"Just tell me," I said. "What were you thinking?" It was a struggle to get the words out. Like they were lodged somewhere deep inside me and I had to push them all the way through my body. Or was it Harlow's body? "How could you just…steal someone's life?"

Mom shook her head, tears forming. "But…she was already gone?" Her words were unsure. Almost like she was asking me. Like she couldn't quite remember.

Dad straightened a bit, blinking life back into his face. But he barely looked alive—his face so pale, the circles under his eyes even darker than the last time I'd seen him. "It was the only way to save her."

"But...you didn't save her. You took her memories. The only thing you saved was her body, but that isn't her."

His forehead crinkled like he was trying to figure out if that was true. I got the sense they'd been sold a concept they hadn't quite bought into.

"Experion had a problem. Harlow's shell of a body was there, and then what? You just happened to want a kid of your own?" I shook my head. "All that trouble for a kid you don't even seem to want."

Mom flinched at my words. "But you're Nova," she said, but she didn't look sure of what she was saying.

I looked at the ceiling. "And I knew it too," I said, talking to myself more than anything. "I knew you were busy and everything, but there was always something off. I could feel it."

Mom opened her mouth to say something then closed it again, swallowing as if her unsaid words tasted sour.

"It was the right thing," Dad said, his eyes not able to meet mine, still searching as if his mind was wading through tar to find his thoughts.

"There's no one that—if they had sat down for two minutes to think about it—would have ever thought this was the right thing." My voice was rising. "It's unthinkable," I said, tears piling up behind my eyes as my voice quivered. "It's cruel."

Mom started crying softly and I couldn't help but think how unfair that was. I was the one who was going through all this, who had no idea how to move forward knowing what I knew, and they couldn't even give me any answers.

Maybe it was too late for answers.

Except...

"Come on," I said to Kade, pulling on his shirt and dragging him into the Memory Room, locking the door behind us.

"What are you doing?" he asked.

"I just want some answers."

"Nova, come out of there," Dad said from the other side, jiggling on the door handle.

"Can you jam a chair under the handle?" I asked Kade.

He maneuvered one of the chairs while I surveyed the wall of drawers.

I had to be smart about this. We weren't going to have much time. The hidden key drawer. If I downloaded the master list of all the Memories first, maybe we'd have a better idea about what we were looking for.

"Maybe you should film this," I said, handing him back his phone.

He nodded.

I flicked the light off. Instantly the drawer with the glowing paint shone in the same little key shape.

Kade made a little surprised noise then started panning across all the drawers, the phone light piercing through the darkness. Kade opened a drawer here and there to show the disks inside. He spoke, narrating the scene. "These are Memories—true Memories—that have been taken from people. The unaltered ones." He panned some more. "There are hundreds of drawers here, each containing Memories stolen... for what? For other people's entertainment.

"How many lives have been taken? Are still being taken. No, they're not killing in the sense we've always believed killing to be, but they are taking people's lives nonetheless. And they are still doing it in the Memory Farm I was taken to." He turned the camera to me. "Nova saved me, and now we hope to save the rest. Please, share this video. Don't let what happened to Harlow Beckman happen to you."

It was unsettling having Kade film the moment. I knew it had to be done—the world had to start understanding what was really going on with EM, but it was so personal too. Like someone had discovered all my secrets and was putting them out there for all the world to see. They were secrets I didn't want people to know, but it was also the only way.

I pulled the key drawer out and picked up the little disk from inside, my hands shaking slightly as I sat.

I held the disk up to my face, studying it closely.

It looked so innocent. Simple and round like a coin but thicker and smoother, rounded at the edges. It looked like something that could have come out of a children's toy. And yet it was so dangerous.

I steeled myself and put the disk into my EM machine, leaning back in the chair, closing my eyes, then pressed Play.

The list was intense. So many Memories to choose from. The Memory directory was laid out as sort of a pictogram, each little square having a picture on it representing what was inside. You could open each virtual drawer to discover more information about each experience—like clicking a link on a webpage.

As expected, most of the Memories were experience based—adrenaline-filled stunts, romantic interludes, trips around the world, and things like that.

Still, something niggled at me. I mentally scanned the drawers again, hoping I'd missed something.

But everything looked the same. The same two walls of drawers the Memory Room had in real life. Nothing was out of place—in fact, nothing was even in this virtual room except the drawers against a white backdrop. None of the other things in the real room were in this version—no chairs, no nothing.

Except...that wasn't entirely true.

The painting was outlined on the virtual wall.

Which had to mean something, right?

Inside the Memory, I looked at the painting and tried to determine if anything was strange about it, but I couldn't tell. I reached up and touched it. The painting swung ever so slightly.

It moves.

Still inside the Memory, I couldn't stop myself from grinning as I imagined putting my hands on either side and lifting it off the wall.

Just like I'd hoped, another chart presented itself—hidden behind the picture. Set out the same as the master list, but this one was much smaller—about a dozen little drawers.

Three jumped out at me immediately.

And all three of them sent dread slithering down my spine.

Experion Enterprises, Harlow, and...*Nova?*

But...what did that mean?

Harlow had been wiped—her—my—memories gone. I just...never thought that my new memories, my Nova memories, had come from someone.

She was real?

I was real.

I had to know who she was.

But would the disk tell me? What if I already had all the Memories in my head? Maybe it was the Harlow Memories I should be more concerned about. The ones they stole from me.

But did I even want them anymore? I still mostly felt like Nova. What if that changed? What if things got worse?

I shook my head and opened my eyes, stopped the directory Memory and brought myself back to the physical world.

Dad was still at the door, knocking. I ignored him and focused on the room.

The painting seemed so obvious now, like I should have known all along that there was something about it. I quickly stood and took it down. Sure enough, the drawers appeared.

"Whoa," Kade said.

I nodded. "The directory showed everything in all the drawers."

I couldn't steady my hand as I reached for the Harlow drawer, barely able to open it. I knew I shouldn't do it. Was I being selfish…too curious? I wasn't that person anymore, I didn't need to know. I certainly didn't need to know right then, but I reached in and grabbed the disk anyway.

I sat, my stomach quaking, my breath coming in choppy bursts.

"What is that?" Kade asked, worried.

It was like my arm had a mind of its own and I couldn't stop it from inserting the disk into my EM player as I sat again.

"It's Harlow."

He reached for me. "Maybe you should wait a second and—"

I pressed Play.

It was like being hit by a truck. I shot back in the chair and my teeth clamped together, biting my tongue.

There was something different about this disk. Something wrong. I quickly realized that instead of one experience being housed on the disk, all of Harlow's memories were on there. It was like her—my—entire life downloaded all at once, at a much faster pace. Enhanced Memories were supposed to put you in the action, make you feel like you were living the experience, but this was very different.

A lightning bolt ricocheted through my head but I couldn't move—it was like the experience had taken over my free will. Once it started, there was no going back. Memory after Memory flooded my mind, fast-forwarded in sequence from Harlow's first thoughts and experiences to the last things she remembered.

And her life had been remarkable. She had been a force in the world—so different from Nova—so vivacious and strong and courageous and...incredible. Everybody loved her and she loved everybody back, truly curious about everyone she crossed paths with. She became everybody's best friend.

As the Memories finally ended, my arm dropped to my side. Tears streamed down my face, though they weren't tears of emotion, even though there were certainly enough of those pinballing through me. They were tears brought on by the sheer physical ordeal. I tasted blood from the bite on my tongue.

I could not slow my mind, barely able to catch a thought. I

understood that I was in my parents' Memory Room but the rest of my awareness was mush, my brain working to stitch all the memories together. To try and differentiate one life from the other. Images and flashes and moments all scrambling together, my brain feeling like it was expanding inside my skull. I grabbed my head, squeezing my eyes closed trying to control the pain.

"Nova! Nova!" a voice sounded, but it seemed far away.

I was desperate to grab hold of my mind. Racing in a thousand directions, trying to split into a thousand pieces. I felt it then—a flash of knowing—Harlow's parents, my parents, were dead—killed in a fiery wreck—and I don't know if I let out a scream or if it was phantom, but as I did, my mind broke and my world went dark.

30

"**N**ova!"
     I don't know how long I was out. It could have
been seconds or hours for all I knew but when I came to, I
was still in the Memory Room and it was still dark.

"Nova!"

Someone was lightly shaking me. "Come on, Nova."

I blinked my eyes open. "Kade?"

And then I noticed it. The pain. It was gone.

Like completely gone. In that way that you almost hadn't
even realized you'd been walking around with this low-grade
ache because you'd gotten so used to it, until one day it went
away and you were so grateful for the relief.

And my thoughts were clear. Like super clear. Clearer than
maybe they had ever been. I was still Nova, but I also had
these other memories inside me. Harlow memories.

It was like I was Harlow too. And somehow instead of everything being confused by having two sets of memories inside me, I had this clarity. Like it was perfectly normal that I was suddenly two completely separate people. There was so much grief—for my—Harlow's—parents and for her old life, but I felt energized too, elated, like my brain had rewired itself entirely and adrenaline was coursing through my veins.

Everything was completely foreign yet so familiar at the same time.

I tried to imagine what my parents had been thinking. How they could have let this happen. What kind of a monster did you have to be to take away someone's life? And at the same time they were still my parents. Every memory I had of them and this life growing up seemed so real. And it was a good life. So many trips to the beach, birthday parties, all the family time we used to spend together. Closeness. Connection. I remembered every moment like it was so real. They loved me. Nova. And I loved them back, but…how was I ever going to face them again?

Face what they had done?

How could *they* face what they had done?

But they didn't though, did they? Not really. They got lost in the Memories instead.

"Nova! What the hell happened? Are you okay?" Kade was kneeling in front of me, his eyes searching my face.

"Yeah, I'm okay."

"What happened?"

"I…just downloaded Harlow."

"Harlow? You're Harlow now?"

I couldn't tell if he was scared or if there was a hint of excitement in his voice.

"No, I'm still Nova. I just…remember her. Remember being her."

"You remember both?"

I nodded. "Except…I don't remember the switch. Like when I became Nova. I have childhood memories, but… nothing from in between."

"Okay, but you're still you, right?"

"Yeah, I'm still me. I think."

"Do you feel like you're both in there somewhere?"

I shook my head. "No, I feel like Nova still. But Harlow is definitely in there. Maybe not all of her, but her thoughts and memories are there."

"That's…kind of cool, actually," Kade said.

I nodded. But there were still so many questions. Like how I became Nova in the first place. I took the Harlow disk out of my EM player and stood, a little shaky. Kade put his hand under my elbow to steady me.

I put the disk back and pulled out Nova's. Mine.

Both parents were knocking at the door now. Quietly— more pleading than angry.

But now that this had started, I needed to know. I inserted the disk and pressed Play as quickly as I could. Kade would probably try to talk me out of it—tell me I needed to rest or something, but I had to do it.

I had to know.

Memories flooded one after the other after the other and I smiled, reliving the moments, relishing in my favorites, an odd sense of joyful nostalgia mingled with the happiness I'd felt as the moments had happened. And then, as the final Memories downloaded I began to understand.

Nova had been a real person and she'd been sick. Like really sick.

Cancer.

She was wasting away. I saw for the first time that she didn't look anything like Harlow. She'd had brown hair, like mine was dyed now, but that's where the resemblance ended. I'd always thought I just liked my hair better brown, but maybe I was always trying to find something...real.

I sat up and blinked, then almost mechanically moved the chair from under the door and walked out of the Memory Room, coming face-to-face with my parents.

They just stood there. And for all the banging on the door they'd been doing, for a moment, they were silent.

Waiting to see what I'd say. Something I'd wanted for so long, but unfortunately, it was coming way, way too late.

"You knew you were going to lose your child," I said.

Mom looked at her hands, quiet. Defeated. Dad stared at me, blinking.

"You started to take her memories and store them away."

Mom was nodding. "I just wanted to preserve them. To preserve her."

Dad looked at her then and it was like something in him cracked. The protective shell he'd been carrying on the outside crumbling away, his face distorting.

"I don't know what I thought I was going to do with them," Mom continued, "but then Experion Enterprises found out about Nova being sick."

"The plan unfolded, almost by chance," Dad added, clearing his throat, a slight defensiveness still in his words.

"And that poor girl..." Mom trailed off.

Dad gently grabbed onto Mom's elbow then, as if to steady her and for the first time in a long time I saw how they had once been a team. Partners. "After Experion extracted the Harlow memories, her mind didn't do well," he said, his voice taking on an almost clinical tone. "They were...losing her."

"The same time as my body began to lose its battle," I said. "A Harlow shell in need of new memories and Nova memories in need of a body."

Mom's tears started again.

They couldn't have been thinking straight. They were simply desperate. It must have seemed almost fated—a dying daughter, but then...a new way to keep her alive, voilà! And I almost felt sorry for her. For them.

Almost.

"Of course, reality always sets in," I said. "Everything started falling apart. Every day when you looked at me, I wasn't the face you wanted to see. I was never going to be her, exactly."

Dad let go of Mom and crossed his arms.

I shook my head. "But it wasn't like you could send me back either."

Mom's sobbing came harder then, regret pouring out of her.

"That's why you use so many Memories," I said, trying my hardest not to sound accusing and disappointed, but failing at both. "I wasn't the daughter you thought I would be."

"Nova, please," my father said, trying to sound fatherly, but the time for fatherly had passed when he decided to trade one daughter in for another.

"I suppose you just needed a break from it all at first, and then...it became all the time."

"It wasn't supposed to be this way. Enhanced Memories were supposed to be nothing but good. We'd created this magical thing," she said, a tiny glimmer of pride breaking through the tears. "We gave people all these experiences, this incredible new quality of life. Helped them learn, helped them live so much bigger..." She got a faraway look in her eyes and dropped her hands. "And then they took over," she said, her voice fading to a whisper. "They stopped listening. We lost control." She glanced up at me. "I wanted to tell you. So many times I wanted to tell you, but they knew our secret and threatened to tell everyone. I'm so sorry, Nova," Mom said, her tears coming again.

Emotions pulled at me. I felt wrecked for what they'd been through—no one deserves a dying child—but at the same time, how could they? What they had put me through—put Harlow through—was unbelievable.

They'd manufactured themselves up a new little daughter.

My heart split seeing them now, trying to imagine what they felt as their Nova wasted away, the desperation that would make someone do this. And I could imagine it. I was losing people too. Losing them.

I realized I had tears in my eyes too. There was no going back now. No saving them.

"I think it's time to get out of here," I said, turning to Kade.

And for the first time, Dad seemed to notice he was there. His eyes flitted to the Memory Room. "What were you doing in there?" he asked.

And it was strange. Even with all that I knew, this was still the same man as before. Nova's father. My father. And my heart ached with grief mixed with a weird sympathy that I didn't know what to do with.

Kade took a step forward. "This was my idea. Nova had nothing to do with it." And I don't know why he said it, because it was the last thing from the truth.

The regret in Dad's face morphed into the paranoia I'd gotten so used to seeing lately, his eyes darting to Kade's phone, then to me, then to the phone.

His hand lowered to the drawer of the side table.

"Dad, this is Kade. He's my friend." I spoke slowly, carefully, like the last time I'd had to talk him down.

But Dad's hand kept moving and Kade didn't know what was inside that drawer and it was like everything was happening in slow motion, but way too fast at the same time.

"Is that a camera?" Dad asked as he slid the drawer open.

That was the way his brain worked now. He saw a phone and thought recording device. Which, admittedly, was entirely accurate.

"Dad, it's just his pho—"

My words were cut off by a shattering, deafening sound followed by a scream.

And Kade went down, his phone shattering in his hand, a bloom of blood spreading in his side. As if watching from far away, I realized only when it stopped, that the scream had been my own.

31

My mother called 9-1-1, and soon people poured into the room. I had a vague notion of my father being taken down. Of someone pulling me away while others went to work on Kade.

Everything was a blur of tears and blood. And faces.

Dad was confused, staring at the gun like he wasn't quite sure how it had gotten there. He opened his hand and let it drop to the floor. Mom's expression was painted with shock as the paramedics rushed past, their expressions intent and serious. And Kade...Kade looked so scared.

"The blood is slowing," one of the paramedics said. "It looks like he's going to be okay. It hasn't hit any major arteries."

Kade groaned, and it was one of the most beautiful sounds I'd ever heard.

They bundled him onto a stretcher and I followed them toward the ambulance.

Police dragged Dad out behind us, taking him in the opposite direction.

I looked back at the house as we reached the ambulance. My mom came out. I'd never seen her so unsure of what was happening. She sat on the front steps and just kept crying.

I didn't go to her.

Instead I got into the ambulance to ride with Kade.

They had bandaged him up. He was stable and talking and he tilted his head, flashing me that crooked smile.

And I couldn't take it anymore—he looked so vulnerable lying there and it felt like forever since we'd had a real moment together, only us with no agenda in the way, and I don't know if it was Harlow's confidence taking over, or if I was acting on pure relief that he was okay, but I somehow found the nerve to lean in and kiss him.

But he didn't kiss me back. In fact, he gently pushed me away.

"Nova, what are you doing?" He looked shocked.

I blinked. "What do you mean what am I doing?"

"This…isn't what our relationship is," he said, looking confused, and maybe a little scared.

And in his look, I understood.

The time he spent underground before I found him. They had taken some of his memories already, the skydiving and who knows what else. Except in that moment I knew exactly what else. What was more intense than memories of falling in love? Nothing can compete with that.

Of course that's what they took first.

My heart dropped out of my chest. I knew what it was like to live in that world of uncertainty, to not be able to trust your own mind, and I didn't want that for Kade. I wanted him to live the authentic life he'd been fighting so hard to have. And I especially didn't want to embarrass him and make things weird between us.

"Uh, sorry," I said. "I guess I got caught up in the adrenaline or something." I looked away, trying not to let Kade see the tears creeping into my eyes.

"Oh um, okay. I uh, you're really important to me. I just… don't feel that way…" he said.

"Yeah no, it's all good," I said, blinking the tears away.

His face morphed into something else, something exaggerated. "And hey, we should be celebrating."

"Celebrating? Kade, my dad shot you. Your phone was destroyed."

But he just grinned even wider. "I know, but not before I got my video uploaded. The whole world is going to know about all of this when they wake up. We did it," he said. "Everything's going to be okay."

But even though he had survived, I knew it was going to be a long time before everything was okay.

Because I was going to have to somehow live with the memory of that night we kissed in the park, knowing it was the only night like that we'd ever have.

epilogue

As the months passed, Enhanced Memories were still a huge presence in everyone's lives, but more laws and regulations were being passed every day to help make sure it remained recreational and not something that would take over people's lives. It was still a problem, but things were getting better.

Black market dens like the one at the club were being shut down. Authentic Memories were outlawed altogether except for in medical instances like with the people at Golden Acres. I was still torn over whether they should still be extracting from memory patients, but most people thought it still seemed to do more good than harm. I stayed on at Golden Acres in hopes that I could keep learning and maybe make the process better someday.

My parents were arrested for the part they played with Harlow and the Memory Farm and so I had no parents left—

Harlow's or Nova's, and that was maybe the hardest part of vowing to never use Enhanced Memories again. Because sometimes I wanted to remember how things used to be. Or maybe I just wanted to forget how they became.

Genie sort of took me in as my guardian, and I was living at Golden Acres. They'd decided they could spare a bed for me at least until I turned eighteen in a few months.

It was definitely weird living with a bunch of seniors, but it was good too. Somehow the world felt right surrounded by Mae's soft smiles, Bea and Ruthie's constant bickering, and my favorite of all, Clyde's stories. He hadn't lost all of himself, thank goodness.

Kade and I still hung out, but things were never like they had been. I thought maybe with time his feelings might grow again, but that seemed to be wishful thinking.

Still, he and Andie were bright spots in most of my days. She'd been so pissed after I left her that night in the club, scared completely out of her mind, but after finding out that Kade had been shot and everything else I'd gone through that night, in true Andie fashion she came straight to my side. And thankfully, she hadn't left since. We were even making plans to find a place of our own next year.

My Harlow memories have continued to mingle and integrate with my Nova side. I'm definitely not all Harlow, but I'm certainly not just Nova anymore either. A new, somewhere-in-the-middle identity had begun to form.

And I finally felt like I was exactly who I was supposed to be.

★ ★ ★ ★ ★

ACKNOWLEDGMENTS

I'm pretty sure I used up most of my words writing this book, so I'll keep this simple. Please know that you are all immeasurably important to me.

Many, many thanks to:

Bess Braswell, the most patient, kind, and championing soul; Anna Prendella, an incredible editor and, more importantly, amazing teacher—you helped me find Nova's story, so a thousand times thank you; Connolly Bottum, an incredible organizer of all the things; and everyone else at the Inkyard family who had a hand in this book.

Lane Heymont, the best agent and, more importantly, emotion wrangler a writer could ask for, and everyone else at the Tobias Literary family for all your support.

My family and friends, especially to my partner, Vern, all my kids, my parents, my sisters, and my extended family (with an extra shout-out to Stacey for always being my first and best reader).

The readers of this book. You are the reason we writers do the things we do (sorry, not sorry).

Much gratitude,

Sacha